SWEET SORROW

SWEET SORROW

SWEET SORROW

Denise Robins

CHIVERS

British Library Cataloguing in Publication Data available

This Large Print edition published by AudioGO Ltd, Bath, 2013.
Published by arrangement with the Author's Estate

U.K. Hardcover   ISBN   978 1 4713 3976 9
U.K. Softcover   ISBN   978 1 4713 3977 6

Printed and bound in Great Britain by
MPG Books Group Limited

CHAPTER ONE

Guy Denver had been motoring all day. For the first hundred and fifty miles after leaving London, he had not stopped. He had driven his car remorselessly, thankful for the first time in his life that it had an acceleration second to none—the long low body beautifully built on a chassis which had cost a great deal of money. Guy Denver had never worried about speed before. He had just wanted a car that looked good and could pass others when he wished to pass them. But today he had felt a demon of despair impelling him to hurtle down the roads at a mad pace. He must get away. *He must get away*—quickly from his thoughts, from his house, and everything in it. From the memory of the woman who had left him in that house. The crushing blow which she had dealt him a few days ago since when he had been a prey to nerves and depression.

He was driving in the direction of Lincolnshire. He had no clear idea where he was going. As much as possible, he chose the quiet by-roads with little traffic. Sheer exhaustion had made him stop for lunch at a small pub, then carry on, mile after mile— mile after mile. Now at four o'clock, darkness was falling. The grey January twilight blotted out the landscape slowly but surely and it had

1

been raining persistently for some time. Guy Denver pulled up his car, felt for his pipe and lit it, then looked around him, conscious that the country was as dreary as his own soul.

On one side of him, there appeared to be marsh; damp, scrubby, low-lying land. On the other, he could see only sheep-walks and rabbit-warrens. Immediately before him a ridge of bold hills which looked through the rain as though concealed by a handful of blue chiffon.

Guy Denver pulled out a map. Where was he? He tried to trace his route, unutterably tired, eyes red-rimmed and sore. God, but he needed sleep! But even if he found a bed, he knew that he would not be able to sleep. He would only think:

'I'm a failure! A failure in my job. A failure with the woman I married . . .'

Dragging his thoughts back to the immediate present, he went on examining the map with the aid of the light from the dashboard. He came to the conclusion that he must be in the Fen district. No wonder it was damp and gloomy. He had reached those lowlands which adjoin the tidal reaches of the Trent and Humber. Those hills beyond must be the Wolds.

Guy put away his map. He sucked thoughtfully at his pipe for a moment. The best thing he could do was to get back on to the main road and find shelter for the night.

2

As he switched on his engine again, a gust of wind spattered great raindrops against the windscreen. He put the wiper into action. The steady droning of it against the glass only added to his gloom.

'Oh, damn, damn everything,' Guy Denver said to himself, miserably, and drove on until he reached a signpost. The rain was shortening the beam of his headlights. He could just manage to see the words :

'To Lyme Purgis.'

Guy had never heard of the place. No doubt it was a small hamlet. But it would probably have a pub in it. He would go on—to Lyme Purgis.

He covered another couple of miles, meeting nothing on the road. This was wild, lonely country. If he had wanted solitude, he had got it. But he wished the rain would stop. It made driving even more tiring than before and it was a narrow road. If he met anything as big as his own saloon, he would have some difficulty in passing it.

Suddenly he saw the dim yellowish light of a vehicle coming toward him. He pulled his car, into the side of the road as far as he could get it, scraping the paint against a scrubbly hedge.

The lights on the other car were poor. And now the beam of his headlights threw up a narrow bridge just in front of him. Just as well he had stopped. If two cars met on that bridge they would block each other entirely.

3

Guy dimmed his headlights and watched the other car come on. From what he could see, it was a small two-seater—possibly a little Morris.

What was happening? The car faltered—seemed to stop. The lights wavered as though the driver was turning the wheel—first in one direction, then in the other. Weary, and with his nerves on edge, Guy felt unduly irritated. He put his head out of the window and shouted:

'Come on! *Come on!*'

Then suddenly, the catastrophe! Something terrible which happened in front of Guy Denver's very eyes. For the lights of the little car seemed to drop, and the *car dropped with them*. Simultaneously he heard a piercing cry. The cry of a woman.

Guy Denver's heart leapt to his throat. He switched his lights full on and leapt out of the car. The rain drove against his face. He brushed the drops away with the back of his hand and stared before him. Then it was revealed to him that one of the piers must have been swept away. The bridge had tumbled in, and the car with it.

'*God!*' A cry of horror came from Guy's throat. He began to run forward. The driver of that car had been a woman. And now she must be in the river—that river, which, swollen by the rains, was tearing across the marshland like a cataract.

4

With his heart in his mouth, Guy came to the edge of the bank and peered down.

Merciful heavens! What a piece of luck. The car was not in the water. It was suspended on the remains of the pier, sideways.

Guy, already soaked to the skin, but no longer tired, scrambled down the bank to the rescue. With some difficulty, in the darkness, he managed to get to that car. Equally, he thought, it was a mercy that it should have been an open car with a cloth-hood and talc side-curtains which were easily smashed in. A girl lay across the wheel, motionless. She appeared to be the one and only occupant. Breathing hard, Guy dragged the unconscious form out of the little car. He laid her on the bank and kneeling down beside her, placed a hand on her heart. He could not see her face clearly. It was a white mask, blotched with mud and rain. But he found that her heart was still beating. Thankfully, he wiped her face with his handkerchief, hoping that she would open her eyes. She did not move. He lifted one of her hands—a slim, cold little hand—and began to chafe it. His own feelings of misery and depression had evaporated. He was very much alive now, and concerned only with the condition of this woman. For all he knew, she might be seriously hurt. He must get her to shelter as soon as possible.

He stooped and, like a fireman, lifted the girl over his shoulder. She was not heavy.

She was small and built on fragile lines. He wondered what the devil she had been doing driving alone through such desolate country at this time of night.

Reaching his saloon, he opened the back door, and placed the girl on the seat, with a folded rug for a pillow beneath her head. He switched on the roof light. Now he could see clearly the victim of the bridge disaster. Why, she was absurdly young—she could not be more than twenty or so. And lovely—yes, even in her bedraggled condition—hatless, lovely, fair silky hair, a tangled mass. Long black lashes spread like little fans on the pale cheeks. The oval nails on the slender fingers were pink and polished. She was rather shabbily dressed but her tweed suit was good. Guy Denver knew good tailoring when he saw it. She wore a leather motoring-coat over her tweeds and a green cashmere scarf. Bending over her, Guy loosened the scarf and patted her cheeks, wishing that she would recover consciousness. What in heaven's name was he to do with her? This was a nice end to his day. The day on which he had walked out on all women—hoping he had finished with them— loathing the very thought of the sex, since the one woman had destroyed all his faith.

Well, the best thing he could do was to turn the car back and go back along the road whence he had come. He was forced to do so now since the bridge leading to Lyme Purgis had broken down.

The rain went on pelting—pelting. A piercing cold wind shivered through Guy despite his thick coat. He drew on his fur-lined gauntlets and climbed into the driver's seat. The sooner he got this poor girl to an hotel, the better.

With difficulty, he turned the long car, then hot and tired began to drive quickly through the night. Now and again he looked over his shoulder at the silent passenger on the back seat. She made no movement.

'Concussion,' Guy Denver muttered to himself.

He reached the signpost which had sent him in the direction of Lyme Purgis. Now, which road should he take? Coming along for the last ten or fifteen miles, he had seen neither farms nor houses. He had better take that right turn. It must lead him to some sign of civilisation. What a fool he had been to drive right into the Fen country with which he was so unfamiliar, and in total darkness.

The next thing that would happen, he thought grimly, was that he would run out of petrol. The indicator on the dashboard showed that he was getting low.

Twice he got out of the car and stared around him. His heart began to sink and a real dismay shook him. God, what country! It was the lowest-lying marshland on either side. And there was water everywhere. The whole damn

7

country seemed to be under water. He had heard that there were floods in the Fen district at this time of year. Well, it was a nice thing to find himself in the flooded part of the Fen country with an unconscious girl on his hands.

With a sensation of helplessness, Guy drove on. Then at last he saw a welcome light glimmering in the distance. He drove toward the light. It seemed to come from a dwelling down a narrow turning which was little more than farm lane, fringed with trees. Perhaps it was a labourer's cottage. Well, no matter. He could not go on any further in the hopes of finding a pub. He might lose his way altogether and for all he knew that girl in the back might be seriously ill.

The big wheels of his car squelched and slithered a bit as he turned down the lane. The road was well under water here. Now and again his back wheels went round with a hissing noise, and he accelerated in vain. But he managed to reach the dwelling whence came that welcome beacon of light.

Jumping out of the car, Guy wiped his eyes with his handkerchief, went up to the door and knocked on it. It was a small grey-stone house—solidly built and of quite good type. Not, he imagined, a labourer's dwelling. There was a well-kept little garden surrounding it and some trees at the back.

No answer to his knocking. He knocked again. Then impatiently pushed the door open.

He found himself in a small lounge-hall which was deserted. Striding through it, he pushed open another door. Darkness here. He felt for an electric switch, then laughed at himself. No electricity here. That single light had come from an oil-lamp burning in the hall. He was certainly a long way from civilised London.

Raising his voice, he called out:

'Hi! anyone here?'

No answer. Only an uncanny silence. And now Guy Denver stared around him, puzzled, wondering if there was anybody in the place at all. He picked up the lamp from the hall and began to walk through the house. To his surprise he found it completely deserted. Whoever had been here, had apparently left in a hurry. In the living-room on an oak trestle table, there was a half-finished supper; some eggs, now cold and stuck to the dish. Bread, butter, ham and a big pot of coffee. The coffee was stone-cold which meant that the person or persons about to eat, must have left here sometime ago.

A coal-fire had obviously been burning, but had now gone out, so that the little house was intensely cold. The furniture was good old-fashioned stuff and there was every sign of comfort. No, it was no farm-labourer's house. But it was very small—two rooms and a kitchen.

Guy Denver passed a hand across his forehead and blinked his eyes.

9

He wondered if he was in a nightmare. The whole thing was curiously unreal—even eerie. This unoccupied, deserted house . . . the stormy night . . . the shattered bridge . . . and that unconscious girl in his car.

Certainly fate had chosen a strange way of helping him to forget his own troubles. Everything that had happened in London receded into the background. He could think of nothing but his present predicament.

There was only one thing to do. He must carry his unknown passenger into this house and shelter here for the night.

It was long past eight o'clock. Four hours since he had taken that turning for Lyme Purgis. Four exhausting hours of battling with the darkness and rain and this sinister countryside.

Guy carried the girl into the house and shut the door behind him. In the living-room there was a sofa. He laid the girl on the cushions, then hunted for alcohol. If he could only find some brandy for her! He needed a drink for himself, too. Rummaging through cupboards in the kitchen, he was disappointed to find nothing but beer. That was all right for him, but not for his companion.

He went back to the sitting-room, took off his coat and knelt down by the sofa. He began to make a more extensive examination of the girl. He had careful sensitive hands. And soon they discovered the wound on her head. A nasty jagged cut across the scalp on which the blood had congealed, matting the fair silky hair. Guy Denver nodded to himself.

'That's it! Concussion, and as near thing as I have ever seen. It's a wonder she was not killed.'

She was very pretty. What a perfect mouth! Faintly rouged, piteously open, showing small white teeth. A firm white chin with a cleft in it.

Guy Denver said to himself:

'I must do something about that cut on her head. If it isn't attended to, it may mark her for life and that would be a pity for one so young and beautiful.'

He took the oil-lamp and walked up the narrow staircase to investigate still further. He found one large bedroom with a big old-fashioned double-bed in it spread with a white counterpane. On a high mahogany chest-of-drawers there was another lamp, which he lit. In the grate a fire was laid. Kneeling down, he applied a match to the paper and soon the dry wood was crackling. He must have warmth for that girl. He hoped he would find a hot-water bottle, too. She must have heat in her state of shock.

He would get her up here and wrap her in blankets. Then he would go downstairs, make up the kitchen-range which was still smouldering and get some boiling water. He must do what he could to that wound on her head.

CHAPTER TWO

Celia Hammond opened her eyes.

For a moment she thought that she was in her bed, at home, in Lincoln. And she had been having a nightmare—she had suffered from them since daddy died. But there was always old Mary, who had been her nurse and afterwards cook, to call for. Mary who would come in, soothe her, pat her hand and say: 'Now Miss Celia, deary, it's all right. You try to sleep again and I'll sit by you 'till you're off.'

Celia's eyelashes fluttered.

'Mary!' she called.

But it did not seem to her that she called very loudly. Her voice was only a whisper. Strange! And now she saw that she was not in her own bedroom at all. How very queer and frightening. She was in a strange room with a sloping ceiling, white-washed walls on which there were some unfamiliar pictures. Unfamiliar china ornaments on the mantelpiece, over which hung a big text:

The Lord Is My Shepherd.'

Celia, coming to consciousness more fully every second, felt her heart beat quickly. In heaven's name where was she? She moved her head and a queer pain made her call out. She lifted her hands and found her hair concealed by strips of linen, forming a bandage like a cap.

12

Suddenly she saw a man come into the room. A slimly-built man in a woollen dressing-gown. He came quickly to the bedside and said:

'Ah! so you're round at last.'

Celia stared up into his eyes, dazedly.

'Where—am I?'

'That, I can't tell you,' he said with a short laugh, 'for I've no idea myself. I'm about as lost as you are. But I can tell you *how* you came here. Do you yourself remember anything?'

Celia thought hard. She could remember leaving the house in Lincoln, yes. Setting out in the little Morris which she was going to sell in London. She had driven all day, then lost herself in the Fen country. She had approached the bridge and after that . . . no remembrance.

'I must have had an accident,' she said.

'You did,' said Guy Denver, and gave her a brief explanation of what had happened and of how he had pulled her out of the car and brought her here.

'So you see,' he finished, 'we're quite alone in this house. And it is quite deserted. I can't tell you in the least who the place belongs to. But no doubt the owners will return to it tomorrow, and if you're fit enough, I'll try to get you to some hospital.'

'Oh!' whispered Celia, weakly, and suddenly became conscious that she was wearing

13

masculine pyjamas much too large for her. How did she get into them? This man must have undressed her . . . who was he? But how frightful . . .! The hot colour tore over her throat and face.

'Did you . . .?'

She broke off, embarrassed beyond words. Guy Denver stopped looking grim and for the first time smiled. He patted her hand.

'That's all right,' he said, 'don't think anything about it. I had to put you to bed. You were in a state of shock, and you needed warmth and looking after. I had to see to your head, too. You see I'm a doctor of sorts—women mean nothing to me.'

And to himself he added:

'Nothing . . . after what Frances did to me—and they'll mean nothing to me, ever again!'

Celia Hammond lay motionless, staring at the man. It was an extraordinary thing to find herself alone in a deserted house with a stranger. And not a little frightening. Except that it made it better to know that he was a doctor. He seemed to have done a lot for her. He was telling her that he had made quite a neat job of her wound, in spite of the fact that his instruments were limited. It was lucky, he told her, that he had left a case in his car. But he felt that she ought to see another surgeon quickly, just to make sure that he had done his work well. With any luck, they would drive off tomorrow.

14

She watched him while he was speaking. With a pipe between his teeth, he stood by the fire at the foot of the bed. Celia, like any other girl, appreciated good looks, and this Dr Denver, as he called himself, was definitely handsome . . . in a rugged way. Crisp, brown hair, springing vitally from an intelligent forehead, narrow grey eyes and firm lips and chin. A man with virility in his face, eyes that one could trust.

Celia swallowed hard. She *must* be able to trust him, or it would be too ghastly . . . at his mercy, here, with her head-wound, her helplessness.

Now he was questioning her. She told him about herself. How, until a month ago, she had been living quite happily near Lincoln in an old manor-house with her father for whom she had kept house since her mother had died. Humphrey Hammond was a retired solicitor. He had given Celia a first-class education but no training for any specific job. He meant well, but when he had died, suddenly of heart-failure, Celia had been faced with disaster. His investments had gone wrong. He had left nothing behind him but debts. She had had to sell up everything, except the little Morris and her personal belongings. She had no relatives to help her and was not going to beg from her friends in Lincoln. So she had decided to go to London and find a job. She had thought she might get a better price

15

in town than in Lincolnshire for her car. She had contemplated spending the money on a secretarial training.

'And now,' said Celia, 'the car's gone, wrecked! And it wasn't insured, except for Third-party Risk. I couldn't afford to take out another insurance when daddy died. So I've nothing. Oh, I wish I had *died*—drowned in that river!'

Guy Denver moved back to the side of the bed. He could not bear that note of anguish in her voice. She was such a child—only twelve years younger than himself—but he felt that she was a mere baby. He took her hand and pressed it between his own.

'You mustn't feel like that, or think that way. You've had bad luck but there's always something round the corner. There's never any need to despair.'

Big tears dripped down Celia's cheeks. She found herself clinging to the doctor's kindly hand, feeling more lost, more lonely than she had ever felt in her life before.

And he was thinking :

'Who am I to preach to this girl when I, myself, wished yesterday that I was dead?'

Fate had played a queer trick throwing Celia Hammond across his path in this fashion. They had each set out on their separate journeys with little hope for the future. And now they were together, like two exiles flung up on a desert island. He had told himself that he

16

would never again make a soft-hearted fool of himself over a woman. Yet he could not bear to see this girl lying here, crying. And she had such perfectly lovely eyes. In the light of the oil-lamp beside her bed, they shone through the tears like golden stars. Now that she was conscious he was more than ever struck by her beauty. That yellow hair and the golden-brown eyes were a remarkable combination.

He wondered how to comfort her. Gruffly he said: 'I'm going to have another look round.'

With the lamp in his hand, he tramped round the small house. And now he made a discovery which was useful. A radio in the living-room. He turned it on. It emitted various squeaks and groans, then gradually he tuned-in to London Regional. Having done so, the light at last dawned upon Guy Denver as to the present situation. For a bulletin was being broadcast. A bulletin given, regularly at intervals in connection with 'the flooding now taking place in the Fen district.'

The announcer's grave voice said :

'All the occupants of houses in Lyme Purgis district and for twenty miles around have been evacuated. Meanwhile the flooding is slowly extending to outlying districts. It is expected to reach its peak at 12.30 tonight. The experts say that it will last for at least three days but much depends on the tides which may keep the flood from subsiding. Meantime, prompt measures

17

are being taken to deal with the situation at Wolden Creek, so that further flooding can be prevented.'

Guy Denver switched off the radio. This was pretty serious. At last he could understand why this little house had such a 'lived-in' appearance. The occupants must have received a sudden warning to evacuate it because of the floods. It was situated somewhere between Lyme Purgis and Wolden Creek.

God, what a position, thought Guy Denver. The rain was still lashing against the window panes. And the experts said that the flood would reach its peak tonight. Little doubt tomorrow the roads would be impassable. He would possibly find his car immersed up to the wheels. And he might be marooned here with this girl for three days.

If he had only known a bit about the Fen district before he ever came this way! But he had known nothing, and cared less.

He went upstairs to the bedroom where Celia Hammond was lying. Poor child, victim of fate like himself. She must be scared, poor pretty thing. He would do everything to put her at ease.

Gently, but truthfully, he told her the situation.

'I must warn you that you may be boxed up here with me until the flood subsides,' he finished, 'but you have nothing to fear so far as I'm concerned. I hope you realise that.'

Celia, her heart knocking a little, looked at him. Instinctively she knew that he was to be trusted. Yet it made the situation no less a delicate one. She said:

'Well—we must just make the best of it.'

He had to admire her for that. She was plucky. With that head-wound and fear of the floods, she might easily have become hysterical.

But Celia's mind did not work that way. She was not an hysterical person. She was a thoughtful and reasonable being and used to looking after her father. It struck her suddenly that Guy Denver looked desperately tired. She wondered if he had eaten anything and asked him about it.

'No,' he said shortly, 'I've been busy attending to you, young woman.'

'You've been grand,' said Celia, 'but how about a meal?'

'What do you want?'

'Tea,' said Celia.

'Very feminine,' said Guy, with that charming smile which wooed his face from sternness and made him look a boy.

'Well, I can find tea—and gallons of water, heaven knows! I'll go and scrounge around.'

After he had gone, Celia lay still, watching the leaping firelight and thinking how good Guy Denver had been to her. To have done all this . . . waited on her hand and foot. He must be a fine person. What was his story? Why did

19

he talk so bitterly? Was he married or single? She knew nothing about him. She wanted to know more.

Downstairs, Guy switched on the radio again. The bulletins went on. The floods were continuing to rise. Guy looked out of the kitchen window while he waited for the kettle to boil. Throwing the beam of a torch on to the ground, he was horrified to see that the water was surging round the little house as though a dam had burst and a river was pouring over the ground. Good God! this was flooding in earnest. There would be no hope at all of driving away in the morning. And if the water continued to rise as rapidly as this, it would soon begin to come in through the cracks, and flood the bottom part of the house.

The grim stark truth hit Guy Denver hardly. That injured girl lying upstairs must be protected. And if it was true that the flooding might go on rising until half-past twelve tonight, the sooner he took everything that was wanted upstairs to safety, the better. There were two more hours to go before midnight.

Ah! already there were signs of water on the kitchen floor and a large pool widening in the hall, coming under the door. It was Guy Denver's first experience of a bad flood and it was not a pleasant one. For himself it did not matter, but that girl . . . well, something must be done, and quickly.

He took tea and bread-and-butter up

to Celia, found some cheese and a bottle of beer for himself, then began to carry up what he considered necessary. Celia heard him tramping up and down the narrow little staircase a dozen times or more. He explained what he was doing and why. It made her pulses leap with fear, but she pretended not to be afraid. She kept talking to him, trying to cheer him on and he talked back to her, grateful for her camaraderie.

'Getting up as much coal as I can,' he called out, 'three buckets already. Must keep that fire of yours going and we may have to cook on it. Bringing up all the groceries, too. We'll soon run out of bread, but we've got some biscuits. Thank the Lord these people have left a full larder behind. Yes . . . I'm afraid the water is coming in now, rapidly! Pretty grim . . . the appalling rapidity of it. I expect my car's well under.'

Then he was finished with the work and back in her room; hot; hair clinging damply to his forehead, pipe between his teeth. He had put everything on the landing outside the bedroom. If it became flooded downstairs, and the radio announcer was right, then they would have to live up here for three days until the water subsided.

He had hoped to bring up the wireless but the batteries on the floor were under water and it wouldn't work any more. He had got his suitcase out of the car. He apologised to Celia

21

for having to come into her room, and it was the only one! This house obviously belonged to a married couple who lived in these two rooms—this bedroom and the one below. He would try not to inconvenience her, he said. He would curl up on the floor with a pillow and a blanket.

Celia lay listening, watching, wondering if she was in some kind of strange dream. It was going to be pretty embarrassing if the pair of them—strangers—had to share this room for the next three days and nights. He met her gaze. He knew what she was thinking. He was thinking it, too. A slow flush crept up under his skin. He was a doctor and a man disappointed in women, but he was only human. And Celia was the loveliest girl he had ever seen. The whole thing was going to be a bit of a strain. Not that he was unable to cope with it. But it would not make his jangled nerves any better.

He continued to do his utmost to put Celia at ease. After making her comfortable for the night, he stoked up the fire, wrapped himself in blankets and an eiderdown, and lay down on the floor.

Celia looked down at him anxiously.

'I feel so mean—occupying this big bed. Oh, will you be very uncomfortable?'

He smiled up at her.

'I'll be fine. Just blow out the lamp and go to sleep, my dear.'

She obeyed him. The room was plunged

22

into darkness except for the glow of the fire. For a moment she lay breathless, heart fluttering, listening to the howl of the wind and the force of the rain which lashed the windowpanes. And on the floor beside her lay a man, breathing deeply, sleeping. A man she had never seen in her life until a few hours ago.

Celia shut her eyes, Then she, too, fell asleep.

CHAPTER THREE

It seemed the most curious thing in the world to Celia Hammond to open her eyes that next morning and see a man wearing a dressing-gown, standing opposite the mirror, shaving. For a few moments she lay watching him, her heart beating strangely. A man shaving in *her* room . . . as though he were her husband . . . quite casually! There he was, dipping his razor into a bowl of water, scraping the creamy lather off his chin. She could see his reflected face in the glass screwed up a little while he shaved. His brown tousled hair stood up on his head like a schoolboy's. How young he looked! Yet not young, for there were deep lines carved upon that thin face. It was the face of a man who had suffered.

Suddenly Guy Denver turned and saw that Celia was awake. He said:

'Good morning!'

Quite casually . . . even cheerfully, and then resumed his shaving. He put her entirely at her ease. As she moved, a pain shot through her head and she put out her two hands with a little cry. Immediately Guy Denver swung round.

'What is it?'

Her golden eyes smiled at him a trifle ruefully.

'I expect it's the cut on my head.'

He came to the bottom of the bed and looked down at her.

'It's sure to hurt a bit. Feels stiff, eh? Well, don't move too much. Keep still. I'm not going to take the bandage off until tonight.'

Celia said:

'I must have slept very soundly. But you . . . were you terribly uncomfortable?'

'No. I slept like a log until 6 a.m. Then I got up and had a look downstairs. It may interest you to know that it's still raining, and that the water is still rising, and that the rooms downstairs are right under. I couldn't get more than half-way down the staircase. It's an amazing sight.'

Celia caught her breath. Anxiously she looked out of the window. How grey and lowering the sky appeared! And that awful rain still spattering at the panes! It was hard to believe that the lower part of this little house was submerged in water. Frightening!

24

Guy read what lay in her mind.

'Don't worry. It won't get up as far as here. According to the radio, the water is due to subside tomorrow and then we'll be rescued, and there's no fear of the place collapsing. The foundations are too good. It's one of these solid little houses —granite!'

'And your car?'

Guy moved to the window and looked down at the flooded garden. He gave a short laugh.

'My car is what might be called "up to its neck". I shouldn't think it will ever start again. You've no idea what the countryside looks like. We're marooned in a sort of lake. It's astounding.'

He slid off the dressing-gown, put on his coat and added:

'Sorry I've got to perform my ablutions in this room, but it's the only one. We've just got to get used to the fact that we're here together for a day or two more.'

Celia coloured and bit her lip.

'Oh, that's all right.'

Guy thought as he had thought last night:

'She's plucky . . . I must say I admire—the spirit of the little thing.

Aloud he said:

'I'm going to make you some tea. I've got a Primus stove outside the door.'

'You've thought of everything,' said Celia.

Said Guy:

'Quite taking me back to the boy-scout days

25

when one had to forage round for this and that.'

He walked out of the room. She heard him pumping the Primus. It seemed to her that this young surgeon must surely be one of the nicest persons in the world.

Later he came back with some tea and buttered biscuits. He sat by her bed and they ate their breakfast as though they were old friends. And now it was inevitable that Guy should talk to this girl about himself. He wanted to. For nearly forty-eight hours he had been fighting a battle against himself, bitter, repressed, antagonistic toward women in general. But to this brave child whom he had rescued last night, he could speak. His story came tumbling out and Celia listened to it, her grave lovely eyes fixed upon him.

It was as she had imagined. Something had hit Guy Denver pretty hard. His wife! The woman he had loved and in whom he had trusted. He described her. Frances was unusually attractive; a brunette with rich warm colouring, dark, black-lashed eyes and smooth dark hair. Hers was the darkness of the South, inherited from a Spanish grandmother. He had been wildly in love with her when they married, but he supposed now that she had only been in love with the idea that he was a rising young surgeon. She must have invested him with a certain romanticism because, before they became engaged, he had operated

26

on her for acute appendix and saved her life.

They had only been happy for six months, then gradually she had grown bored—and she had not failed to show it. She had been reared in a rich home, used to a gay society life. To have a husband who was at the beck and call of everybody, and a slave to the hospital, had soon become an anathema to her. The inevitable had happened. At the end of a year she met a man who fell in love with her and then . . .

It almost hurt Celia to see the look in Guy's eyes when he talked of that hour when he had discovered that Frances had run away from him. He had come home from his rounds, he said, and found a letter telling him that Frances had left him for Paul de Poiret, a French novelist of some considerable repute. A man whom Guy knew, vaguely, and whom, he told Celia, he imagined was the sort of brilliant amusing companion whom Frances desired.

So crushed had he been by her lack of thought for him, her breaking of all their mutual vows, he had felt he could not stay in his house. He cancelled all his appointments. Told his secretary to tell everybody in the medical world that he was ill. Then he had driven away from London.

'And found you . . . and this . . .' Guy finished, with a laugh which had little mirth to it.

Celia sighed.

'Well, I thought 'I was pretty miserable when I drove in this direction,' she said, 'But it's nothing to what you must feel. I'm so *terribly* sorry.'

Guy put his pipe in his mouth.

'Don't pity me, for God's sake.'

The pain in his voice stirred her to a yet deeper pity, but she said nothing, realising that sympathy was abhorrent to him He began to pace up and down the room, smoking his pipe. Restless, moody. She watched him, wondering how best she could help to ease the torment in his mind. She began to talk about his work:

'Won't that be an anodyne to you?' she asked him, 'it's wonderful work—operating— the most marvellous in the world.'

Guy Denver shook his head.

'Is it worth it? Wearing myself out for other people and nobody to work for now that Frances has left me. With all this beastly thought of divorce facing me. God! I don't feel I want to go back. I'd rather stay here.'

A tiny smile lurked at the corner of Celia's mouth.

'You won't feel like that when you run out of tobacco, and you can't light that cherished pipe of yours.'

Some of the deep depression which had been weighing upon Guy's soul, while he spoke of his wife, lifted. There was something so simple and charming about Celia.

28

'You're right,' he said, 'and I haven't much of the tobacco left. I must go slow with it . . .' he pocketed the pipe, 'and I never even asked you if you minded the smoke in here. Very inconsiderate of me.'

'I don't mind it at all,' said Celia.

Indeed, she rather liked it. There was something thrilling and attractive about seeing Guy Denver in her room, smoking his pipe. He was such a grand person! How in heaven's name could that woman have left him? Surely he was worth waiting for—until the end of a day's work? What an utterly selfish and heartless person Frances Denver must have been. It was so criminal to destroy the faith of a man like this one . . . to strike at him a blow that could bring him to the pitch of feeling that even his beloved work was not worth continuing.

Said Celia suddenly:

'You've got to go back to your job. And *of course* you will. It would be awful to think of you doing otherwise. All your patients must miss you terribly.'

Guy, hands in his pockets, gave her a faint smile. She was rather a darling, he thought, lying there looking so pretty and nun-like in her white cap-bandage, solemnly lecturing him. He said:

'Perhaps you're right. We'll have to see.'

And then he got off the subject of himself and began to be domesticated and busy. There

29

was the breakfast to clear away and the room to tidy. Celia, hating her inactivity, was forced to lie on her pillows and watch him. It seemed all wrong that he should be doing these things. But he would not let her move. Perhaps tomorrow, he said, she might get up for a bit. Today she was to keep that head of hers quite still.

So the strange day went on. It might have been slow and boring. Yet it was not so. They found much to talk about to each other. And then there was the lunch to get. Guy excelled himself, opening tins of this and that, which he thought might tempt his patient. He looked after her so well that she was not conscious of any discomfort. At awkward moments he did not allow her to feel embarrassed. He brought her warm water for washing in. He was tact and delicacy itself. He reminded her continually that he was a surgeon and used to this kind of thing. And by the end of that day Celia knew not the slightest feeling of difficulty or fear with this man who was fated to lead such an intimate life with her.

The flood went on pouring across the Fens, remorselessly. The water rose in the little house . . . up . . . up . . . until the staircase was submerged and now it was impossible for Guy to get downstairs at all.

When evening came, Guy felt a very real anxiety about the position. But he did not betray it to Celia. They grew very used to each other. They felt that they had known each other many years when yet another day came to an end.

That night after supper, they talked of other things than themselves. Guy had always been a good conversationalist and Celia proved herself a ready listener. He found also, that she had ideas of her own . . . sensible views about love and marriage. She had never been in love, she told him. Never wanted to fool around with men because she was so sure the day would come when she would meet the absolutely right person for her. And for that reason she wished to wait . . . to keep herself. Guy recognised the fact that in the nature of this girl was a deep sense of loyalty, as well as courage. *She* would never let a man down once she loved!

She refused to allow him to say that his own faith was totally destroyed. A human being must never entirely lose faith, she declared. No matter how hurt he was, he must not look *into* his personal grief, but outside it, remembering all that he could do for others. By keeping his trust with the medical world and the patients who believed in him, he would regain his self-confidence, she said, even though he no longer cared to place his faith in any individual woman.

Guy listened to her, marvelling at her wisdom and sagacity. She was such a child and yet such a woman. She had read a lot, thought

31

a lot. He marvelled at her.

What had life got to offer *her?* Nothing much. She was alone and without prospects. Yet she had lost faith neither with the world nor with herself. He began to feel that he must take a leaf out of her book.

Later, by the light of the oil-lamp, beside, he dressed the wound on her head. He was bound to hurt her a little, even though his practised fingers were sensitive and gentle. He saw her bite her lips and the colour leave her cheeks. But she did not murmur. He said:

'You're the bravest child!'

That brought the pink surging back into her cheeks again. She realised, suddenly, that his admiration was immensely satisfying to her and that the pain did not matter any more.

That night, when, once again they had to share the communal room, and Guy slept on the mattress beside the big bed, Celia lay awake for a long time with many queer exciting thoughts chasing through her brain.

It was no longer a stranger who lay there quite close to her, breathing quietly in the darkness. It was a friend. Someone she knew very well. Someone whom life and a woman had hurt and whom she, Celia Hammond, had talked to and comforted a little. It brought him curiously close to her. And she no longer felt lonely as she had felt yesterday when she drove away from her old home. There was Guy Denver in the world . . . her friend. She had a warm crazy little feeling of gladness that this thing had happened . . . that she was exiled with him here in this flood, and that tomorrow she would wake up and find him still here with her.

Came yet another dawn . . .

The flood swept on its relentless course. The water rose so high that Guy Denver had a few anxious moments wondering whether it would come into the room in which he and Celia were living their isolated life. But it did not do so. And on the third day the water began to subside. The rain ceased. The sun came out. Guy stood, that afternoon, at the open window, letting in the fresh brisk air, knowing that there was nothing more to fear.

'This is rather like Noah must have felt in the Ark when the flood ceased,' he said, turning to Celia with a laugh.

'It's certainly good to think it's all over,' said Celia.

She was up now, dressed in the tweeds which he had dried for her, on that first night of the rescue. She was stronger, able to walk about and do her share of the domestic work. It was she who made *his* tea and prepared the meals. She would no longer allow him to be 'cook and bottle-washer'!

Later that day, Guy took off her bandages, put on a small dressing, and assured her that the cut was going to heal very nicely. She had nothing to worry about.

'It'll be nice to be able to do my hair again,' said Celia.

He watched her slip a comb carefully through the soft hair, then roll it into shining curls with her slender fingers. And suddenly he said:

'What a very lovely person you are, Celia. Has anybody ever told you that?'

It was the first time he had paid her that sort of compliment. The personal note in his voice had a strange effect upon her. She felt her whole body grow warm, her heart leap in her breast. She made a joking reply, but to herself she thought:

'What's happening to me? My God, I mustn't allow myself to fall in love with this man. After his experience with his wife, it would never do.'

And Guy Denver was thinking:

'One day, some fellow will love this girl very much . . .'

And almost immediately that idea was followed by a bitter reaction. No woman was worth loving . . . not even Celia Hammond. Once Frances had been soft and sweet, and he had *believed* in her. He would never allow himself to *think* of another woman from now onward.

He was a bit curt with Celia that night. She noticed it but said nothing. Neither did she let him know that there was a sinking feeling in her heart when she contemplated the fact that soon their communal life in the flooded house must end. Yes, it would all be over and Guy would go back to his work. She would go her way and perhaps never see him again. Well, perhaps it was all for the best. For she knew herself; and she realised that she was as near to falling in love as she had ever been before. In love with Guy Denver who could never be more to her than a memory. The central figure in the strangest episode of her life.

CHAPTER FOUR

For two more days, Guy and Celia stayed together in that little stone house. For two days the floods went on subsiding, and the water seeped away until finally they were able to leave the room which had been their home for four days and four nights, and go downstairs to the ruined rooms below.

Came the moments when the owners of the little house returned to it. A young farmer and his wife, pathetically anxious to see what havoc had been wrought in the little dwelling from which they had escaped.

They were astounded to find that there had been occupants there during the flood. A little perturbed to find that all their supplies of food were gone. But not for long. Guy had a way with him which soon put the young couple at their ease, and when they realised that he was a well-to-do London surgeon, and saw the cheque he wrote for them, they were soon smiling.

The farmer's wife said to Celia:

'You poor dear . . . you and your husband must have had a shocking time.'

Celia met Guy's gaze. Her throat felt dry. She laughed, conscious that her face was burning to the roots of her hair.

'We aren't married,' she said abruptly.

The owner of the house froze a little.

'Oh!' she said.

Guy felt unduly annoyed. Drat the woman for looking at Celia like that. At the same time he began to wonder what the rest of the world might think when it became known that he and this pretty girl had been marooned here for nearly five days and nights.

For the next hour, he was very busy making arrangements with the farmer. His saloon must be towed to a garage; Celia's poor little run-about must be dragged off the ruined bridge, and, as soon as possible, arrangements must be made to take them to the nearest town.

'It had better be London for both of us,' Guy told Celia.

She nodded.

'Yes.'

'You meant to go there in the first place, didn't you?'

'Yes.'

Her voice was low and her face averted. He saw that she was distressed and worried. He felt a sudden warm desire to protect her. She was his protégée whom he had saved from an accident and from the flood. She had nobody in the world and he was not going to let her feel destitute. He took her arm and said:

'You're not to look like that, my dear. I've got a plan for you.'

The friendly protection of that arm did much to raise Celia's drooping spirits. He was smiling down at her. How utterly charming he was when he smiled. *Too* charming for her peace of mind. She was fast beginning to recognise that fact even though she kept her feelings encased in steel armour.

'What plan?' she asked him.

He told her. He would need a secretary when he got home, because Miss Bryant, his present one, was leaving. Why shouldn't she, Celia, take up the job?

'But I'm not trained!' she said, her heart leaping at the prospect of remaining with him.

'Then I'll get a temporary secretary and have you trained,' said Guy, cheerfully. 'I'll find you somewhere to live, and you shall take a course of shorthand and typewriting. I shall hold the job open for you. That'll give you something to work for, won't it?'

Celia looked up at him with eyes starry bright.

'It sounds too good to be true.'

37

'We'll make it true.'

'Then you *are* going to go back to your work after all?'

'Yes,' said Guy, 'I am going to go back to my work.'

He knew as he said those words that he owed his new-found desire to re-create himself and carry on with his job, to this fair-haired girl with the brave brown eyes who was the most gallant person he had ever known.

It was impossible for them to get to the station for yet another twenty-four hours, the main road being impassable, but the next morning the farmer came back for Guy and Celia in his car and took them to the nearest town.

Sitting in the train with Celia, going down to London, leaving the Fen country behind them, Guy Denver felt very different from the stricken, hopeless man who had driven away from his home. It was as though those few days with Celia Hammond had been an oasis in the desert. A quiet interlude during which courage had renewed itself, and peace had returned to him. He felt fit now to cope with life. Even to get through the unpleasantness of the divorce. And the thought of Frances was no longer a crushing pain. It was as though she were dead to him. His love had died, too, with his faith in her. She no longer counted. It was only his work that counted. And Celia Hammond had given him back to that work.

38

A shock awaited them both when they saw the newspapers. The farmer had not been long in broadcasting the news and the reporters had made the best of the story. There were headlines:

'FAMOUS HARLEY STREET SURGEON AND GIRL MAROONED IN HOUSE IN FLOOD DISTRICT.'

There were photographs of Guy. Photographs of Frances, although the papers did not mention much about the surgeon's wife. They embroidered richly the *'romantic story of Mr Denver's five days and nights in the flooded house with a beautiful girl whom he had rescued from the river.'*

Celia thrust aside the papers and looked anxiously at Guy.

'Isn't it rather a pity that it's been broadcast like this? It doesn't matter about me. But you . . .'

'These reporters want murdering,' said Guy savagely, 'they just love to get hold of a thing like this and make the most of it. I don't mind for myself, I assure you.'

But Celia knew that he did. A surgeon has a reputation and an important one. And in a moment when he was going to petition for a divorce against his wife, it was very urgent that there should be no slur on his name—no scandal attached to him.

Celia Hammond realised during that

39

journey to London, exactly how important anything concerning Guy Denver had become to her. She realised, too, that to serve him now would be her idea of complete happiness. She was hot with indignation about those newspaper reports. Nothing definite . . . just subtle allusions . . 'handsome surgeon and pretty girl, marooned.' She knew what the world might think. How wrong the world was! If they but knew the respect with which Guy had treated her. If they but knew how far romance was from his mind.

When they reached London, Celia said:

'Don't you think I'd better say good-bye to you? Do you think it will do for me to come to your place now?'

'I'm going to give you a job,' said Guy stubbornly, 'and first of all I'm going to settle you somewhere while you're being trained. And before anything else, you're going to come along to my house and have a really decent meal which you need after all that tinned-stuff we've been living on. I'll put you into the hands of my housekeeper, Mrs Mortimer. She used to be an old nurse of mine. She'll look after you. You need looking after, you know. That cut on your head hasn't healed yet, my dear.'

Celia had no volition of her own, in that moment. She was just perfectly happy when Guy Denver put her in a taxi and drove with her to Harley Street. He meant everything in the world to her now. She knew it. And she *wanted to* be in his keeping.

She was afraid that she looked a wreck. Her tweed-suit wanted pressing. Her hat was out of shape. She could do with a shampoo and set. She was certain that Guy must be used to very smart, well-dressed women. His wife was chic and beautiful. Celia had seen that, from the photograph of Frances in this morning's paper. (Strange, but she hated violently, actively, the thought of Guy's wife . . . she would hate *any* woman who had hurt him . . .)

Guy felt like a man waking from a dream when he put his latchkey into the lock of his front-door and opened it. How queer to be back . . . and here by his side was a girl who must forever call for his admiration and his friendship, after their recent experience together.

He walked with Celia into the hall. She was enveloped at once by a sense of warmth and luxury. This was a beautiful house full of beautiful, expensive things—the home of a prosperous surgeon. The home from which he had escaped because he had found it unbearable.

He called out:

'Mrs Mortimer . . . Mrs Mort-i-mer!'

The door opened. Into the hall came not a housekeeper, but a slim dark woman dressed in a rich mink coat and wearing a smart hat with a black spotted veil. Guy and Celia stared at her. Celia's heart gave a tremendous leap, then sank to its very lowest. For she knew at once who this woman was. She recognised her from the photograph. It was *Frances,* Guy's wife!

Guy looked at his wife as though at a complete stranger. In a slow icy voice he said:

'Why are you here?'

Frances Denver cast a quick, curious glance at the girl, then drew nearer her husband.

'I'm glad you're back, Guy. I've been worried about you.'

'Why are you here?' he repeated.

She said with a frown:

'Please don't speak to me like that, Guy. Come into the consulting-room. I've got a great deal to say to you.'

He stood his ground.

'I have nothing to say to you. You left my house with Paul de Poiret. Why aren't you with him?'

'Really, darling, you're so crude,' Frances said with a nervous little laugh, 'and we really can't discuss our personal affairs in front of a third person.'

Celia said:

'I think I'd better go, Dr Denver.'

'Not at all,' he said, harshly. 'I don't quite know what this is all about, but I'll be with you in a moment. Meanwhile, I'll get my housekeeper to give you some coffee.'

Celia looked at him in an agony of

embarrassment. He appeared oblivious of it, and of the frown directed upon him by Frances. The last thing he had expected was to find his wife in this house. One thing stood out in his mind . . . the sight of her renewed neither his love nor any vestige of pleasure. Rather the reverse. He almost disliked her. It was queer.

Mrs Mortimer came up from the basement and took Celia to the morning-room. Drawing off coat and gloves, Guy followed Frances into the consulting-room. There she raised her veil and smiled.

'That's better. Now we can talk. I suppose that's the girl with whom you were marooned? All very romantic, Guy. I read about it.'

'I want to know what you're doing here,' he said.

'Isn't it obvious,' she said. 'I've come back to you, Guy.'

He looked at her without emotion.

'In the circumstances, you can scarcely do that, can you?'

'Don't jump to conclusions. You see, I didn't go away with Paul. The very day I left this house, I realised my mistake and came back, after all. You rushed off in such a hurry, or you would have found that I was back the night you vanished. You have nothing whatsoever against me, except that I *wanted* to leave you. Paul has returned to Paris—and here I am.'

Silence. With a slightly dazed feeling, Guy Denver looked at his wife. Once the sight of her sitting there on the arm of a chair, looking at him from beneath those incredibly long black lashes, would have moved him. He had always been moved when Frances chose to be charming. He could smell her familiar perfume—rather heavy and overpowering. He could sense her wish to reinstate herself in his favour. What had gone wrong between her and her lover he did not know. Perhaps de Poiret had decided that he did not want her. The fact remained that she had returned to him, Guy. *And he did not want her.* That was the plain unvarnished truth. He no longer wanted her and the fact that she had *intended* to leave him and ruin his life was as much a crime in his eyes as if she had really gone.

'It's too late, Frances,' he said. 'There can be no question of you remaining with me. Everything between us is finished. *You* finished it. You finished it when you left that letter for me, asking for a divorce.'

Frances Denver stiffened. Her eyes darted angrily at him, rapier-bright. Then she gave a little laugh:

'So that's how the land lies, my dear Guy. You don't want me any more? Have you by any chance fallen in love with that girl with whom you have been spending the last few days . . . *and* nights? For if so, there may still be a divorce. Only this time the petition won't

44

be against me. Instead, it'll be against *you!*'

CHAPTER FIVE

Guy Denver stared at his wife. It took him a few seconds to gather what she meant. Then a slow, angry flush crept up under his skin. He said:

'You must be crazy. You have no possible evidence on which you could divorce me.'

Frances made a little *moué* with her lips and shrugged her shoulders. Unwrapping the mink coat, she rested her slender manicured hands on her waist. At twenty-five, she was at her best—her figure in that wine-coloured tailored suit, was perfect. And once the perfection of it had made Guy Denver's pulses thrill when he realised that all that rich beauty was *his.* Today it almost repelled him. He was beginning to see only the mean, calculating soul within her.

'My dear Guy,' she said, 'you cannot deny that you were shut up alone in a house for nearly five days with a young and pretty girl. At least, fairly pretty,' she added spitefully, 'a bit shabby. Not quite your style, Guy.'

His hands clenched. He, of all men, knew the value of restraint, but it was hard for him not to lose his temper now. It was clear, too, how greatly he disliked to hear Celia Hammond spoken of with malice.

'Don't let the question of "my style" come into this,' he said, grimly, 'and don't even imagine that you have any cause to suspect me of infidelity. You know perfectly well that I met Miss Hammond by chance and that we were forced to remain in that house because of the flood.'

Frances swung a shapely leg and admired the texture of the gossamer silk stocking, and the trimness of her ankle.

She murmured:

'Darling, *really!* How do I know anything of the sort? Lots of men have secret love affairs. How do I know that you and Miss Hammond are not, shall we put it, *old* friends?'

Guy Denver began to shake.

'Frances, don't drive me too far. You know damn well that that girl was a stranger to me until I rescued her from the river.'

Frances yawned.

'Sounds a good story and the papers made the best of it. But your names are linked and if I chose to be nasty . . .'

'If you chose to be nasty, you could make things very unpleasant both for me and for her, I admit,' broke in Guy, 'but I think you had better remember that it is *you* who walked out of this house last Monday—and left a note telling me that you were going to de Poiret. So I shall ask *you* to leave this house, and at once, my dear Frances.'

For an instant she kept silence. Behind her

46

casual mask, Frances Denver was anxious . . . anxious for herself. She had no intention of telling her husband what had really happened with Paul. It was too humiliating. Paul had been such a marvellous lover . . . so full of extravagant praise and passion for her. She counted on him. And for once her reason had forsaken her. She had been mad enough to leave that letter for Guy, and run to Paul's flat, fully believing that he would take her away. Not so! She had stayed in that flat with him in vain all the afternoon. There had been one 'scene' after another. Tears, reproaches, kisses, a wild emotional upheaval, ending in Paul telling her gently but firmly that although he found her charming, he had no intention of being made a co-respondent in a divorce case. Finally, he had driven her, sullenly defeated, back to her home, only to find that Guy had received her farewell-note—and had gone.

She had a few days and nights alone now in which to review the situation, and although still madly in love with Paul and infuriated by his cowardice, she had come to the conclusion that in throwing away Guy, she was throwing away something pretty good. After all, he had a big position and she did not have a bad time as his wife. The fact that she had fallen out of love with him and had grown bored was unpleasant, but things might be worse. Besides, her people would not be too pleased at her folly. No! She had decided that she must settle down with Guy again and wipe out the past.

It was something of a shock to discover that Guy felt so cold and hard about her. He had always been so much at her feet . . . she had fully anticipated that he would welcome her back with open arms.

Of course, there was this flood-business . . . and the girl who had come back to the house with him. What *was* there between those two? In all probability, nothing. She knew Guy and his high standards and principles. He seemed to like the girl, but he was chivalrous. Oh! yes, she knew him. Always out to protect the innocent and help the unfortunate.

Guy said:

'You told me you were going to de Poiret. Why did you come back?'

Her long lashes veiled the resentment in her eyes.

'Changed my mind. Decided I was a fool. I thought you'd be glad.'

His hands were trembling. He pulled his pipe from his pocket and began to search through the drawers of his desk for a tin of tobacco. It irritated Frances to see him do that. Guy and that darned pipe of his . . . it was like an anchor to him! It bored her to tears to see him smoking it, and yet . . . there was something quite attractive about Guy . . . especially this new, hard Guy, who was not so ready to give in to her. Frances liked things she

48

couldn't get.

Said Guy:

'When you walked out of the house and left that letter behind, you did something to me, Frances, that can never be undone. You killed something inside me.'

She slid off the arm of the chair and came close to him. 'Aren't you being rather dramatic? I acted in the madness of the moment. And if you still love me . . .'

'That's the point,' he broke in, 'I don't know that I do.'

She flushed scarlet, then bit her lip.

'Rather a sudden change!'

'Have you no understanding of what you did to me?' he demanded. 'Good God, I trusted you. I've got no more confidence in you. I gave you everything . . . everything in my power to give . . . and you treated my love so lightly, that you contemplated walking out on me with a Frenchman full of fine phrases and cheap emotions.'

Frances wanted to say something back, furiously, but she controlled herself.

'Well, I didn't go with him, and that's that. But you and that girl . . .'

'Be quiet about me and the girl,' said Guy, savagely. He stuck the pipe in his mouth and lit it, then took it out with an angry gesture and surveyed his wife. 'You know darn well that there was nothing between us. She was like a patient to me. I had to look after her and that's

49

the beginning and the end of it.'

Frances was pale now, conscious of very uncomfortable feelings. Part of her wept passionately still for Paul . . but she was thwarted . . . baulked . . . he had gone back to Paris, away from her. The other side of her, the sensible, far-seeing Frances . . . wanted to be reinstated in Guy's favour and start life with him again in this house. She was not at all anxious to fall between two stools. Whatever happened, she must use that girl. It was a stroke of luck for her that Guy should have been marooned with Celia Hammond in that flood.

Frances walked across the room and put a finger on the bell.

'What are you doing?' asked Guy.

'I'm going to ask Miss Hammond to join us.'

'What the devil for?'

'You'll see!'

'Look here,' began Guy, 'I won't have her dragged into our affairs . . .'

'I'm sorry,' interrupted Frances, coolly, 'but she is already *in* our affairs.'

For a moment Guy was nonplussed. He was a clever doctor but, like so many men, not much of a match for a designing woman's wit. For a moment he really did not know how to tackle this domesticated problem. But he did realise conclusively, that never while he lived, could he love Frances again. Indeed, he almost hated her in this hour. She was repellent to him. God, what right had she got to walk back to this house, take control of it, dictate to him and cast ugly aspersions against that poor child who had been marooned with him. It was iniquitous of Frances . . . vile!

Five minutes later, Celia was in the room. Celia refreshed by a cup of Mrs Mortimer's best coffee, hat in hand, revealing that pale gold head of hers, one side of which was marred by the dressing on the wound.

Celia looked questioningly and with some embarrassment at Guy. He looked back at her, conscious suddenly of all that she stood for. All that was good and honest and brave. And it was a strange thrill to remember their days and nights together in that little stone house; of how they had talked and laughed together and become friends. All his protective instincts were awakened. He felt enormously tender towards Celia. She was young and courageous and he was not going to have her insulted or hurt by Frances.

Frances said:

'I sent for you because I felt you owe me an explanation. I just want to know, Miss—er—Hammond, your object in coming back to my house today, with my husband?'

The direct question was a bit of a shock to Celia. She did not really know how to cope with Guy's wife. She had never for an instant anticipated her being here, neither did she know even now why Frances Denver had come back.

Said Guy:

'You have no right to cross-question Miss Hammond, Frances.'

'Every right . . .' began Frances.

Then Celia spoke:

'I can tell you straight away, Mrs. Denver . . . I came here because Dr Denver very kindly offered to help me get a job.'

'I see,' said Frances. Her dark piercing eyes were running up and down the girl, cruelly. She recognised the fact that Celia Hammond was beautiful in her fair slim fashion . . . that her taste in tweeds was good, even though the suit was old and worn. And that she had exquisite hands and feet. All very calculated to attract a man.

'Look here,' said Guy, impatiently, 'it's no good mincing matters. Celia and I are friends, Frances, and friends we're going to remain, whatever you like to say or do. That's enough!'

'Quite enough,' said Frances. 'Has Miss Hammond seen the papers?'

Celia went hot, then cold. She began to see daylight. Frances Denver was jealous of her. She had returned to her husband and she was jealous . . she wanted to make the best . . . or rather the worst of that flood-story and place a rotten construction upon it.

'Mrs Denver,' Celia said, 'I don't think you have any cause to question my friendship with Dr Denver. He saved my life and looked after me when I was ill with this . . .' she touched her head. 'Then he brought me back here, meaning to help me because I am in some difficulties about my future. But I can look after myself. I always intended to, and I think it would be better if I just leave the house and say good-bye . . . to you both.'

It was in that moment that Guy Denver knew how much he wanted Celia to stay. He was suddenly aghast at the thought of her walking out of his life, taking with her that sweet friendliness, that wonderful encouragement that she had given him to face his life again. His mind felt dazed. But through it swept a burning resentment against his wife. He moved toward Celia. 'I won't have you turned out. If anything, it is my wife who should be leaving this house.'

'How dare you,' said Frances, furiously.

Celia looked up at Guy. Her heart was beating so that she could scarcely breathe. It had become an agony for her to be in this room with him and the woman he had married. For her, it was an instant of all-revealing love . . . her love for him. She would have given so much to drive that dazed, miserable, anxious look from his face and see him as he had been in the little cottage . . . smiling . . . a boy again . . . enjoying a breathless adventure in the flood.

She loved him. And because she loved him, she must protect him. He was a doctor with

53

a reputation. This wife of his, for reasons best known to herself, had come back to him. Whatever happened, for the sake of his beloved work, he must not be allowed to do anything indiscreet or irrational now.

Celia said:

'I must go. Obviously I must. Mrs Denver is quite right. Thank you for all you did for me, Dr Denver. Good-bye.'

'I can see you're sensible,' began Frances.

But Guy did not hear what else his wife had to say. Celia was walking out of the consulting-room. Following that slim, brave young figure with his gaze, he knew just how little he wanted to see her fade out of his sight—and out of his life. Good God! what had come over him? Was this what was called *rebound*? A new, obliterating emotional experience with the young girl who had been shut up with him in a flooded house? A mere child who had shown courage and endurance and who had given him back the will to work. And all this coming on top of his lost faith in his wife. And now there was nothing but conflict and disaster . . . because Frances had come back and Celia was going, forever.

Guy laid his pipe down on the desk and hurried out of the room. He closed the door behind him, shutting Frances in. He followed Celia into the hall, took her arm and made her face him.

'I won't have you turned out like this.'

54

'But I must go, of course,' she said, breathlessly, 'you can see it would never do for me to stay.'

'I didn't intend that you should stay actually in this house. But I meant to fix you up in a good room somewhere, and by heaven, I will.'

Celia's breath came quickly. Her shining golden eyes looked up at him in a bewildered way. He looked grim and stubborn . . . (oh, she liked that line of the jaw and the way his lips set and all the strength and determination that poured from him). But she was not going to let him ruin everything out of his desire to show her kindness.

She said:

'You see, we didn't expect to find Mrs Denver here.'

'No, and she has no right to be here,' said Guy, savagely.

'What happened?'

'She changed her mind and came back to me.'

'Then, of course, you've got to give her another chance, haven't you?'

The cool thoughtful words smoothed down some of Guy Denver's flaming anger against Frances, and the whole scheme of things. That was what this child could do to him . . . calm him down, show him the way . . . guide him out of a maze. It was astonishing, her ability to do these things to him. Just with a word and a brave look from those marvellous eyes of hers.

He said:

'I suppose you're right. Yes, I suppose so.'

'Of course. Your whole future depends upon it. If she wants to begin again, you can begin with her, and build up life afresh.'

He stared down at her.

'What leads you to say these things to me?'

She would like to have answered with the truth . . . to have told him that she had learned to adore him during the days and nights of their exile. That he was a god to her and because of it, she would never allow him to step from the pedestal—*for his own sake.*

'You've been so good to me,' she said. 'I'm your friend, aren't I? You said so, and it wouldn't be very friendly for me to do anything that would injure your reputation. Our names are linked . . . they oughtn't to be . . . and your wife is quite right to remind me of it.'

Guy drew a long breath. Suddenly he picked up Celia's right hand and kissed it. It was an action of pure homage. It filled Celia with a suffocating sense of ecstasy and of pain. The touch of his lips on her hand . . . how utterly wonderful!

'Bless you, Celia,' he said, huskily, 'you are indeed my good little friend, and I am yours. And no matter what my wife or anybody else says, I shall not desert you now. I'm going to find you a home and I shall help you get a job after you've taken your secretarial course. Or even before. I might find you something you could do straight away.'

'Don't worry . . . I'll be all right,' she began. He interrupted.

'No, I shall look after you, Celia. I said I would and I will.' He drew a notebook from his pocket, scribbled something on a leaf, tore it out and gave it to her.

'That's the address of an old patient of mine. She'd do anything for me. She lets rooms . . . just off High Street, Kensington. Go to her and tell her that I sent you. I'll communicate with you—phone you there sometime tomorrow morning. Will you promise me that you'll go to that address?'

Celia took the piece of paper and nodded.

'If you really want me to.'

'I do. Your welfare is of great importance to me. I want you to think of me as your friend.'

A queer kind of joyfulness seized Celia as she heard those words. She looked up at him—into those clever handsome eyes, which she knew from now onwards, must haunt all her days and her nights. She said:

'Thanks awfully. I shall always think of you as my friend.' Then she was gone. The big front door closed behind her as she stepped down into Harley Street.

Slowly Guy Denver turned and walked back into his consulting-room. The conflict within him was dying down. He felt calmer, more himself. It soothed him to know that his little friend of the flood was not going to be alone, without friends or prospects, in London. And now to deal with Frances . . .

Frances had taken off her coat and hat. She was standing in front of the fire, smoking a cigarette. When Guy re-entered the room, she threw the cigarette into the flames and came quickly toward him. There was a soft look in her eyes—an invitation such as he had not seen from Frances since the early days of their marriage. She said:

'Guy, I want you to know that I'm sorry for what's happened. I want us to start again.'

He stood immovable. There was not one thrill to his pulses. It was almost a shock to him to realise how little Frances meant to him any more. He thought of her with Paul de Poiret. She had not gone away with him but she must have been in his arms at some time or another. Guy was utterly repelled by the thought of the woman whom he had loved and trusted, in the embrace of that suave Frenchman. Yet if she was sorry . . . if she really wanted to come back . . . what right had he, Guy, to refuse her? He had certain responsibilities which he could not shelve, no matter what havoc she had wrought with his feelings. But he was conscious that she had blackmailed him . . . yes, it was a case of moral blackmail . . . after the way she had threatened him . . . and threatened that grand girl who had just left the house.

In an ice cold voice, he said:

58

'You've come back, Frances, and for the moment I suppose there is nothing to be done but for me to accept your gesture. But I do not feel the same toward you and never shall. I tell you, what you wrote in that letter to me killed my love . . . I went through hell . . . and all my old feeling died in me.'

The softness left Frances' eyes. She was not good at being thwarted. She had received one humiliation from the hands of her lover and she did not want another from her husband. Through her teeth she said:

'You seem to have been speedily consoled in that flood!'

He remained cold. He was no longer going to allow himself to be angered by her innuendoes.

'We shall get nowhere if you say things like that.'

'You're being simply beastly to me,' she flamed.

'Did you expect me to be charming? No, Frances, you'll have to give me time. I cannot possibly forget what you *intended* to do . . . even though you did not do it.'

She gritted her teeth. 'And I'd like to know what you did in that house with that girl?'

He did not reply. Turning his back on her, he sat down at his desk and began to look through the correspondence that was piled on the blotter.

On the memorandum-pad were a dozen

messages.

'Would Mr Denver ring up the hospital?

Lady Ashbridge wishes Mr Denver to see her.

Dr Pawltry would like Mr Denver to telephone him etc., etc.'

He was wanted here, there, everywhere. As he read the messages, and began to open letters, Guy realised the singular importance of his work. There were operations waiting to be done. Lives to be saved. The sick to be helped and comforted. Little Celia was right— work must go on and life must go on, despite one's personal grief and disappointments.

He felt suddenly strong, glad to be here, ready to face life again. And with a pair of clear brown eyes shining at him through the darkness, encouraging him, bidding him carry on.

He was not going to let Frances get him down any more. He knew her now for what she was. Vain, selfish, out to get her own ends, ready to strike at him like a snake. He despised her. But he had no right to turn her out of this home if she wished to remain. Neither would he ever risk her striking at Celia, too. He could see that Frances, having failed to get her freedom one way, might seek another method of getting it . . . through him.

He heard her voice:

'So you've made up your mind to be vindictive?'

He looked up at her with a grim smile.

'Isn't it you who would like to be that?'

Frances pulled a lipstick from her bag and applied it to her mouth, her fingers shaking a little with anger.

'Oh, I don't care. Say what you like. Here I am and here I shall remain.'

'Quite,' said Guy, and slit an envelope open with his paperknife.

She drew nearer to the desk and put a clenched fist on it.

'I've got to protect myself. Everybody the length and breadth of Harley Street knows about you and that girl in the flood. If you have anything more to do with her . . .'

'Will you kindly leave me alone. I want to work,' he broke in.

Frances swallowed hard. Her mortification was acute. She had a sudden uneasy feeling that it was not going to be easy to get her husband back where he used to be—eating out of the palm of her hand. Dropping her voice to a lower note, she said:

'I admit I did you a wrong, Guy, but surely you'll be decent enough to give me another chance?'

He looked at her stonily.

'Only time can tell what will happen between you and me, Frances. Meanwhile, by all means let us have peace.'

With that she was forced to be content. But her mind was working busily. She was wondering how and when she could get a cheque out of him for clothes. How she could get him to finance a trip that she wanted to take with some friends down to the South of France . . . what she could do to make her life exciting and attractive, now that Paul had left her. And as she picked up her coat and hat as she walked out of the consulting-room, she thought:

'I'm not going to let Guy have the upper hand. I believe he's keen about that girl and I shall watch him. *I shall watch him* until I'm in the position to dictate to *him,* again.'

CHAPTER SIX

No. 22 Vincent Street, W., to which Guy Denver had sent Celia, was one of those tall narrow basement-houses which had once been occupied by the rich and had now become shabby, dilapidated, with dusty windows bearing cards which said: *'Apartments',* or *'Room To Let'.*

The house occupied by Miss Fuller, Guy's patient, was as shabby as the rest, but cleaner. It was at the corner of the street and because one could see the back of Barker's, Miss Fuller, who ran what was really a boarding-house, liked to say that her house was not in a back street, but actually *in* High Street,

Kensington, itself. Therefore, it was of a special refinement!

Miss Fuller, despite the servant problem, managed very well, gave plain but adequate food to those who lived in her house, and prided herself that respectability was the keynote of the place.

The fact that Miss Hammond came on recommendation from Mr Denver was sufficient to ensure Celia being accepted and well looked after. For, as she said almost as soon as the girl arrived:

'There never lived a better man than the doctor. One of God's own gentlemen and he saved my life when I was in the hospital and charged me little for it—God bless him!'

Celia was in the exact mood to appreciate a second person's warm feeling for Guy Denver. So she took the faded, the worn-out, the shabby little Miss Fuller to her heart and was glad to become a member of her household.

It was far from an inspiring household. It was dark and crammed with ugly furniture of the Edwardian period. It reeked of cabbage water and fried onions. The dining-room in which meals were served at regular hours to all guests, looked out over a sooty piece of ground which Miss Fuller, herself, called the 'cat-run'. It was darkened by thick Nottingham-lace curtains and a long pair of faded red chenille which framed the window.

Miss Fuller took pride in her table. She had

forsaken tablecloths for mats, which she hoped gave an air of 'the new age' to her table, aided by cheap-coloured glass, and highly-coloured china. She tried to make things bright for her guests and during meal-times was unfailingly bright herself, always with a little word for each boarder.

Celia was plunged into the middle of the life at No. 22 Vincent Street, almost immediately, because she arrived at the lunch-hour and Miss Fuller said she must eat before she saw her room (the said room was to be the lop-back' because it was the only one vacant, but Celia was promised that she should have a front one as soon as possible).

The price was to be thirty-five shillings a week, including meals, which was exactly what Celia could afford. Not that she could afford it for long, she told herself, ruefully. She had to pay for her secretarial training, and the money which she now had in the bank would certainly not keep her for more than six months. And economy was especially necessary because her poor little car had gone to ruin. She had hoped to sell that, and put the proceeds to her account.

Celia felt slightly dazed during lunch at the long table surrounded by strangers. She felt abominably homesick. So abjectly lonely that she hardly knew how to bear it. How could this life be borne after that other life with her father in their Lincoln home? It seemed years since she had left Lincoln. And those days and nights with Guy Denver in the flood . . . what a curious interlude they had been . . . the strangest lull in her life.

No, lull was not the word. For those days had been eminently exciting. Intimate, even happy days. With Guy Denver for her friend.

She could think of nothing but Guy; remember nothing but his face, his voice, and that kiss upon her hand. Dazed and miserable she sat at Miss Fuller's table, toying with the meal placed before her.

There were eight guests including herself. Two married couples, a young foreigner, a very old man with a beard who sat opposite her and continually passed her condiments which she never used, and beside her another girl of her own age. Celia stole a glance at this girl and was a little frightened by her appearance.

She was a tall raw-boned creature with the square-jawed face of a boy, and black short-cropped hair. She wore a badly fitting skirt, a red jumper, obviously home-knitted and a scarf which didn't go with it. She spoke once or twice to Celia in a deep voice which betrayed a slight Lancashire dialect. Celia thought her crude and uninspiring. Then suddenly the young woman made a joke and smiled at Celia, and that smile transformed her rugged face and made her look suddenly feminine and quite attractive. It was such a singularly sweet smile, showing a set of dazzling teeth. She followed up the joke by saying:

'Don't laugh. You needn't. It's only my fun.'

Then Celia suddenly liked her. Timidly she said:

'Have you been here long?'

'A year. And a year *too* long, when I'm hankering for a cottage and a few hens, and the chance to breathe God's fresh air.'

'I come from Lincoln,' said Celia. 'We had a lovely garden.'

'Then you'll miss it,' said the other girl. 'Poor kid. You'll miss it, and your home-life, too. What's your name?'

'Celia Hammond.'

'Mine's Janet Leith—known to my friends as Jan. Have you come to stay?'

'For a bit.'

'Well, that'll be nice,' said Jan, finishing the last spoonful of her suet pudding. Then, glancing at Celia's plate, she added: 'Hey! you've eaten nothing. I've been watching.'

'Not very hungry.'

The big Lancashire girl stole another look . . . this time at Celia's face. And she saw two big tears in a pair of eyes so lovely that they almost took her breath away. Gosh! she thought, what a lovely kid she was, and so small and slight . . . so delicate-looking . . . showed breeding . . . not the ordinary sort of person they got at No. 22. And she looked so sad! What were those tears about? Jan had a maternal instinct so strong that it always

66

made her the inveterate friend of those weaker than herself. She could never resist a weeping child, or the old and infirm, or stray animals. She put out a hand and patted Celia's knee.

'Go on, eat up the suet. You can't be slimming. You're only half the size I am, and look at me . . . inclined for a second helping.'

Celia tried to smile, but she did feel so lost, so hopeless. Yes, it was the hopelessness of the future which was suddenly affecting her, robbing her of her courage. There seemed nothing to look forward to. When she had left the Fen country with Guy Denver this morning, she had somehow imagined that a new and wonderful vista was opening up for her. She was going to have a job—a marvellous job as *his* secretary, as soon as she was trained. But that had been before the thought of the woman who was his wife, had disturbed her. She had looked upon Guy as a lonely man whose wife had run away from him. Very different was the situation now. Frances Denver had returned to him. What was more, she looked upon her, Celia, with suspicion and dislike. She could make something hateful out of those lovely, innocent days and nights in the flooded house. Celia remembered her, as she had seen her two hours ago in her husband's consulting-room. Beautiful, chic, in her fur coat, with that haughty, insolent expression on her face and practically ordering Celia out of the house. And Celia *hated* her. Not because

67

of any injury she had done her personally, but because of what she had done to Guy . . . and what she might do to him in the future. That hard, cruel woman could never be the right person for a man so sensitive, so good . . .

The tears began to trickle down Celia's cheeks. Horrified, she wiped them away and rose from the table.

'If you don't mind, I'd like to go to my room,' she said to Miss Fuller.

'Oh dear . . . I haven't quite finished serving lunch,' began Miss Fuller.

Then Jan Leith came to the rescue.

'I'm an old trooper here, Miss Fuller. I know my way about. Let me take Miss Hammond to her room. What number?'

'No. 8,' said Miss Fuller. 'Thank you, Miss Leith.'

Celia found her arm being taken by a firm, kindly grip. And now the tears were coursing fast. She went blindly up the narrow staircase with Jan half guiding her, talking cheerfully about nothing in particular. Then she found herself in No. 8, and through the hot tears, saw what was to be her home for the present. Nothing very homely about it. Utterly different from the cheerful sunny bedroom up in Lincoln where she had been another Celia altogether . . . a Celia who had scarcely been aware of the hardships, the griefs that life could hold. Just a square ugly room this, with a window overlooking the 'cat-run', a cheap oak suite . . . that horrible yellow, shiny oak . . . a worn-out hair-carpet with linoleum 'surround', and the one modern touch—a divan bed with a cretonne cover. The walls were washed in an ugly pink distemper, and hung with badly-painted water-colours. There was a gas-fire, with a shilling-in-the-slot meter and an old-fashioned wash-stand, behind which was nailed a piece of coloured matting. On the mantelpiece in a china vase were stuck some faded purple 'everlastings', a pathetic attempt at floral decorations. It was bitterly cold in her, and when the door shut, the draught poured underneath it, making the cord of the roller-blind flap dismally against the windowpane.

Celia looked around her, seeing everything yet nothing. There was her suitcase on the floor. She must remember to get her trunk from King's Cross. A good thing she had sent it on by rail, she thought drearily, instead of putting it in her poor little car. The trunk might have gone to perdition in the river, that night, and with all that she owned inside it.

Jan Leith said:

'How about putting a match to this fire? It's freezing.' Celia drew the back of her hand across her eyes and gulped.

'It'll want some money in the meter, won't it?'

'I've got a bob, if you haven't,' said Jan. 'I'll run to my bedroom and get it.'

'No—I've got one,' said Celia.

The next moment Jan had lit the fire. Then she lifted Celia's suitcase on to a chair.

'Let me help you get unpacked.'

The kindliness of the big Lancashire girl stole through Celia like a ray of sunlight through the darkness and depression of this moment.

'How kind you are,' she whispered.

'Not a bit. But we all need a pal sometimes. You look as though you need one here and now. Life's not being too good for you at the moment, you poor kid, hey?'

Celia took the keys from her bag and unlocked her suitcase, 'Oh, I expect it might be worse,' she sighed.

'I always say that,' announced Jan cheerfully. 'Whatever happens to me, I try to think it might be a darned sight worse. We might all be dead if it comes to that. Buck up! You never know what's round the corner and it's an ill-wind that blows no good and all that. I never knew I was going to have a holiday today until the boss announced that his wife had died and he was shutting up the office to go to the funeral.'

Celia found herself laughing through the tears.

The next moment she was unpacking with Jan, listening to a gay stream of humorous chatter, and forgetting her depression. One couldn't be depressed for long with Jan. She was like a sea-breeze, Celia thought. Rough and ready, but with a heart of gold. Soon the little room was quite warm as the gas-fire roared into a hot glow and finally the two girls drew their chairs up before it, sat down and smoked cigarettes produced by Celia, and exchanged a few confidences.

Jan told Celia that she, too, was alone in the world, and she, too, had once known the joys of family life, up North. She had lost both parents, and her brothers and sisters had married and gone away, so she had come down to London to work. She had been brought up to a furriers trade, and found a tolerably good job in a wholesale furriers, near St. Paul's Churchyard. She had to sort and choose skins before they were made up. It was hard work, but not uninteresting, and there was always a chance, she told Celia, that one day she would be the head of the department in which she now worked.

'Of course, it wouldn't do for you,' she remarked to Celia. 'What *you* should be is in the showrooms, showing off the stuff. You'd look a treat in silver-fox capes and mink coats, with that lovely skin of yours and your fair hair.'

Celia smiled and shook her head.

'I don't think I should want to be a mannequin. I prefer the idea of secretarial work. I'm going to take a training.'

'Oh, I haven't the brains for that sort of thing,' said Jan, 'but then you've had

71

education, I can see it. Of course, I was at Public School myself—not Eton or Harrow, mind you—just the Council!'

Celia smiled. There was always an irresistible twinkle in Jan's eyes.

'I'm glad you're here,' Celia said, impulsively, 'it'll make all the difference having a friend in the place.'

Jan flushed and because she was embarrassed, talked a lot of nonsense to hide it. But through it, she conveyed to Celia that she was pleased and flattered.

And then it was Celia's turn to talk, and Jan Leith heard the strange story of the disaster on the bridge and of that great adventure in the flooded house.

'Lord!' she exclaimed, when Celia finished, 'why, *of course*. The girl in the flooded house with the well-known surgeon. I read it in the papers. Good Lord . . . that was you!'

'Yes, it was me,' said Celia.

'All alone with the doctor all that time . . . and in one room . . . well I never!'

The colour surged into Celia's face. She had a sudden blinding vision of Guy, sleeping on the mattress on the floor . . . beside her bed . . . of Guy waiting upon her, bringing her improvised meals . . . of Guy's sensitive fingers dressing the wound in her head . . . of their talks and their jokes and the life they had shared so happily.

Jan was saying:

72

'Tell me all about it. What was he like? Well-known chap, wasn't he?'

'Yes, a surgeon in Harley Street. He was very wonderful, Jan. If I'd been his own sister, he couldn't have treated me better.'

'Well, I'm surprised he didn't fall for you.'

Celia's heart missed a beat.

'And it's to be hoped you didn't fall for him,' added Jan, with a shrewd eye on Celia's tell-tale colour.

Celia said hurriedly:

'We were just friends—good friends. He—he's married.'

'Married men are the worst,' said Jan bluntly.

'But not men like Guy Denver. Oh, I expect lots of people think things. The papers were ghastly . . . they like to put a romantic construction on everything because it makes sensational reading. But there was nothing like that, Jan. I want you to believe me.'

'But he sent you here, didn't he? Didn't Miss Fuller say at the table that a doctor had recommended you to her?'

'Yes.'

Jan Leith formed her own conclusions. She threw her cigarette-end into the fireplace, and for a moment sat with her thick dark brows knit, then she said:

'I'll tell you something, Celia. You want looking after. You're too darn young and pretty to be alone in this big, bad world. I'm

73

the same age as you are, but I'm not pretty.
Men don't fall for me and if they did, I could
take care of myself. I know them. They're a lot
of wolves and you're just a lamb. Don't you go
falling for anyone who's married. You're the
sort who should have a nice young boyfriend
to take you out, give you a good time and then
marry you, one day.'

Celia shook her head.

'I don't want a boyfriend, Jan.'

'Well, watch out, my dear. I'm a bit cynical
about men. I had a little pal who got let down
mighty badly; and I've never forgotten it. She
was a blonde like you and too softhearted,
and he was married . . . pah! I've no use for
married men who come round young girls.'

Celia stood up and her lips set a little.

'I know you're trying to be kind, Jan, but
please don't criticise my friendship with Mr
Denver.'

Jan also rose and stuck her thumbs in the
belt of her skirt. She surveyed Celia from
beneath her frowning brows.

'I know! You want to say I'm interfering
and impertinent. Perhaps I am. I don't mind. I
always say what I think. I'm that sort. And I'm
your friend whether you like it or not.'

Celia softened again.

'I do like it . . .' she held out a hand which
Jan grasped '. . . and you can say what you like.
But don't misconstrue my friendship with Guy
Denver. There's no need.'

'Well, I'll be round if I'm wanted,' said Jan. And now, how are you going to spend the afternoon? Like to come out with me and do a cheap flick and a cup of tea at the Corner House?'

Celia was on the verge of accepting that generous and kindly invitation when there was a knock on the door.

Miss Fuller's voice said:

'Miss Hammond . . . you're wanted on the telephone downstairs, please. And if I'm not mistaken, it's dear Dr Denver, because I know his voice.'

Celia was astonished and even dismayed by the way her heart leapt. She avoided Jan's eye.

'I'll come at once, Miss Fuller,' she said, and ran out of the room and down the stairs.

Jan Leith shook her head and followed a trifle gloomily.

'Darn these married men,' she thought, 'I like that kid and I'd hate to see anything rotten happen to her. Darned if I won't take her under my wing and keep her there, whether she likes it or not.'

Downstairs, Celia spoke to Guy:

'Yes, I'm all right. Miss Fuller's going to look after me . . yes, I know I shall like being here. Thank you for sending me.'

'Is the head all right?' asked Guy in that low attractive voice which had become so familiar to her.

'Quite. It just hurts a bit if I move too

sharply.'

'The dressing ought to be changed tomorrow morning,' said Guy. 'I'll look in and see you soon after ten.'

'Oh . . . ought you to trouble . . . ?' began Celia.

'Of course,' broke in Guy. 'I stitched up that head of yours and I've got to see my work through. And by the way, I think I may have good news for you tomorrow about a job:

'Oh, how marvellous! What?'

'A doctor . . . great pal of mine . . . and his wife have a small girl of seven. She goes to a day-school in town. Her mother's just had another baby and she wants somebody to take the little girl to and from school and out for walks and that sort of thing. I thought it might suit you. It would be a daily job and you could do your secretarial training in the evenings. It would mean that you would be earning money, meantime.'

'But it sounds marvellous,' said Celia . . . 'I'm terribly thrilled.'

'After I've seen Davis again, I'll be able to tell you definitely. When I mentioned it to him this morning, he said he felt sure his wife would consider you for the job.'

'It's terribly good of you,' said Celia.

They discussed the possibilities for a moment.

Celia yearned to ask Guy how he was . . . how things were progressing with his wife

. . . how he felt about getting back to the old routine of work . . . but she could not. She did not feel she had the right to question him about his private life any more. There was that woman there . . . that woman in his house. His wife! Yet Guy went on talking to her as though he found it hard to ring off. And when he did say good-bye, he said:

'Sleep well, little Celia. You won't have a stranger snoring on the floor at your side, tonight. At least, I hope not!'

She caught her breath and laughed.'I certainly won't.'

'Till tomorrow,' said Guy.

Celia hung up the receiver. It was not a white, tear-stained young face that Jan saw now . . . Jan, coming down the stairs into the hall . . . but a radiant face with golden eyes glowing. It confirmed Jan's worst suspicions that this young girl was in love with her companion of the flood. But when the two girls went out together that afternoon, Guy Denver's name was not mentioned.

CHAPTER SEVEN

Guy Denver was a little bewildered and disturbed by his own sense of pleasure that following morning when he saw Celia again.

She sat on a couch in Miss Fuller's sitting-room whilst he, coat off, sleeves rolled up, leather case of instruments and dressings open beside him, attended to the cut on her head. The wound, he declared, was healing nicely, and would soon give no further trouble.

Their meeting had been ordinary enough. Just a smile and a handshake between them. Yet when he had looked into her eyes he had realised what it meant to him to be back in contact with her. He had missed her, last night. Missed that funny little stone house, their communal room, their picnic-meals—the whole of their strange intimate adventure.

He had felt suffocated in his big luxurious house, waited on hand and foot by excellent servants, sitting in a dinner-jacket at his table eating a lavish meal, with Frances opposite him, chic and beautiful in a new dinner dress, and in a mood to be pleasant to him.

Yes, it had all suffocated him. He had felt it to be unfriendly and cold. Frances sought only what she could gain for her personal ends. None of them in that house cared whether he lived or died . . . whether he failed or continued to succeed in his career from now onwards. But here in Miss Fuller's shabby sitting-room, so inadequately warmed by a spluttering gas-fire, he had reached some sort of home again. Celia was here. Celia asking him in that soft voice of hers about his job . . . Celia showing real anxiety for his welfare . . . Celia always so anxious that their friendship should not socially embarrass him.

He felt human again. And after he had done the dressing, and put on his coat, out came the cherished pipe. He sat, puffing at it, talking to her in the way that he bad talked all last week . . . as one friend to another. The boyishness came back into his eyes. He lost the sense of strain. He joked about Miss Fuller and the house. He said:

'She's a grand old girl, really. Prides herself on coming from an aristocratic family, you know. Rather pathetic. I like her. Is she looking after you?'

'Yes, and so is a girl called Jan Leith . . . from Lancashire . . . . she's been awfully kind to me.'

'Who wouldn't be kind to you, Celia?'

Her pulses fluttered.

'And you? Are things all right for you at home?'

His lips and eyes hardened again. He took his pipe from his mouth and pressed a thumb into the bowl.

'Can't say that. There's a wall between my wife and myself, Celia. A wall which she put up when she left me. I don't feel it'll ever be knocked down.'

Silence. Celia was conscious of an almost guilty pleasure in what he told her. She loved this man. Oh, God, but she knew it beyond all doubt this morning, now that she saw him again. She knew it from the rapture which she experienced at being in the same room with him, at hearing his voice, being near to him. How could she want that wall between him and his wife to be broken down? She would not have felt like this if Frances Denver had been different . . . if she had been a good wife. But she was cruel and exacting . . . she would ruin anybody who stepped in her way . . . indeed, she *had* very nearly ruined her.

'You do feel you can go on with your work, don't you?' Celia asked.

'Yes, I'm up to the neck in my job again. I oughtn't to be here now. I mean, I'm due at the hospital.'

'Then you must go quickly,' said Celia, rising.

He put away his pipe and smiled down at her. Conscientious little Celia! She would never influence a man in the wrong way. She would seek only for his good. That wasn't like Frances. Ye gods! Frances had always loathed his job and been jealous of it . . . she would encourage him to keep any hospital waiting if it suited her book to do so.

'I'm seeing Davis at the hospital,' he said. 'He's my anaesthetist. He's going to give me a message about this job for you. Then I'll ring you.'

'But you won't have time.'

'I shall have time for that, my dear,' he said as he closed his case of dressings.

She stood silent a moment, looking at

80

him. If he only knew, she thought, what his presence in this house meant to her. How he transformed this cold dark shabby room . . . like a god, making magic for her. She was badly in love now, and she was both glad and sorry. Sorry because that love must remain forever locked in her breast. Glad because it was good to love like this . . . to pour out all her emotions upon somebody who seemed to her so utterly worthy of love. But he belonged to another woman and he must never know it. . .

She wanted to go outside and see him off, but it was pouring with rain. A grey depressing January morning. She had to be content with watching him through the window, noting the easy grace with which he walked . . . Not the Guy of the flooded house, in his homely tweeds. But the London surgeon . . . complete . . . black coat, striped trousers, grey Trilby and the brown handsome head. He turned to wave and smile to her, before he stepped into the long shining saloon which stood at the kerb. Celia waved back, her whole being on fire. After that beautiful car had driven away, Vincent Street became a lonely, depressing place once more. Celia thought:

'I oughtn't to see him any more, feeling like this. He doesn't feel the same as I do, so it doesn't matter to him. But *I* oughtn't to see him.'

It seemed incredible to her now that that

elegantly-dressed young surgeon who was just going to give his valuable opinion in consultation at a big London hospital should be one and the same as the man who had been marooned with her in the floods. Incredible that she had ever seen him wash and shave, and brush his hair, and sit at her bedside, smoking and talking to her.

Celia went round the place in a sort of daze for the next few hours. Dazed by the poignancy of her own fast-developing passionate love for a man whom she had not known a week ago.

She wished Jan were here. But Jan was at work today and would not be back until this evening. Finally Celia went down to King's Cross, got her trunk and brought it back to No. 22 Vincent Street, and tried to pass away some time unpacking her things.

Homesickness seized her as she pulled out the old familiar possessions. A framed photograph of her parents . . . another of the lovely old house and garden in Lincoln . . . a painting of her favourite Cairn terrier who had been her special pet for years and had recently died. It hurt her to see these things—even the clothes she had worn at home . . . the books she had brought with her. A dozen and one objects which reminded her of that former happy life. Once again courage seemed to fail her and she found herself lying on her bed in tears, dreading the future. Yet she could not be wholly unhappy because there was Guy

Denver in the world. The memory of his touch and of his smile and the way he had turned to wave at her before he got into his car just now, was still with her.

Celia admonished herself for her weakness. She dried her tears, tidied her room and got herself into a better frame of mind.

Better not let Jan Leith come home and find her like this or she would question her in that blunt piercing way of hers and discover what she felt. And no one—*no one* must know about her feelings for Guy Denver.

It stopped raining after lunch and Celia, used to fresh air and exercise, went out for a long walk in the park. She returned to find that Guy had been on the phone which gave her a crushing sense of disappointment because she had not been there to answer the call. However, after tea, Guy telephoned again. And once again the world became a brighter place for Celia. He had bright news for her, too.

Mrs Davis, the wife of Dr Ian Davis, to whom Guy had spoken, would be only too glad if Celia would go round to see her about helping daily with the little girl.

'Go and see her this evening,' Guy suggested, 'and you might start your job at once. The sooner you do something, the better. It must be so dull in that place.'

Said Celia:

'It's so terribly good of you, Mr Denver.'

'Since when have I been "Mr" to you, my young friend?'

Delighted and thrilled, she corrected herself.

'Guy, then.'

'Well, go and see Mrs Davis and good luck to the job.'

'I can't thank you enough.'

'I've a lot to thank you for, if you did but know it,' he said, shortly. 'Let me know how you get on. I may run in and see that head of yours tomorrow.'

Celia wished she had the strength to say:

'Don't come . . . don't come . . . because I love you with all my heart and soul, and I oughtn't to see you any more . . .'

Instead, she said:

'What time?'

'I've got an operation early,' he said. 'I'll have to come round about lunch-time.'

Then he added:

'And don't forget those night-classes for your secretarial training.'

His interest in her welfare was infinitely precious to Celia. She went up to her room carrying with her the memory of his voice, saying:

'Good night, my dear.'

Dear Guy! Grand friend! But how impossibly sweet was this love that was breaking into blossom deep in her heart. A sweetness which could only become an agony unless it was quelled in time. She *must* quell it. She must school herself to look upon Guy as he looked upon her—in a purely platonic light.

She called at the Davis's house that evening. She did not see the doctor. But she was received by Mrs Davis who was in the middle of a Bridge party and who gave Celia a very hurried interview.

Marjorie Davis was a tall, good-looking woman in her early thirties. She had rather a dictatorial manner, although she was quite pleasant to Celia. As the wife of a well-known doctor, she led a full, busy life, was tremendously social and although fond of her children, had not much time to attend to the details. Her six-weeks' old son was in the hands of a capable nanny. Now she wanted a daily nursery-governess for little Diana. Her husband, she said, had told her that Mr Denver had suggested that Miss Hammond might fill the bill.

'He saved your life, or something, didn't he,' said Mrs Davis, vaguely. She was very vague about facts and had not concentrated on the flood-story that had been told her. She liked the look of Celia. She was decently dressed, rather pretty and obviously a lady. One needed that sort of person for one's daughter. Accent and manners were so important.

Rapidly she explained to Celia that her duties would be to come and take Diana to her day-school at nine o'clock every morning,

85

look after her clothes and mending, and in the afternoons take her for walks or to her riding or dancing-classes. In fact, to take her completely off the nannie's hands.

'You would have your meals up in the nursery' said Mrs Davis, 'but I suppose you wouldn't mind that?'

'Not at all,' said Celia.

'Will a pound a week suit you to start with, anyhow?'

Celia made a rapid calculation. A pound a week would certainly be something toward her keep, and if she got her meals here, she might make arrangements with Miss Fuller to lower the price of her room. Anyhow, it was a job and something to keep her going, so she accepted it gladly.

'Well, that's all right,' said Mrs Davis generously, 'you might start on Monday, after the week-end.'

Celia left the Davis's house and walked down Welbeck Street feeling slightly more pleased with life. Her first job and Guy had got it for her! It was rather marvellous. She got back and told Jan all about it. Jan congratulated her and followed up the congratulations with a typical remark:

'It'll be all right so long as Diana's Papa doesn't take a look at you, and Mama doesn't shoot you out of the house quickly. You're so darned pretty, and I don't trust these married men.'

'Oh, shut up!' Celia laughed and kicked the point of her shoe gently against Jan's ankle. 'You and your complex about men!'

'I'm right,' said Jan, 'keep away from them unless they're young bachelors.'

Celia maintained a somewhat guilty silence. For she knew that she had only one clear thought in her head . . . and it was not so much her new-found job as nursery-governess to Diana Davis, as the knowledge that tomorrow morning she would be seeing Guy again.

CHAPTER EIGHT

Guy Denver looked out of his dressing-room window that Saturday morning and saw that the weather had changed. All day yesterday it had been raining. Today the sun struggled bravely to lift the pall of the winter gloom. It was very cold but there was a crispness in the air which made him long to get out of town into the country. With regret, he thought of the hard day's work in front of him, in hospital wards, the hot odorous atmosphere of operating-theatres, in nursing homes, or, in his consulting-room seeing his private patients. He had a distracting vision of driving away from it all, back into the direction of the Fen country . . . Those lonely marshes would be lovely in the sunlight . . . and of course Celia would be there, driving with him.

But that wasn't the way in which his mind must work. Guy pulled himself up sharply, completed his dressing and walked into his wife's bedroom.

He had not had a very happy evening with Frances last night. She was undoubtedly piqued because he did not wish to rush back to her arms. She could not understand that she had hit him a mortal blow when she had made that decision to leave him for the Frenchman, and it was a blow from which he had not recovered. He could never see her now without thinking of Paul de Poiret. Her very smile which used to beguile him, seemed treacherous. Yes, he was always wondering now what lay behind it . . . how soon she would choose to betray him again . . . for in her mind and her heart, if not in actual fact, she had already once betrayed him.

After dinner last night she had suggested that they should take a holiday, go away together 'for a second honeymoon'. He had not fallen in with that idea. First of all because he could not bear the thought of taking Frances away at the moment. There could be no 'second honeymoon' for him, and secondly because he wished to throw himself into his work. Work was the real anodyne for trouble. That was what Celia, brave little Celia, had told him, and he knew it to be true.

Frances taunted him at intervals about

Celia. She had ugly jeering things to say which made him white with anger, but he said nothing. He chose to treat Frances with cold disdain—even indifference—and that, of course, maddened her.

'You're not the same man since you came back,' she said last night. 'The company of that girl seems to have affected you strangely.'

To which Guy replied:

'Nothing of the kind. It is your own conduct that has affected me, Frances.'

He had lain awake a good bit of the night thinking about the position between his wife and himself. And toward the early hours there crept into his mind the uneasy feeling that perhaps he was being too hard on Frances. Perhaps she really, sincerely, did wish to show some affection for him. If so, what right had he to repress such an instinct in her?

He decided to go and say good morning to her in a more friendly spirit.

Outside her bedroom door, he stopped to fasten the strap of his wrist-watch. As he did so, he heard his wife's clear, rather high-pitched voice. She was talking on the telephone . . . She mentioned the name Rina. He knew who that was. Rina Millgard, wife of Sir Charles Millgard, one of London's leading oculists, and counted by Frances as her 'best friend'. If there was one woman in London whom Guy disliked, it was Lady Millgard. She was a blonde with beauty and wit, and

89

a character which Guy despised. She was much younger than her hard-working notable husband, and it was well known that she spent his money like water, neglected him for the foolish, extravagant crowd gathered about her, and was altogether a bad influence for Frances.

Guy was about to turn the handle of his wife's bedroom door when something which she said, very clearly, reached his ears and checked him.

'My dear Rina, you can't imagine what he's like ... very up-stage, out to humiliate me. I don't really care a damn, as you know. Only as Paul let me down, I can't afford to have a smash-up just now ... I'm going to try to put over the good-little-wife-act for a bit. But I don't altogether trust this girl who was in the flood with him ... yes, she's damned attractive and I'm going to keep an eye on her...'

Guy Denver waited to hear no more. He was a man who loathed eavesdropping, but every word that his wife had said to Rina Millgard, had been so significant and rang so blatantly true, it made him sick ... sick to the bottom of his soul.

It was not that he loved Frances any more, nor had much respect left for her. But what he had just heard removed from him the last hope that there could be any real reconciliation between them. Frances did not really care 'a damn' about him ... That was what she'd said

90

to that wretched woman who made poor old Charles Millgard's life a hell. They were birds of a feather, all right. She didn't care, and she was 'putting over the good-little-wife-act' . . . Added to which, Guy knew that de Poiret had let her down. That was the truth. She had come back, because her lover had quitted on her. Not a pretty story.

Guy made a poor breakfast. White and tense he sat alone in the big gloomy dining-room, wishing to God there was some way out of this mess. Life with Frances was going to be barely tolerable after this. It was horrible that he should have heard what she had said to Rina Millgard. Horrible to know how treacherous a woman could be—and that woman his wife. But he could do nothing about it. He did not even intend to let her know what he had heard. She was back, the possibility of the divorce had blown over and because of his medical career, he must avoid scandal. He would have to go on with this sham of a life . . . knowing that he was less than the dust to the woman with whom he lived . . . knowing that she meant nothing to him, although he had once adored her.

After breakfast, a message was brought to him by Frances' maid. Madame wished to see him. He could not face Frances. She would be smiling and doing that 'good-little-wife-act'. (Would he ever forget that?) His mind was a daze of misery and shame. He preferred to do a day's work before seeing or speaking to Frances again He told the maid to tell Madame that he had to rush out to an urgent operation, and would see her tonight.

Throughout his work that morning, Guy was conscious, not only of deep depression, but of the wish to see Celia Hammond. She meant a lot to him, his little friend of the flood . . . He felt vaguely that she might give him some sort of strength and courage to carry on. She was so utterly different from Frances . . . never in a thousand years would she betray a human being. He knew that. He had grown to know so much about her during those days and nights they had spent together.

He remembered what his wife had said to Rina Millgard about 'keeping an eye' on Celia. He felt enraged by that. What right had women such as Frances and Rina Millgard to mention the name of a straight, decent girl like Celia Hammond? They weren't fit to lick her boots. And he wasn't going to allow Frances to upset Celia's life. No! neither would he permit her to destroy the friendship that had risen between them.

Guy was in a mood very unlike himself when he called at No. 22 Vincent Street to see Celia. He had meant to see her at noon, but had been delayed at the hospital. She had waited in all the afternoon, afraid of missing him. When she saw him, she was disturbed. He was not the calm, quiet Guy whom she knew. He was a nervy, restless, unhappy man, with deep discontent marked in those handsome eyes of his.

After he had dressed the wound on Celia's head, he paced up and down Miss Fuller's little room, pipe in his mouth, hands in his pockets. He said:

'I'm fed up, Celia. *Fed-up*, this evening, my dear.'

She sat watching him with her grave golden eyes, her heart beating fast as it must always beat now when she saw Guy Denver . . . when she heard his voice. She was anxious for him. She said:

'What's happened? Why do you feel like this?'

He swung round to face her.

'Life's not too good when you strike the rock-bottom of dishonour in those you have once loved and trusted.'

She did not answer. She could only guess that he was referring to Frances and wondered if anything fresh had happened . . . But Guy was generalising. He mentioned no names.

'Everything's a bit of muddle in my mind, Celia. It has been since I returned home. And it's getting worse instead of better. There are moments when I feel it isn't worth while carrying on.'

Celia shook her head.

'That isn't so. That must never be so with you. Another kind of man, in a different

93

position from yours might feel like that—but not you. You do so much for humanity. That in itself must make it worth while for you to carry on, no matter how little you get out of it, personally.'

He took the pipe from his mouth and gave her a brief smile.

'Wise little Celia! I knew you'd talk to me like this. It's like a trickle of cool water in a burning desert, my dear. You soothe and help me. I knew you would.'

She flushed. Her long dark lashes swept downward to hide what lay in her eyes . . . the agony of her love for him. But his praise was wonderful to her.

'I can do nothing to help you, really,' she said. 'But I do hate to hear you even suggest that nothing is worth while any more.'

'So you would have me live my life for others and cease to worry about my personal life, eh?'

She bit her lip.

'It doesn't sound right. I know everybody should have some kind of inner personal happiness. But if things go wrong, I suppose service to others is a way out—a cure for despair.'

'Despair is the word,' he said, grimly. 'I've been feeling that all day, Celia.'

She was shocked.

'But you mustn't . . . you *can't* . . . Oh, you must never feel like that! You're so good to

94

everybody else. Life ought to be good to you for a change.'

The distress in her voice penetrated the shadows in his soul. Suddenly, impulsively he put out a hand and took one of hers.

'Celia, you're a grand child! And life *is* good to me—giving me such a friend. I suppose the world would say I'm a man of many friends. Certainly I know hundreds of people. But there are few I get to know very well. Certainly no other woman outside my home whom I know as well as I know you. When I saved you from the river that night, I saved something that was destined to be very precious to me.'

Her fingers trembled in his. She changed from red to white and did not answer. He went on:

'We got to know each other very well in that little house, didn't we? One can scarcely be shut up in a single room with somebody for days and nights without becoming well acquainted with their weakness and their strength . . . the good in them and the bad. I have yet to find anything bad in you, Celia.'

'That compliment is returned,' she said, breathlessly.

Her heart was near to bursting with happiness because of the things he was saying, and the clasp of his hand about hers. She did not really understand why this clever, successful man should like and need her, but she could see that he did and that was enough

95

for her. She was enchanted by the knowledge.

Suddenly he became aware of the fact that he was holding that slender hand so fast and so long. He dropped it quickly and took refuge in the pipe again. God, but it was sweet to hold that friendly young hand. *Too* sweet, perhaps. He had better beware! He was in a weak and foolish state and he knew it. Knew, for instance, that he would give a lot to be able to take Celia out in his car this moment, drive her miles out of London, go on talking to her . . . listening to her . . . gathering strength and courage from all that was strong and brave in her.

He got off the personal note and began to discuss the job which she was to start with Mrs Davis on Monday.

'I hope it will be a great success,' he said. 'And what about tomorrow? What will you do all day tomorrow? You're not used to London. You must loathe it. London's frightful on a Sunday.'

Celia stood up and walked to the window. Drawing aside the curtain, she looked a moment out at the street lamps which glittered through the dusk. The black night-clouds were rolling behind the chimney-pots. It was freezing fast and the cold air coming through the window made her shiver. She said:

'I don't think I *do* like London very much, but Jan Leith said she'd take me out. We're going to walk on Hampstead Heath, or something.'

Guy knit his brows. He thought of his own plans for tomorrow. He knew exactly what Frances required of him. She was expecting him to take her in the car down to Brighton for a lunch-party. They had already promised to go to some friends who lived in Hove. There he would be sitting in an over-crowded, over-heated room, listening to a lot of aimless chatter with people who had so much money that they did not know how to spend it. Whilst the true brave people of the world, like Celia, and her working girl-friend, took a bus-ride and walk on Hampstead Heath.

He longed to take them both out in his car . . . give them a slap-up lunch somewhere . . . spend money on them. And he would love to do something for Celia, in particular.

Gruffly he said:

'One day, soon, I'm going to come along and take you out.'

She turned and faced him, smiling a little oddly.

'I don't think that's possible, much as I'd love it.'

'You're thinking of my wife. Well—I'm not going to be dictated to by her,' Guy said, harshly.

The colour burnt Celia's cheeks.

'I'm thinking not only of her, but of everything. You know our names are already linked by those rotten papers. You must be careful.'

He put his pipe in his pocket and moved toward her.

'You consider everything—everybody but yourself. You're grand!'

She tried to speak, to laugh the compliment off, but could not. Inside her a voice was crying:

'Don't say these things to me . . . go away, please. I love you so much, I can't bear it. And I can't *bear* to see you looking so hurt, so unhappy . . .'

The next moment Guy's hands were on her shoulders. He was drawing her close to him. Then he kissed her. On both cheeks, and finally her lips. The merest touch . . . almost passionless . . . and almost at once his hands fell away from her. He said:

'Bless you, my dear. I'll be ringing you up . . . I'll see you quite soon.'

He picked up his case, hat, gloves, and was gone, almost before she had time to speak to him. She was left standing there, like one transfixed, both hands up to the cheeks which he had just touched with his lips. Her whole being was on flame . . . she trembled violently . . . . clamouring for the closer embrace, the longer kiss which must not be given or received.

The bitterness and sweetness of it was too much for Celia. To know that he liked her so much . . . to know that she liked him all *too* much . . . to know that every instinct within her must be quelled and repressed . . . and that she must look after *him,* as well as herself because he was lonely and depressed and in need of her . . . He was much older than she was . . . a doctor . . . a prosperous man. Yet he seemed to her a mere boy, broken, lost, clutching at the hand held out to him. It was all too much . . . *too much . . .*

Jan Leith came into the room to find Celia crying her eyes out on Miss Fuller's sofa. And immediately Jan was there to console, both arms around the slight quivering figure.

'Lamb! what is it? What's come over you? Why are you crying?'

Celia turned and buried her face against the broad shoulder of her new-found friend. She said:

'Oh Jan, *Jan.*'

Jan said, grimly:

'You've just seen the doctor, hey?'

Celia nodded, dumbly.

'Is that place on your head all right?'

'Yes.'

'Then what's *wrong.* Did he do or say something to upset you?'

Celia whispered:

'No, *no.*'

Jan Leith looked over the fair, bowed head through half-shut eyes. Her rugged face was harsh and angular in the electric light. She thought:

99

'It's the doctor . . . this kid's in love with him. I know it . . . if he does anything to hurt her, he'll pay! I'll make him. It isn't fair!'

CHAPTER NINE

Celia sat in the nursery at the top of the Davis house reading *Snow White and the Seven Dwarfs* to little Diana who, the day before, had seen the Disney film with her mother, and was enraptured by the whole story.

She was also enraptured by her new companion. Celia was grand fun. Not always saying: 'Don't do this or do do that' and grumbling and scolding like Nannie. She treated one sensibly, like a grown-up, and Diana looked forward to getting back from school and going out with Celia. Their association was a great success and had, so far, lasted a week.

In between the story of *Snow White,* Celia's thoughts strayed a bit from Diana and this spacious, beautifully furnished nursery, which was the child's special room. They strayed persistently and had done so for days . . . always to the memory of Guy Denver.

She had not seen him since that last visit when he had kissed her good-bye. She had fretted about it, puzzled about him, alternated between being ashamed of her love for him and proud of it. She wanted passionately to see him, yet felt it was better not.

She wondered why he hadn't visited her again or even telephoned, which he had promised to do. She had even begun to wonder whether he had wearied of their association, decided he had done enough for her and had no particular further interest.

Such a thought made Celia profoundly unhappy, despite the fact that she reminded herself that he was a married man and she had not the least right to care whether he saw her or not.

She was thankful for this job. At least it gave her something to do and money to earn. And she had grown fond of Diana, who was a charming, imaginative little thing.

Diana began to hum the song:

'One Day My Prince Will Come! . . .'

'Sing it for me,' she coaxed Celia.

Celia had a good ear for music and remembered the tune. Smiling, she crooned it for the child.

'And how thrilling that moment will be
When the prince of my dreams comes to me.
He'll whisper I love you . . .'

As she sang her face crimsoned and her

101

eyelids closed. She could feel Guy's hands on her shoulders and his lips against her cheeks. The pain of her thoughts grew almost unbearable and she ceased singing abruptly.

The door was pushed open. A big man with curly hair and a ruddy, jolly face, walked in. Diana sprang into his arms with whoops of joy.

'Daddy!'

'Hullo, you rascal. What have you been up to . . . ?'

His gaze strayed to Celia who stood up as he came in. Celia liked Dr Davis. He was always ready with a friendly word, and moreover she liked him because he was an enthusiastic admirer of Guy, and Guy's work.

Ian Davis said:

'I heard a very attractive song being sung in a very attractive manner. How about singing it for father as well as child?'

Celia laughed.

'I couldn't. I was only amusing Diana.'

'You seem to amuse her very nicely,' said Dr Davis. 'I've never known the child to be so happy.'

'I'm glad,' said Celia, 'I like being with her, Dr Davis.'

He turned his attention to his small daughter and began to tease her. Celia moved away and prepared to tidy the room and put away some of Diana's books and toys. In a few moments, Nannie would come to bear Diana off to bed and Celia's day's work would be over. She was thinking :

'Will I find a message from *him*? Has he phoned today . . . ?'

Mrs Davis swept into the room, still wearing fur-coat and hat, for she had just come home. She was looking fussed and a trifle cross.

'Oh, Miss Hammond . . .' she began. Then, as she saw her husband, she paused and raised her brows . . . 'Oh, you're up here, Ian.'

'Hullo, my dear,' he smiled at her. 'Come and join the merry party. Miss Hammond's going to sing to us. We've got a first-rate crooner in the house, if you did but know it . . .'

'No, I didn't know it,' said Marjorie Davis, coldly.

Celia stood by embarrassed and a little uneasy. Mrs Davis seemed cross. But why? Surely she didn't object to Dr Davis being up here?

Mrs Davis said:

'Take Diana in to see baby, will you, Ian? I want to talk to Miss Hammond for a moment.'

Dr Davis, always a genial, amiable man, obeyed orders and, with a smile and a jest, bore Diana off to the night-nursery where his son-and-heir was being put to bed.

Mrs Davis shut the door after them and turned to Celia.

'You've been here just a week, haven't you, Miss Hammond?'

'Yes, Mrs Davis.'

'Well, I'm afraid I must tell you that the arrangement we made isn't very satisfactory. You're entitled to a week's notice, but I hope you won't object if I ask you to take your salary in lieu of the notice? I mean, you need not come back tomorrow as I'm making other arrangements for Diana.'

Celia stood very still. The flush left her cheeks and her heart knocked in a strange way. There was something in Mrs Davis' manner and eyes which were hostile and distinctly unpleasant. Celia was utterly bewildered.

'I don't quite understand,' she said. 'I thought Diana and I were getting on so well. Dr 'Davis remarked just now how happy she was . . .'

'I daresay,' said Mrs Davis, icily.

'Have I done anything wrong?'

Mrs Davis was silent a moment. She was not at heart an unkind woman nor, as a rule, a jealous or a suspicious wife. Indeed, she was rather annoyed that things had turned out like this, because they had been very satisfactory until today. For she had thought that she had found in Celia just the right person for Diana. But this afternoon she had had an enlightening conversation with the wife of the surgeon, her husband's colleague, Mr Denver. Of course, she knew Frances Denver quite well. And Frances appeared to have something very definite against the girl. She had said:

'I think you ought to know, dear, that you

are letting your child associate with that young person who was shut up in the house with Guy in the flood, and has been chasing him ever since. Of course, I don't say it was her fault that she was marooned with Guy, but from what he says and from what I've seen for myself, she's a typical man-hunter. And I must admit she has made the best of what happened with Guy. She's pretty and plausible and men like her. But be on your guard. You might find her shut up with Ian somewhere, if you're not careful...'

That had been the beginning of the conversation and by the end of it, Mrs Davis had come to the conclusion that she would be more than foolish to keep Celia in the house. She had been foolish to engage her in the first place, she thought, after all that stuff in the paper about the flood. On the other hand, she felt a trifle mean and uneasy, now when she was giving notice to Celia. There was something so quiet and defenceless about the girl. How wounded those large brown eyes looked! Still, that sort was often the worst, Marjorie told herself, and she must take Frances' advice. After all, if Guy Denver hadn't been interested in the girl, he wouldn't have taken the trouble to recommend her. It was all a bit fishy!

Celia was demanding explanations. Marjorie Davis grew a bit more fussed and finally gave away the truth.

'I'm not too pleased about all this publicity over you and Mr. Denver. I saw Mrs Denver this afternoon and . . .'

'I see,' broke in Celia, and now her heart was galloping and her face was fiery red. She saw in a flash what had happened. This was the work of Guy's mean, spiteful wife. Frances had discovered where she was working and had done this thing to her—out of sheer malice.

'Please don't trouble to explain any further. I quite understand,' said Celia, in a choked voice, and turning, began to collect Diana's books.

Half an hour later she had left the Davis' house in Welbeck Street for good and all. She did not dare tell the child that she was not coming back, or there would have been a scene. With two weeks' salary in her purse and burning resentment in her heart, Celia went back to Vincent Street. Through a chill, foggy evening she rode in a bus, wondering what she was now going to do.

It was the first and last time Guy could be permitted to find her a job. It was easy to see that he was not to be allowed by Frances to help her. And she had been so pleased with her work and attached to the child! It had seemed a pleasant way of earning her living. Now, she could do nothing without a training. It was a bit hard, really . . . to be made to feel that she had done something *wrong* in that flood . . . that Guy had done something wrong,

106

too. Oh, it was beastly, *beastly!* Celia felt choked at the thought.

Janet Leith was not at home to hear the story of her dismissal. She was out with a friend from the business where she worked. So Celia ate her supper by herself—feeling lonely —in a wretched frame of mind. She looked so pinched and miserable that the kindly little Miss Fuller asked if she was ill.

Celia said:

'No,' and retired to her room. It was so cold, so depressing up there. So *very* depressing to think that she had been turned out of her job because Frances Denver was jealous of her. Did Guy know? No, possibly not.

Celia did not light her gas-fire. She had to save the shillings now. It might be ages before she got another job. The future looked blank and cheerless and Celia quailed at the thought. She lay down on her bed and pulled a rug over her and shivering, buried her face in the pillow.

'One Day My Prince Will Come! . . .'

She whispered those words that she had sung to little Diana, and the tears began to flow. Her lips formed the name:

'Guy! Oh Guy!'

At that precise moment Guy Denver was having a few extremely unpleasant words with his wife.

Just before dinner, he had had reason to telephone Ian Davis. He had asked, casually, how Miss Hammond was getting on in her job. He had asked it casually but inwardly had been hungry for news of her. He had wanted to see her so many times that week, but had dared not visit her, knowing that he wanted it *too* much; feeling that it was best to keep away. She had figured far too constantly in his thought and their friendship had grown to be far too sweet.

It had been a week of hard work and suppression, and little comfort in his own home. He hated being at home now, knowing how treacherous his wife had been, and how loveless must be the rest of their lives together.

What Ian Davis had had to say about Celia had come as a shock to Guy.

Davis thought Miss Hammond a grand girl, he said, and had imagined she was getting on remarkably well with Diana. And he had been amazed, he said, to hear tonight that his wife had given Celia notice.

'These women, old boy,' Ian had laughed down the phone. 'Your missus said something to mine about the girl and upset her properly. I don't quite understand what it's all about. Too busy to worry. Old Marjorie has her whims and I always leave the domestic arrangements to her.'

Those few words had been enough to tell Guy what had happened. In a cold fury, he had questioned Frances. She, smiling, sarcastic, had not tried to conceal the fact that she had been the cause of Celia's dismissal.

'I knew what that girl was like when I saw her. She was out to catch you and hold on to you once you got back to London, and I felt it was giving a friendly warning to Marjorie Davis.'

'It was iniquitous of you . . . you had no right.'

'My dear Guy!' broke in Frances with a drawl, 'may I ask why you're being such a champion for Celia Hammond? Does she interest you as much as all that?'

Goaded beyond all endurance, he answered: 'I'm sufficiently interested in her not to treat her in a fashion which is totally undeserved. She's a decent girl—and a very brave one—and I wanted to help her get a job. But you, who have everything in the world you want, prefer to see her turned out, jobless, out of sheer spite. I can see no other reason why you did this. You have been spiteful to somebody who hasn't done you the least harm.'

Frances looked at him through her long lashes and shrugged her shoulders:

'The more angry you get about it, the more you convince me that I've done right. You're keen on the girl, that's the truth of it.'

He had not dared answer her. But those crude words: 'Keen on her' burnt into his imagination. Perhaps it was true. But at least

Frances had no justification for getting the girl turned out of the Davis's house. And who and what was she to judge after her own conduct? For years he had been utterly loyal to Frances. Never allowed the thought of any other woman to enter his head.

Not once since he had overheard her telephone conversation with Rina Millgard had he lost sight of the fact that Frances was just using him for her own ends. Her jealousy of Celia was in any case unfounded, and not in the least because she was fond of him. Merely because she did not want him to pay attention to any other woman. *And* because her lover had let her down!

At the thought of Celia's state of mind . . . for she must be suffering cruelly over the injustice of this treatment . . . Guy had no compunction in going to see her at once, that very night. He felt that it was up to him to try, at least, to undo some of the damage Frances had done Celia. He must find her fresh work . . . and apologise to her for the humiliation she had received at the hands of Mrs Davis.

He left the house, took his car and drove to the Langham Hotel. From there, he telephoned to Vincent Street and asked to speak to Celia.

Celia was still lying on her bed, alone and cheerless, when that call came through. Then she was up and downstairs in a flash, her whole being transformed. She was altogether surprised when Guy said:

'I want you to take a taxi at my expense and come straight to the Langham Hotel, Celia. You've had dinner, haven't you? . . . Yes, so have I. I'll give you some coffee here and I want to talk to you.'

His voice sounded terse, but there was an urgency in it which did not allow her to refuse. Besides, she did not *want* to refuse. She wanted with all her soul to see him.

She rushed upstairs, changed into a black tailored dress which had a coat with an imitation leopard-skin collar . . . her one smart outfit . . . put a small black velvet hat on her fair head and went forth to the Langham, travelling luxuriously in a taxi as Guy had bidden her. Not that she intended to let him pay for it. She would rather go without lighting that fire in her room for a couple of days, and spend the money on this taxi which would take her quickly to *him.*

The suffocating pleasure that she felt as she drove to the hotel frightened her. God! she mustn't feel like this about a man who belonged to somebody else . . . and an eminent surgeon at that . . . it was madness, sheer madness. And whatever happened, she must conceal her feelings from him. She did not quite know why he had arranged this meeting so suddenly, but she had a vague idea that it might be connected with Mrs Davis' dismissal of her.

As soon as she saw Guy, she knew that this was so. He met her in the lounge, shook hands with her in a conventional fashion, but the look in his eyes was not conventional. It was deep, significant, and full of bitterness.

'I've brought you here to apologise to you, Celia,' he said at once. 'I know what's happened and how it happened, and all I can say is it's outrageous. An insult both to you and to me.'

She said nothing. Her heart was beating too fast and her emotions were too much at fever heat. It was marvellous to see him again. He was wearing a dinner-jacket. He looked so very attractive, she thought. He chose a secluded sofa and table in the lounge, and she sat and listened and watched while he ordered coffee and a liqueur-brandy for himself. She found herself remembering that other Guy, with hair ruffled and shirt sleeves rolled up, bringing tea and biscuits to her bedside in a little stone house in the middle of the flood. And her heart ached with the remembrance. For he had been bitter and miserable then—at first—but he had so soon become a gay boy, happy and jesting. And now there was no happiness about him. He was weighed down with depression and burning with resentment against the injustice of things.

'My wife was responsible for the business and I told her exactly what I thought about it,' he said, 'and I assure you, Celia, I'm not going

112

to accept such conduct toward you. I shall not rest until I've found you another job.'

'No, no,' said Celia, 'you mustn't do that. It won't do for you to show any sort of interest in me. I can find a job by myself. My friend Jan will help me.'

Guy Denver, holding his brandy in both hands, warming the liquid, rolling it a little round the glass, looked with some amazement at the girl. She was unlike anyone he had ever met. He had come up against hundreds of women in his profession. He thought he understood feminine psychology. But this young, staunch creature, this slip of a girl with her brave brown eyes and determined chin, she was made of such fine stuff that he mentally bowed his head before her. She was anxious for him—for his reputation—and she obliterated her own wishes. She had nothing— less than nothing to look forward to. But she refused his help because the rendering of it might be an indiscretion for a man in his position. How many women would act in the same way?

'Celia,' he said, 'my dear, you're a very grand person. I know nobody whom I admire more, and I cannot and will not allow my wife or anybody to stop me from lending you a helping hand.'

She did not answer. But the colour swept up under her cheeks. His praise made her heart twist with a queer pain of misery and

113

happiness. He watched her, saw that hot colour come and go in her face and was a little shaken by the quickening of her own pulses. She looked lovely in that black dress, with that small black velvet hat on her fair shining head. He remembered he had thought her beautiful when he had first seen her, lying unconscious in her car on that terrible night of the flood. Tonight with that bright colour, and that quaint little way in which her lips suddenly pouted as though with shyness and embarrassment, she was enchanting.

Oh! the warmth of her presence! After the chilling atmosphere in his own home, the bitterness of the feeling between him and his wife, it did Guy good to be with Celia.

'Look here,' he said, suddenly, 'we're not going to sit here and argue. I'm going to find you another job and that's that. And now, when we've finished our cigarettes, how about a short run in my car?'

'Well . . .' began Celia, helplessly.

'It's a nice foggy night,' he said, with a smile which drove all the sternness from his face, 'cold and beastly and typical of the dear old country. But we'll drive out of this infernal city for a bit—shall we?'

She knew that she should refuse. Yet she wanted passionately to go with him. And he seemed to want her to say 'yes'. She could feel that she gave him some degree of happiness, although why, she could not think. With shining eyes she said:

'All right! I'd love to.'

A while later she was seated beside him in the luxurious, smooth-running saloon. They drove down the Embankment, over Battersea Bridge, through Clapham Common, heading for the wide road that led to Croydon Aerodrome.

Guy had no real idea where he was going. But he found an extraordinary satisfaction in putting his foot on the accelerator, sitting here at the wheel, his pipe in his mouth, and with Celia's warm, sweet presence at his side.

A little way beyond the Aerodrome, he pulled up. The fog was fairly bad here. He took the pipe from his mouth and said:

'Not too good, is it? Rather foolish to go on, perhaps.'

'Very,' said Celia, and laughed, 'we've already been in a flood together, we don't want to get lost in a fog!'

'I can't say I'd mind.'

Her throat constricted. Under the rug which he wrapped around her, she could feel her knees shaking a little.

'No—it might be fun.'

'It was fun in that little house, once your head was better, wasn't it? Do you remember our meals—Lord! I've never known a biscuit and a bit of cheese could taste so good.'

'It was lovely, really,' she said.

Guy drew in his breath. In a blinding flash

115

of revelation, it struck him that those hours had been all too lovely. At the time he had been too full of bitterness against Frances to let any real tenderness enter his heart for Celia or any woman. But now he knew that was all changed. He felt unutterable tenderness for this girl in the car beside him—and more than that. White-hot, urgent, came the knowledge that he was in love with little Celia, and in desperate need of all the sweetness and peace and comfort which she and she alone, could give him.

For an instant, spell-bound by his own thoughts, he sat very still. Then he moved his elbow sharply and it accidentally caught Celia's head. He heard her cry of pain. He turned round to her, aghast.

'My dear! your bad head—I'm terribly sorry—how clumsy of me!'

She put up her hand and straightened her hat which had almost been knocked off.

'It is still a bit sore.'

'You poor darling!'

Unconsciously he used the term of endearment. And having said it, and seeing her face twisted with the pain that he had caused her, something in him seemed to break. He caught her in his arms.

'Oh Celia!' he whispered.

She was unprepared for that sudden embrace. But it was so piercingly sweet that she could not have drawn away from it just

116

then for all the world. He felt her go limp against him. And the next moment his lips were on her mouth. He kissed her, not as he had kissed her before—in friendship—but in love—passionate, pent-up love. Under the spell of that kiss they were both lost. They clung deliriously together in the darkness of the car with the vapouring whorls of mist curling around them. Her lips answered his. For the first time in her life, Celia was conscious of the wonder and potency of passionate love between a man and a woman. She adored this man. She knew it. And for these few glorious moments, she could not control it. Her arms went round his neck, her hands feverishly caressed his head and his were warm and urgent about her shoulders, touching her cheeks, her throat, her hair.

Then the moment of madness passed. With a sudden sense of shock, Guy Denver realised what he had done—what he was doing.

'Oh, my dear!' he whispered, and drew back his head, drew away from the tempting sweetness of her. Taking one of her hands, he drew it up to his lips and sat there like that, in silence for a moment, with that small kind hand against his mouth.

Celia neither moved nor spoke. She was only half-conscious. Just then the force of her feelings were much too much for her. Eyes tight shut, trembling violently, she sat, waiting for him to speak.

It was some time before he found words. His thoughts were in bitter conflict. The one side of him, the human man crying out for love and companionship, for all that Celia could give him, wanted to make love to her and go on making love to her. Indeed, Guy felt tonight that he would willingly drive away with her, never to return to his home. But the other side of him, the doctor, the conventional, practical man warned him that he was treading on dangerous ground. It was sheer madness for a man in his position to do a thing like this. And he was married, too. In actual fact he owed no further fidelity to Frances, but on the face of things, he was still her husband. And he was in such a position that the least breath" of scandal would ruin him.

Why, in heaven's name, he asked himself desperately, should it have come to this? Why had he fallen in love with Celia Hammond? Without asking, he knew that she loved him in return. Her absolute surrender to his caresses had told him so. Yes, they were in love. He must have loved her since that last night when he had slept on the floor beside her bed, in that little house in the flood, knowing that it was to be their last. And he had loved her since the hour he had seen her walk out of his house, sent away by Frances. He loved her for her sweetness and her courage; for the courage she had given him and the faith in woman-kind which she had restored to him.

At last he spoke. Holding her hand tightly between both of his, he said:

'This puts a new complexion on things, my dear. I'm in love with you. Do you realise that?'

She struggled to think clearly but found it hard with all her emotions at fever-pitch. What he said made the blood rush wildly through her whole body. He loved her . . . Guy loved her . . . the brilliant, notable Harley Street surgeon, loved *her*, Celia Hammond. And she was nothing and nobody. It seemed like a fairy-tale. She said:

'I *can't* believe it's true.'

'But you knew it when I kissed you,' he asked quietly.

'Yes.'

'And do you love me?'

'Yes, oh yes, *terribly*.'

His pulses leapt.

'Celia darling child—'

They were in each other's arms again, heart to heart, his passionate kisses sapping all her powers of resistance. But only for a few moments. Then sanity returned and she pushed him away from her.

'You mustn't—you mustn't do this. Oh Guy, you know that you mustn't!'

'I know that I have no right,' he said, 'but it doesn't stop me from loving you.'

'It's madness. We can never allow it to happen again.'

'Oh, my God,' he said on a sudden note of despair, 'can't you see what's happened, Celia? We've found out that we love each other, and it's going to make everything *hellish*.'

'No, no, it's too heavenly for that. It mustn't be allowed to be hellish, Guy. To me, it won't be. It'll be heaven to know that you feel like this about me. Darling, I can't understand why you do.'

'I didn't know it till now.'

'I've known that I've loved you for days.'

He looked down into her eyes and read the exaltation in them. And he, too, was exalted. That was what Celia did to a man. He could not feel ashamed of loving her, only raised up by it.

'My darling,' he said, 'I can't quite think clearly at the moment, but I do know that I'm glad that I've discovered my feelings. I assure you, Celia, that when we first met I didn't think it possible for me to love again. I was so embittered by what my wife had done to me—I thought I'd finished with love for all time. But you've given me back everything— everything that I imagined had gone out of my life forever.'

'You've done more than that for me,' she said. 'You've made me the proudest person in the world. I can't *believe* that you love me.'

'But I do, I do, my darling.'

'And I adore you, Guy. But it means that we must never see each other again.'

120

He drew back from her, a sense of shock and depression replacing his ardour.

'It can't mean that, Celia. It would be too cruel.'

'But it must. You're married and you've got your reputation as a doctor to consider. We must never, never meet again.'

'Never? My God,' he said, in a hollow voice, 'my *God.*'

She, too, was no longer in the clouds. She had come down to earth and to reality, with a crash. She was conscious only of pain.

'We've got to both be strong, Guy, haven't we?'

'You always have been. I've never known anyone so brave and fine.'

'I'm neither. I feel dreadfully weak. I feel like asking you to drive me away and never take me back.'

'That's what I want to do,' he said.

She clenched both her hands. Through her teeth she said: 'Oh, no, *no!—don't* let's even think of it. Take me home, take me home quickly, please.'

'Why should I?' he asked suddenly, savagely, 'My wife let me down. I know just what her feelings are for me. I know just what my life will be worth, as lived with her. I—'

He stopped and suddenly put his head between his hands. Celia, close beside him, could feel his strong body shaking. For a moment she battled with herself, the hardest

121

battle of all, because it was against her own instincts and that most tremendous force in the world—woman's love for man With all her heart she wanted to say: 'Take me . . . take me away . .', and instead, she repeated:

'Take me home, Guy, you must!'

It was for him. It was to save him from doing anything rash in a moment's madness. For she knew that it would ruin him to allow this love which had just entered his life to come before honour and reason.

At last Guy Denver raised his head. His face was haggard and his forehead wet. He took out a handkerchief and wiped the dew from it. For a few moments he, too, had been going through a ghastly struggle. All that was human in him yearned toward this girl. All that was in him rebelled against returning to the wife who had let him down so shamefully. But at last he was master of himself. The battle was won, not only because *he* shrank from letting down his profession, dishonouring those who believed in him, but because he loved Celia. And loving her, he had no right to do anything that might damage her. He said:

'You're right, my dear. I will take you home—now—at once.'

She did not answer. She felt suddenly weak, almost near to fainting. She leaned back in the car and shut her eyes. As Guy started up the engine and turned the car round and they began to drive home slowly through the mists, Celia felt wave after wave of pain pass over her. There was still so much need for strength. She knew that Guy was in love with her, and a man in love can be persuaded. She might touch his arm and beg him to stop and reconsider his action and tell him that she could not do without him, and perhaps he would change his mind and drive in the opposite direction. But she must not do it. She must never see him again. For she might not always be as strong as she was tonight, caring for him with all her heart and soul.

'By the time they reached Vincent Street, they were both white, tense, silent. They had both struggled to master their emotions and had gained control. But they were suffering, and they knew it when at length they came to say good-bye and looked into each other's eyes.

In hers, Guy read all the pain and grief of a woman hopelessly in love. In his, she saw that same pain coupled with a man's stern bitterness.

Guy spoke first. Taking her hand in his, he pressed his cheek against it.

'Darling, I've got to leave you. I don't want to. *You* know that. *But I've got to.* I think we both realise it.'

'Yes,' she whispered.

'I love you,' he said, 'you need never doubt that. I think I shall always love you. But I can't take you away, Celia. It wouldn't be fair to

123

you, or to those who look to me to do the right thing.'

A little shudder passed through her body.

'I know it, and I'll never ask you to.'

'You're so brave,' he said, 'it hits me much harder, I think, because you are so brave. If you cried or implored me, it would be easier to leave you.'

She felt the ache of hot tears against her eyelids and forced them back.

'I'm not brave. I'm a coward in my heart. I can't bear the thought of not seeing you again.'

'I shall see you again. I shall come and see you and find you a job. I've said that and I shan't go back on it. I may not be your lover, but I can always be your friend.'

She shook her head. She knew perfectly well that mere friendship between them was forever finished. A man and a woman in love cannot meet on platonic terms. It is too much against every instinct in them both. Guy wanted to help her. It was his most urgent wish to do something for her. She realised that. But she also realised the folly of another meeting. For it might mean they could not bear a second parting and then what would happen to Guy? She had so little to lose. But he had everything . . . and not one breath of scandal must be attached to his name. Never through her, should the stigma of disgrace rest upon Guy Denver.

'I shall come and see you, perhaps

tomorrow,' he said, feverishly.

She neither argued nor protested then, but she knew in her heart that this must not be allowed to happen. He leaned forward as though to kiss her and she drew back.

'Please don't. I couldn't bear it.'

'Oh, my darling,' he said, and crushed her hand to his lips.

The next moment, she had jumped out of the car, slammed the door and ran up the steps into the house.

After the door had closed upon her, Guy Denver sat for a moment with both eyes shut, fighting for control. Pulling his pipe out of his pocket, he put it in his mouth. His teeth closed savagely on the stem. He wondered how he was going back to his home, how he could leave Celia now that he knew that he loved her. Wondered how he was going to do his duty to a wife who only used him for her own ends. Wondered how he could carry on with his practice—with his life—knowing that Celia Hammond meant more than life to him, now.

He found the house full of lights and laughter. Frances was 'throwing a party'. Several of them were dancing to a radio-gramophone. He caught sight of his wife for a moment, dancing with a tall young man with a mass of blue-black hair and an ivory face. He looked Italian. Frances favoured foreigners. He danced exquisitely, and Frances circled round the room in his arms, looking up at him

125

as though she had found someone new on whom to concentrate her emotions.

And she was his wife. She was the woman who stood between him and that perfect angel whom he had left in Vincent Street!

It was almost too much for Guy Denver. He turned away from the drawing-room and from the sight of Frances and her gigolo. Going up to his room, he locked himself in, lay down on his bed and buried his haggard face upon his arm.

CHAPTER TEN

Janet Leith came back from her evening out, opened the door of Celia's bedroom just to say good night to her little friend, and was aghast to hear a sound of pitiful sobbing issuing from the bed. Immediately she switched on the light, dropped her mackintosh and umbrella, flung off her hat and advanced to the bedside.

'Celia!' she exclaimed, 'why, lamb, what on earth's the matter?'

The face that Celia turned to her was pitiful, swollen with weeping. Her handkerchief was a crushed wet ball. Her eyes were tragic. She sat up in bed and put out a hand to Janet.

'Oh, Jan!'

The elder girl seated herself on the edge of the bed and gathered the forlorn figure

126

into her arms. Celia looked such a child, she thought, compassionately—a mere kid with her wet face and her fair silky hair tumbled over her eyes.

'What is it, young Celia?' Jan might have been talking to a small sister then, her warm Lancashire heart aching at the sight of so much grief.

'Everything's gone wrong, Jan.'

'You've seen your doctor again, hey?'

Celia pressed her face against Jan's shoulder and nodded. Jan was always right.

'You're in love with that man, aren't you, Celia, and you can't deny it?'

'I don't deny it now,' Celia admitted. 'But the worst thing of all—or the best—whichever you like to call it, he feels the same way.'

Jan nodded. Her homely face was very grave.

'So that's it. That's the outcome of those days and nights you two spent shut up in the flood.'

'Not only that. There's something special between us. Some special link. I think I knew it the moment I met him. He's taken a bit longer to find it out.'

'He's a dirty dog to have told you.'

Celia drew away, hot in defence of the man she loved.

'No, you're not to blame him. It just tumbled out tonight. He took me out for a drive and we were both miserable. You

127

see, I was given the sack this morning and he resented it—that hateful wife of his is responsible . . . '

Celia's story of her dismissal tumbled out. Jan listened with wrath and indignation in her heart.

'There are some women,' she said, 'who ought to be put up against a wall and shot. They're traitors to decent womanhood. Mrs Denver seems to be one of them.'

'It was sheer spite, Jan, because she knows I haven't done anything wrong.'

'And of course your doctor was upset, knowing you've been chucked out, hey?'

'Yes,' said Celia, and pressed her eyes against Jan's comforting shoulder again.

'It's certainly a bit of a mess—hard on you both.'

'But you mustn't blame Guy any more than me, because we admitted that we loved each other.'

Jan stroked the fair young head.

'I don't blame you, really—either of you. But it's no good breaking your heart for a married man, Celia. It doesn't work. Not from his point of view, or yours.'

'Do you think I don't know that,' said Celia, in a heart-rending voice.

'Poor lamb, I bet you do.'

'We said good-bye. We had to. And I oughtn't to see him again. I mustn't.'

'Quite definitely you mustn't,' said Jan,

emphatically, 'it would never do. I know you. You're genuine and you say he is, so I'll believe you. So if you're both genuine, it's all the more reason why you shouldn't meet. If it got too strong for you, what would happen? He'd want to take you away and that would wreck you *and* his career.'

Celia drew away from her friend and buried her face on her pillow.

'It's his career that I worry about. Not myself. Oh, Jan, if he was plain Mr Smith down the road and his wife had treated him so badly, and he wanted me to run away with him, I believe I'd do it. I'd sacrifice anything- for him, if I thought I could give him happiness. But being a doctor—why, it's out of the question! I'd *die* rather than be the cause of hurting his good name.'

'I believe you,' said Jan.

'So I must leave here tomorrow,' said Celia.

Jan knit her brows.

'Leave here tomorrow! Lordy, why so?'

'Because he knows where I am,' said Celia, feverishly, turning her unhappy young face to her friend, 'and he can't bear to think I've been thrown out of my job through his wife. He wants to help me. He'll come here to see me again. I know it would be fatal for both of us. I've got to go away and leave no address behind me.'

Jan pondered over this. She was very certain of her young friend's sincerity, but she could not be so certain about Guy Denver. She did not know him. The only thing she did know was that he was married and in the medical profession, and that this love between him and Celia could end in nothing but disaster if it was permitted to expand. Obviously Celia must be got away. But to leave Vincent Street and Miss Fuller's boarding-house at a moment's notice was a bit drastic. Where would they go? Where would they find anything so cheap and yet so good? Jan was thinking in the plural. Instinctively she coupled herself with Celia. For she knew that she would never allow her friend to go away alone.

She said:

'If you're both so much in love that you can't bear to meet, I agree with you—the sooner you get away, the better. It's lucky we've the week-end facing us. We'll have to throw ourselves on Miss Fuller's mercy and ask her to let us both go. And if she wants a week's notice, we'll have to pay for it.'

Celia stared at Jan.

'But you—you don't have to go as well.'

'Chump!' said Jan, gruffly, 'do you think I'd see you go off by yourself in this condition? What you want is a motherly wing and I'll spread mine over you even though my feathers are moulting a bit.'

The ghost of a smile curved Celia's sad lips.

'You're an angel—an absolute angel, Jan. It would make things so much easier if you came,

130

but it isn't fair . . .'

'Oh, rot! Now the point is, where do we go, and what do we do—I mean, what do *you* do? You've got to get a job, young Celia.'

'I daresay I'll find one in time,' said Celia, with a long sigh.

'Meanwhile, you want some sleep,' Jan rose to her feet. 'Try and get some now, and don't do any more crying tonight.'

Celia put a hand across her eyes.

'I don't think there are any more tears left.'

Jan bent down and kissed her.

'Poor kid! Good night, and we'll face Miss Fuller and the world tomorrow. There isn't much I can say except, you'll get over it. That's one comfort. Time helps us to get over almost anything.'

Long after Jan had gone, Celia lay awake, dry-eyed, staring through the darkness, pondering over those words.

You'll get over it.'

No, it wasn't true, she never would get over this as long as she lived. Guy was her first, her last love. Until tonight when he had held her in his arms, she had not known the meaning of the word. But she loved him with a white-hot fervour and a depth which could not be annihilated by time. She did not really know how deeply he cared for her. Perhaps he was just clutching at a straw of comfort . . . a lonely, broken-hearted man, finding solace in the charm of her youth, her looks or that something in her personality which appealed to him. Perhaps if he did not see her again he would get over it. Men were different from women, anyhow. Love was not everything to them as it was to women. They had their careers, their practical lives to lead. Guy would throw himself into his job and keep, perhaps, just a small memory of her in his heart.

But she—she was forever his. She would never forget, never cease to love him. And she would forever be proud that he had loved her, and that for one brief hour he had shown her the splendour, the rapture of being loved by him.

She could feel his kisses burning deep into her lips and his urgent hands upon her. She could hear his voice saying:

'I'm in love with you . . . I have no right . . . but it doesn't stop me from loving you . . .'

How she longed to see him again! To leap into his arms and hear those words reiterated. Yet tomorrow she must go away where he could never find her, where they would be lost to each other and removed from temptation's path.

Celia sent up a voiceless prayer to heaven.

'Help me, God! Help me to be strong . . . help me to do what is best for *him!'*

It was late before she slept. And she awoke early, with the first dawning consciousness only to be swept back to pain and a bitter sense of loss. She had gained so much last night in

Guy's arms, only to lose it at once. It was desperately hard.

But she was terrified that he might come to see her about a job and reopen last night's discussion.

Jan was a tower of strength. It being a Saturday, she got back at half-past one and was able to give her full attention to her young friend. Celia had spent the morning packing, both for Jan and herself. Miss Fuller had accepted the notice from the two girls with regret, because she liked them. But fortunately for them, she demanded no payment in lieu of notice. Fortune favoured them. That very morning, an elderly married couple had applied for rooms and the two single rooms vacated by Jan and Celia were re-let.

Celia prayed dumbly all that morning that Guy would not try to get in touch with her. But that prayer was not answered, for Guy telephoned an hour before she left Vincent Street for good and all.

She could have told Miss Fuller to say that she was out. But the temptation to speak to him was too strong. She loved him so poignantly. She must hear that beloved voice once again, if for the last time.

She spoke to Guy as calmly as she could manage. He was telephoning from one of the hospitals.

'I want to know how you are today, my dear.'

133

'Quite all right,' was her answer, even though the blood was draining from her face and her knees felt so weak that she could hardly stand up by the telephone.

'I am, too, Celia, but only up to a point.'

'Are you working hard?'

'Up to my ears in it.'

'That's good,' she said, 'work is good for one.'

'And that's what I want to see you about. You've got to have a job. I'm going to run in to see you this afternoon.'

She tried to answer. Every nerve in her was quivering, every instinct leading her to say:

'Yes, yes, when?'

Guy went on:

'I'll have to take my chance because I've got so much to do today. I don't know when I'll be free.'

Still she made no answer. She could not tell him that she would not be here, that he would find her gone. The tears were rolling down her cheeks, but he could not see them. He said:

'Hullo! Hullo! are you still there, Celia?'

'Yes,' she said, steadily.

'My dear, I just want you to know that I meant every word that I said to you last night,' came his low voice.

She had a blinding vision of him, of that thin handsome face and of the clever, kindly eyes smiling down into hers, of the clever sensitive hands holding her close to him. Her mental agony was such that it became a physical thing, hurting her very body. She managed somehow to say:

'Thank you . . . thank you. I meant what I said, too.

'God bless you, Celia. I'll see you later.'

'God bless you,' she whispered and hung up the receiver. For an instant she stood there, two clenched hands against her cheeks. She thought:

'You won't see me later, Guy. You can't, you mustn't. But I wish I could die! *I wish I could die!*'

Jan came down the stairs carrying a suitcase in each hand. 'Hi, Celia! Are you ready?'

Celia swallowed hard. Summoning all her courage, she turned to Jan with a smile.

'Quite ready. Do we sport a taxi this afternoon?'

'We do,' said Jan, 'unless you want me to imitate a coolie and carry a couple of trunks on top of my head!'

'Have you seen Miss Fuller for me,' asked Celia, surreptitiously removing the tears from her cheeks, 'have you explained that for personal reasons I do not want Dr Denver to know where we're going?'

'I've told her and she understands. And if he does call today, she can't tell him because she doesn't know herself. Nothing urgent is liable to come for me, any more than for you, so we needn't tell her where we are for a few days.'

Celia walked toward the door. She cast a brief glance into Miss Fuller's little sitting-room. There on that sofa she had sat beside Guy and he had dressed the wound on her head. There, for the first time, he had kissed her, and she had known that with every drop in her body, she loved him.

The bitterness of going away like this, of removing herself so utterly from him, taxed her endurance to breaking point. Without Jan she could never have got through it. It was Jan who had hustled her out of the house and into the taxi. Jan who took charge for the rest of the day. Celia was in a condition of mind to be led whither Jan willed. She had no volition of her own. She did not care where she went, or what happened to her. Her mind was just a red-hot flame of love for Guy and of hopeless longing. Let Jan take her wherever she wished, and arrange what she thought best. It mattered to Celia not at all.

Jan, with her usual common sense, had made enquiries that morning amongst her fellow-workers, and discovered a boarding-house over the other side of the Park, in the Bayswater district, where she and Celia could find a harbour. A girl whom Jan knew had lived there for some time and seemed comfortable. The terms were about the same as at Miss Fuller's, and the place was clean, even though bigger and less homely.

By tea-time, Celia and Jan were installed

in two small, rather dingy little rooms at the top of a gaunt and depressing house in the charge of a certain Mrs Miller. Mrs Miller was a fat, untidy woman with a small and meagre husband whom she called 'Bert'. The name Bert was screamed through the house all day. He seemed a general factotum.

'Bert, open the door, Jenny's cooking. Or

'Bert, bring up that tray . . .' Or

'Bert, run down to the "Crown" and get Mr Jones a pint of bitters . . .'

So Bert fetched and carried, and Mrs Miller, whom he addressed as 'Maudie', puffed and blew and shouted her commands.

It was the noisiest house Celia had ever been in. The boarders seemed noisy, as well as the Millers. One practised a wailing violin . . . one played a gramophone, a series of sentimental crooning dance-tunes . . . in one room there was a small child who continually screamed, either with pleasure or fury.

But here the girls were, and here they unpacked, and once more put a shilling in the slot, and sat smoking their cigarettes over a gas-fire in which the asbestos was broken and the flames seemed to give out little heat.

Jan worried about Celia. The girl looked so drawn, Jan was afraid that she was going to be ill. It was obvious that she was labouring under considerable nervous strain. There were no more tears, no more mention of Guy Denver, but Jan knew perfectly well what was going on

137

inside her. And Jan's heart ached for her. Jan had never loved a man like this, but she could see what it meant and how it must hurt, and she thought it a cruel stroke of luck that Celia should have given her heart to somebody who was already married.

She insisted on Celia going to bed early that night, and having supper brought up to her. Jan carried it up, herself. And Jan slipped out, down the street, and brought a shilling's-worth of flowers to decorate Celia's mantelpiece.

'We'll soon be at home here,' she said in her gruff cheery fashion, 'and we can't complain of being lonely, either. I don't know whether I'm listening to that darned violin or to the baby's yells, do you?'

Celia responded to the jest and made one in return. But later, when Jan had bidden her good night and left her alone, she lay as she had lain the night before, tearless, staring ahead of her, with sleep a very long way off. She was thinking:

'Guy, where are you? Guy, have you been to see me? What did you do when you found I'd gone? Will you mind very much? Will it hurt you as it hurts me? Oh, God, I hope not for your sake.'

She even wondered during that night of mental conflict and torture, whether she had done the right thing in running away. If he needed her, shouldn't she be with him. Despite his position, his wife, oughtn't she to give him her love if he wanted it?

But always the answer to those questions was: *'No!'* It would never have done for her to have remained, for her to have allowed the love between them to increase. She must try to forget him and take it for granted that she, in her turn, would be forgotten.

What pain there was in loving so much . . . so hopelessly . . . what ghastly pain! She had not thought it possible to feel so mentally and physically alone.

And forget she could not. She felt him with her there, felt his spirit beside her and knew that somewhere in London tonight, his thoughts were with her. Possibly they were as anguished as her own, reaching out through the darkness and silence, trying vainly to find her.

She whispered:

'I'm with you, darling. I'm with you!'

From below drifted the strains of a song sung in a throaty crooner's voice . . . another record being played by the insatiable owner of the portable gramophone. An old favourite and a very poignant one for Celia in this hour.

'Night and day . . . you are the one . . .
Whether near to you or far
It's no matter, darling, where you are
I think of you, night and day . . .'

Celia put her hands to her ears to shut out

139

the sound. Great gasping sobs convulsed her thin body. She thanked God she had had the strength to run away this afternoon, because she knew that if at this moment she heard that Guy was waiting for her outside this house, she would have leapt from her bed, dressed, rushed down to him, never to leave his side again.

But Guy Denver was not outside that house in Bayswater. He was in his own warm, luxurious home, sitting in his consulting-room, going through his own secret purgatory.

At six o'clock that evening, he had called at Vincent Street, only to receive the shattering news that both Miss Hammond and Miss Leith had gone away earlier that day and left no address.

After the first shock, Guy had questioned Miss Fuller closely, but the little woman, no matter how much she wished to oblige her cherished doctor, could not tell him what he wanted to know. She did not know. Miss Hammond had left no address, she said, and seemed particularly anxious that no messages should be forwarded. It was a bit of a mystery, Miss Fuller admitted, but there it was; the girls had just vanished with their belongings.

Sitting here tonight, at his desk, staring at letters which he did not see, Guy pondered over the whole thing again and again. He had been tortured by it the whole evening. Celia had run away from *him*. That was obvious. For she had known that he meant to call today to see her. She had run away, not because she did not love him but because she loved him too much. Just another proof of her courage and her integrity. It overwhelmed him. He loved her more than ever for doing it But he was fully alive to the fact that her action shook him to the core.

It didn't seem possible that Celia had just walked out of his life and that he would never see her again. Impossible that never again might he take that slim, sweet body of hers into his arms and see those dark tender eyes of hers shine like stars into his own. Never again must he know the exquisite bliss and solace of being loved as passionately as he loved; nor enjoy that dear companionship which meant so much to a man.

He had found Celia, just for a little while and then lost her again. She had left him with the loveliest of memories. But that was all, and Guy cried within himself that it was not enough. A man could not live on memories. it was starvation diet. It was condemning him to bitter loneliness within himself for all time.

Yet what else could they have done? If she had stayed, he would surely, in the long run, have wanted to take her away. He would have wanted to cast off the shackles of his home and his miserable marriage, and find peace and happiness with this girl who had grown to mean so much to him Gladly he would have bartered this mansion, his success, his money, for that little stone house up in the Fens . . . a house in which he would be nobody, but where he could laugh with Celia, hear her laugh, and regain his boyhood in the sweetness of her youth.

Guy rested his elbows on the desk and put his weary aching head between his hands.

'It's too much,' he thought, drearily, 'too much!'

He was so anxious for her. For he knew that she had nothing, and that her only friend was that Lancashire girl who, after all, could do little for her. Where had they gone? Where would that poor sweet child sleep tonight? What life would she lead in the future? She had taken herself beyond his reach so that he could not help her now. And of course she had gone for his sake—he knew that. He worshipped her for it. But he would have given years off his life to know what she was doing and how she would fare.

This was another grief and bitterness which he owed to Frances. It was Frances who had taken Celia from her job with the Davis's and driven her away.

Frances had nagged him all through dinner, because he would not give her the money to go down to Monte Carlo for a fortnight with Rina Millgard and some of their useless friends. But he had been adamant with her.

'Your job is here in the house with me,

142

Frances,' he had said. 'You're my wife and you've asked to remain here as such, so you must stay and run the place and play fair, if you can. You want me to play fair with you, don't you?'

She had shrugged her shoulders and showed a complete indifference to him and his feelings. Then she had wanted to drag him to a poker-party, and he had refused, not only because he hated gambling in any form, but because he was so tired. He had done several big operations that day, besides which he was emotionally exhausted.

The one star in the darkness was his memory of Celia and her love. Out of her perfect, unselfish love for him, she had left him because she wanted him to carry on with his job and play the game. Well, for her sake, by God, he'd do it, he thought. But he wondered, that night, why love must be bought at such a bitter price and how many dreary weeks and months and years they must both go on paying.

CHAPTER ELEVEN

During the weeks that followed, Celia did not get another job. She had no desire, as she told Jan, to spend her life looking after young children at a domestic servant's wage. She wanted something more for the future than

143

that. And largely because Guy Denver had suggested it, she took a secretarial course. Day after day she attended the classes, flung herself assiduously into the job of learning shorthand and typewriting. She was already proficient with the latter because in the years before her father's retirement she had done some typing for him.

But there was nothing much save anxiety in the heart of Celia during those weeks of her training. She was having to pay for it and keep herself at the same time and she knew that her savings would not last forever. Added to which she could not be certain of getting a job. She knew that there were hundreds of trained secretaries trying vainly to get the sort of post she wanted. It was all dull and dreary with nothing much to look forward to. And overshadowing all was the continued pain of loving the man whom she must not see and from whom she could not even hear.

It was so difficult to be brave. Sometimes the longing in her to go to the nearest telephone-kiosk and ring up Guy Denver was almost uncontrollable. She knew, instinctively, that he would want to see her, that she had only to get in touch with him to arrange a meeting. But she must not. For his sake so much more than her own. So whenever the thought of him came into her mind she tried to blot it out and put an iron heel on that crushing sense of loss and longing.

144

Being only human, there were moments when her courage deserted her and misery was uppermost. In those moments, Jan was the big rock of refuge. Jan, who hated to see Celia grow thinner and whiter, did everything she could to help her friend. As soon as she thought that depression was getting the upper hand, she dragged Celia off to see a new film or took her to the gallery in a theatre, or a cheap seat in a music-hall. Anything that might take her mind off that hopeless love-affair which Jan knew was causing so much agony. On one occasion Jan said:

'I wish to the Lord I could find a crowd of nice young men who'd come and amuse you. Maybe you'd get a suitable boyfriend to cheer you up.'

But for that sort of remark Celia only had a faint smile and a very emphatic declaration that there could be no young man in the world who would 'amuse her'.

'And I don't want a boyfriend, Jan. There's only one man in the world for me. If I can't have him, I'll have no one.'

With another sort of girl, Jan might have argued . . . protested that everything gets better in time and that she was much too young and pretty to live and die an old maid, etc. But with Celia, somehow, she could not bring out such arguments. She could see for herself that Celia was different . . . that she loved not just for the moment, but for always

145

. . . and it seemed to her the greatest tragedy. Celia was meant for love and laughter, and not this strain and sorrow.

At the beginning of March, a stroke of luck came Celia's way—something that at least broke the dreary monotony of her present existence, although it brought her no nearer her heart's desire.

By mere chance, coming out of the Underground at Piccadilly Circus one afternoon, where she was about to do a small, piece of shopping for Jan, Celia ran into an old friend. The son of a Lincoln solicitor who had been a friend of her father's.

Celia had known the Maddens since she was a child. This young man, Timothy Madden, had always paid her a good deal of attention. In fact, there had been a time when Celia's people had wondered whether she might marry him. But from Celia's personal point of view there had never been such a possibility. She had never even kissed Tim Madden. All the sentiment had come from his side. Then he had left Lincoln and started work in London, and it was over a year now since she had seen him.

Meeting him today she was conscious of more pleasure than she had ever felt before at the sight of Tim. He was someone from home. A link with the past which had been peaceful and happy. She hailed him eagerly.

'Tim!'

He put out a hand and gripped hers, obvious pleasure lighting up his face.

'Good heavens above, if it isn't Celia!'

'Just imagine running into you,' she said with a little laugh. He went on holding her hand, shaking it warmly. He was delighted to see her. He had heard from his people that the Hammond home had broken up after the old man's death and that Celia had gone away. But no one knew what had happened to her.

Her indifference to any overtures of affection from him in the old days had left him with little expectation of winning her when they were both in Lincoln. He had always admired her and had by no means forgotten her despite the fact that he had neither seen nor heard from her for so long. The sight of her this afternoon was a bit of a shock to him. She was the same lovely Celia with her fairness, her slenderness, those brown lovely eyes which at one time had disturbed him vastly. But she had changed. She was so thin, and she looked so ill and sad. He remembered Celia with laughter on her lips, and a prevailing sense of humour. She used to be the most amusing person at any party up in Lincoln—never at a loss for a jest.

'I'm *terribly* pleased to see you,' he said, dropping her hand at length. 'But what on earth has been happening to you? It must be a good twelve months since we last met. What are you doing? Are you living in London?

Look here . . . come and have a cup of tea and let's talk.'

Celia was glad to do so. Despite the fact that she had never been sentimentally inclined toward Tim Madden, she had always liked him. He was a genial, open, friendly young man, apt to be a bit too hearty and congenial at times, which, she remembered, had annoyed her up in Lincoln. But he was a solid reliable person, and it had been generally accepted in her circle of friends that Tim Madden had a first-class business brain and would go far.

Certainly he looked as though he was on the top of things, she thought. He was smartly groomed—the complete 'man-about-town' with his well-cut blue overcoat, silk muffler, grey felt hat and grey suede gloves. Under his arm he carried a neatly rolled umbrella and a folded newspaper. He was not exactly good-looking, but arresting because of his height. He stood well over six-foot-two and had a pair of attractive blue eyes which knew how to look at a woman—his best feature in an otherwise blunt, ordinary face.

Celia was feminine enough to be glad that she had put on her best black suit and hat in which to do her shopping, and secretly hoped that he did not think that she looked too shabby and dreary. She would hate Tim to write home and tell them all that he had found her so. She had always held her head up high in Lincoln and was proud.

In a very little while, however, Tim Madden lifted her out of her depression. He swept her off to tea at The Piccadilly Hotel and made her eat plenty of hot buttered toast and cakes, telling her that she looked as though she wanted feeding up. He talked nineteen to the dozen in his cheerful fashion, and brought her to the pitch when she could forget her miseries and exchange reminiscences about the past, and laugh with him.

He was full of himself. Doing extra-ordinarily well, he said. She remembered that he had been studying as an architect when she left Lincoln. Now he was fully qualified and with a big firm in the West-End. At the age of twenty-seven he was beginning to build up a bit of a reputation for himself, he informed Celia. He was making money, and had excellent prospects for the future. He lived in a small flat near Marble Arch, played a lot of squash in his spare time—he had always been fond of sports—had a small car and 'tootled into the country at the week-ends', as he put it, and life was pretty good one way and another.

'And of course,' he laughed to Celia, 'there is always the odd girlfriend. Not that I've ever found one as charming as my old pal, Celia.'

She sat looking at him with envy. What marvellous spirits! How wonderful to be prosperous and gay and pleased with life, and to have no crushing disappointments or sorrows. Certainly, Tim Madden was to

149

be envied. Then he ceased to chatter about himself and made her talk. And that was a different story. She had nothing very cheerful to tell Tim and what she did tell him of the life she had led since her father's death and the sale of her old home, horrified him. He ceased to laugh and joke. His square rather rugged face took on an unusual gravity.

'Good heavens! I had no idea things were as bad as this with you, Celia,' he said.

She bit her lip.

'I suppose they could be worse.'

'I don't quite see how. I'm shaken to the core, my dear. They all thought at home that Mr Hammond had left you some money.'

'Practically nothing, Tim. He was very much in debt.'

'It's tough,' said Tim. 'It would have been tough for a man but it's dashed awful for a woman—a mere kid like you.

'I'm no kid, Tim.'

He lit a cigarette and looked at her critically.

'A slip of a girl. And what a story! Shut up in that house during the flood with this doctor fellow. It must have been awful.'

Her heart began to thump as it always did at the thought of Guy Denver. The painful colour stole into her cheeks. She said:

'No, it wasn't awful. He was terribly kind.'

'Anyone would be kind to you,' said Tim, and said no more about the doctor. He was not really interested. But he had an absorbing desire to help Celia. He couldn't see a friend from home in this plight. Let alone the girl whom he had once thought of marrying. Only *thought* . . . of course he had been a bit 'browned off', as he called it, by her chilly treatment of him. But now he didn't mind how she regarded him. He wanted to be her friend, and he said so.

'I'm going to get you a job, Celia. And when I say a thing, I mean it.'

'It's good of you, Tim, but I'm not fully trained yet. I've got months more of this shorthand.'

'Rubbish! I'll get you a job where you don't need shorthand.'

'But how—where?'

Tim Madden invented a job there and then. He could afford to do that sort of thing now. He stood very high in the firm of Rotherford & Sons, Architects. Not only because he had made such a success with his plans for that block of flats in Brixton, but because his uncle was a partner. He'd get hold of Uncle Bill and see that Celia was installed in the firm right away.

'I need a typist,' said Tim, grandly. 'No, not a shorthand-typist. There are plenty of those knocking about. I want an intelligent girl to do odd secretarial jobs. You're just what I've been looking for. The angels must have sent you straight from heaven.'

Slightly dazed, Celia shook her head at him. 'I don't believe a word. There can't be such a vacancy. You can't be wanting a thoroughly inefficient girl in your office.'

'You're not inefficient. From what I can remember, you've always shown a keen spirit and a tidy mind, to say nothing of the fact that you look lovely. And I can't bear plain girls around me.'

She had to laugh.

'You were always a dear old fool, Tim.'

'Always a fool about *you*, Celia.'

'Oh, that was long ago.'

'It's got nothing to do with this job, anyhow,' he said generously. 'Now listen! You come along to Rotherford & Sons tomorrow morning. Our offices are in Cockspur Street. I'll give you the number. Go up in the lift to the top floor, and you ask for my noble self, and I will grant you an interview, Miss Hammond.'

'Do you really mean it?' said Celia, dizzily. She felt dizzy. It was pretty good to think that she would be given a real job in a good office, long before her training was over, and under the patronage of one of her oldest friends. Tim was really a dear. She could forgive him for being facetious. When he actually wrote down an address for her, handed it to her, and made the appointment with her for ten o'clock tomorrow, she began to feel that her luck was really in. There *was* a vacancy, Tim assured

152

her, and she should fill it right away. Salary? Well, he'd start her at two-pounds-ten a week, and if she made herself indispensable (which of course she would) he'd see that she got much more.

Celia was overwhelmed. Her eyes filled with tears as she thanked him. That made Tim Madden very uncomfortable. Celia was not a 'crying girl'. His memory of her was of a cool, self-possessed young woman who teased him and derided his amatory advances. He was both moved and distressed by the sight of her tears. He patted her hand in a brotherly fashion.

'I can't bear to see you looking unhappy, Celia,' he said. 'You've been through a rotten time. We must try to make it cheerful for you in the office.'

'It all sounds too good to be true,' she said.

'It's such a mercy that I ran into you. Look here . . . why not dine with me tonight? Let me take you to a show or something.'

But Celia shook her head. If Tim was to become her employer, she was not going to start her job on these grounds and she told him so.

'No entertaining your typist, Tim. I'm going to be Miss Hammond and you're my boss and going out together won't work.'

'Hey!' he protested, 'just as standoffish as ever! Still Celia of the frigid heart, huh?'

She was silent a moment. The beloved

153

face of Guy rose before her, choking her with a thousand memories—the pain which was scarcely bearable. Frigid heart! God, if Tim only knew—only knew how she loved Guy, would always love him!

Tim was grumbling.

'You're so darned attractive—aren't you *ever* going to unfreeze?'

Then Celia said:

'Tim, I may as well tell you, I'm not frozen—I'm just the opposite. I'm terribly, terribly in love with someone. You might as well know it. Only . . . she turned her face away from him, the muscles in her throat working 'only he's married and it's no use.'

Tim Madden cleared his throat.

'I'm sorry. You do seem to have tough luck all round, poor little thing,' he said gruffly.

There was an embarrassed pause, then back came Tim's natural geniality. Picking up her hand he squeezed it and said:

'Well, never say die. You mustn't feel too down and out. I don't know anything about the chap—but I feel—jealous. Wish I had his chance. However—for your sake, I suppose I ought to hope the wife will slip on a bit of banana skin and break her neck!'

Celia found herself laughing again.

'You're such an idiot, Tim.'

'I'm all for idiocy,' he said, 'in every direction. But, honey, I've got to leave you now. It's been so lovely talking to you—I've completely forgotten a most important date. There's a blonde waiting for me at Oddy's. You see, I'm faithful to blondes, in memory of you.'

Celia walked with him out of the hotel, feeling slightly more light-hearted. And she was genuinely excited at the thought of that job. What a lot she would have to tell Jan tonight. Jan, of course, would say that she was foolish not to dine with Tim —not to take any chance that came her way. But she didn't want *that* sort of chance. She needed work but not a man to amuse her. There was no room in her heart for anybody except Guy—the unquenchable memory of Guy.

Tim reminded her of her appointment with him in the morning, bade her good-bye and hurried off to meet his blonde. Celia walked through the grey March twilight, managed to do her shopping just before the big stores closed, then took a bus back to Bayswater.

'I've got a job,' she kept telling herself, 'I'm going to get two-pounds-ten a week. A *start* in life and no need to go on spending all my capital!'

She began to think of all the things she'd do for Jan when she got her first week's salary. She'd buy her that new hat at Swan & Edgar's which Jan coveted and had refused to buy for herself. She'd buy her some silk stockings, too. Real silk, not artificial! She wanted to do many things for dear Jan who had been so unforgettably kind to her.

Celia's mind was buzzing with plans as she walked down the Bayswater Road and turned into the street in which she lived. Just as she reached her boarding-house, she heard the hoot-hoot of a car coming up behind her. She turned and glanced over her shoulder. The March night was cold, and inclined to be foggy. For a moment Celia saw only the dim long shape of a private saloon-car. Then it came quietly alongside her, and pulled up at the kerb. At once she recognised it . . . and the man at the wheel. Every bit of colour drained from her face. Her heart missed a beat with shock and astonishment. She almost dropped her bag and the parcel she was carrying. She stood there clutching it with ice-cold fingers, staring speechlessly. Then her lips formed the name:

'Guy!'

Guy Denver stepped out of the car. He wore an overcoat and muffler but he was hatless. Drawing off his driving gauntlets, he approached Celia, and stood before her, looking down at her with eager, hungry eyes.

'Celia! At last!' he said.

The colour surged back into her cheeks, violently. She breathed so fast that she could scarcely speak.

'Guy! How . . . how did you know . . . how did you find out . . .?' She broke off helplessly.

He seized both her hands.

'Oh, my dear! Come into the car. Come and let me drive you somewhere where we can talk.'

She hesitated only for the fraction of a second. After the weeks of separation it was such heaven to see him that she could not for the moment be sensible, practical or even discreet. She felt only the wildest longing to do as he asked. The wildest excitement of seeing him once more; at hearing his voice; feeling his fingers, strong and warm, convulsively gripping hers.

There was no resistance in her. She allowed him to lead her to the car. She found herself driving away with him, intoxicated by the familiar odour of tobacco and of brilliantine that clung to him . . . feeling his arm press against hers . . . glorying in the knowledge that she was with him again after the long grief and pain of their separation.

'Oh, God,' she said weakly, 'I didn't expect this.'

'I had to see you,' he said. 'I *had* to.'

She shut her eyes tightly.

'How did you find out?'

'Miss Fuller.'

'She promised not to . . .'

'Don't blame her. I went round the other day and bullied and wheedled, and you know the old thing will do anything for me. I *made* her tell me. Apparently you had to let her know where you were, because of some

157

important correspondence that arrived.'

'Yes . . . our family solicitors were writing to me . . . I had to sign some papers . . . I'd given them Miss Fuller's address and she forwarded letters to me. But I didn't want you to know . . .'

'For a time I didn't want to know, either,' he broke in, 'at least, I thought it might be best if I didn't know. But after five weeks of hell, I couldn't stand it any more. You've been brave, Celia—braver than I've been, my dear.'

'Oh, Guy, you don't know, you don't know how I've suffered.'

He took his eyes from the road for a second and flung her a warm, intense glance.

'My darling!'

The way in which he said that, in which he looked at her, was too devastating for Celia. Half choking with emotion, she drew nearer him and leaned her head against his shoulder. She was conscious suddenly of immense fatigue—a weariness of the spirit rather than of the body. She had struggled so long against her feelings for this man. Now just for a few moments she gave way to them. Oh, the peace, the blessed peace of leaning against him like this, and of being in his beloved presence!

'My dear,' he said, 'the main reason why I couldn't bear things was because I didn't know what had happened to you. I think I could have stood it, if I'd known you'd had a job and were well and reasonably happy. But I thought of you, unemployed and living a wretched existence on your own, and I couldn't bear it. It was too much. I *had* to make sure you were all right before I could go on.'

She could not answer for a moment. She was too deeply moved by the thought that he cared so much about her. He was driving on and on.

'Where are we going?' she whispered.

'Anywhere,' he said, 'out of London. Just for an hour or two I must be with you. No, don't deny me, Celia. I know it's all wrong and yet it isn't. It's utterly right than should be with you. I love you. I've had time to realise how much and I know just how much you love me. Running away as you did was proof of it. I know that you did it for me. I can never forget that. I adore you for it. But I must be with you for a little while, even though I realise it may be for the last time.'

'Jan will wonder where I am,' said Celia, helplessly. 'She'll be worried to death. I must let her know.'

'Phone her,' he said, 'phone her and tell her the truth. I don't mind her knowing that you're with me.'

'And . . . your . . . wife?' The words stuck in Celia's throat.

'I left Frances at her poker club. And she doesn't care a damn where I go. Sometimes I don't know why I carry on, except for all the obvious reasons. Law, honour, reputation

. . . and the rest of it! But it's a mockery of a marriage, Celia. I think Frances literally hates me these days because I'm not the sort of fool I used to be, at her feet. And God knows I feel very little but scorn for her. Sometimes I ask myself if I'm doing the right thing in remaining with her.'

Celia struggled to find words. Her mind was so dazed and chaotic by this sudden and unexpected meeting with Guy that she found it difficult to talk intelligently.

And when he spoke thus about Frances and his marriage, she felt as he did . . . that such a marriage could not possibly be right. Yet it *was* a marriage. He and Frances were bound to each other. He could not leave her without injuring himself and his medical reputation, and that seemed to her the all-important thing.

Tonight it was of very secondary importance to Guy Denver. During these weeks of separation from Celia, he had been working at fever heat. He had achieved fresh triumphs of surgery . . . he was at the top of the tree in his profession . . . On the surface he had everything that a man could want. Yet he had nothing. Nothing without Celia. He was a lonely, embittered man. And she . . . God alone knew what she had been through, he thought. He was shocked by her appearance. She was so painfully thin and tragic-eyed.

'How's the head?' he asked, tenderly.

She answered:

160

'Completely healed. Sometimes I look at the little scar. I love it because you stitched it up . . . it's your mark on me . . .' she tried to laugh, but the laughter broke in her throat. The wild hot tears surged into her eyes and she hid her face against his sleeve, kissing it passionately, achingly. And she was absurdly happy when she saw him take the familiar pipe from his coat pocket and put it in his mouth. Somehow, that homely-looking brier pipe was part of Guy and immediately changed the sophisticated London specialist into the Guy who had washed up dishes with her during the flood. The Guy whom she had learned to love. He laid a hand over hers, pressing it hard.

'I refuse to feel a criminal because of this hour,' he said, 'It can't do any harm to anybody. I know you'll argue that it's dangerous and that it mustn't be repeated. I expect I'll agree with you later on, and promise not to come near you again. But I had to know that you're all right, Celia. Oh, God, my darling, tell me that you are. Tell me everything about yourself.'

She lifted her head.

'There isn't much to tell.'

'What have you been doing?'

She gave him a brief outline of her existence since she had left the job with Mrs Davis.

'And now I've met this friend of mine, Tim Madden, I suppose I can safely say that I've got a good job which I start tomorrow,' she finished.

'I'm jealous of Tim Madden,' said Guy. 'Damn it, why should he be able to help you and not I?'

'Oh, darling, don't feel that way. I know you'd have found me work if I'd let you.'

'I'm only too glad, really, that you've been given a decent chance,' he said. Then, lover-like added: 'Is this fellow in love with you?'

'Not seriously. In fact, not at all. He did have a sort of penchant for me, once. But he's not really serious where women are concerned.'

'But you're different from every other woman. He might become serious about you.'

'Oh, darling,' she said again, 'you needn't be jealous of Tim. He's never appealed to me, and anyhow no man could, now. There's nobody for me in the world except you.'

'I like to hear you say that.'

'It's true. Even though I never see you, I'm absolutely yours, forever.'

He could not doubt her sincerity. A feeling of mad happiness surged through him. It was so good to be beside her, to hear the warmth in her vibrant young voice and to know that all that he felt for her was amply returned. It was so good to be loved . . . even though that love was a hopeless one . . . so very good to a man who was starved of love and happiness . . . a man who had to share a house with a woman-like Frances.

162

They were on the outskirts of London now, on the open road.

'We always seem to drive in a fog,' said Guy with a brief laugh. 'It's pretty misty tonight.'

'I don't care,' she said.

'Neither do I. Oh, darling, darling, it's good to be with you. Celia I must hold you in my arms or go crazy.'

'I feel the same,' she whispered. 'Hold me, Guy, *hold me.*'

He pulled up the car, switched off the engine, turned to her and swept her into his arms. Then he set his lips to her mouth.

The long kiss which they exchanged was almost unbearably poignant. They clung to each other, shaken, drowned by an overwhelming wave of love and longing. For a long time Celia stayed thus, lying against him, her arms around his neck, his hands caressing her and their lips meeting again and again . . . urgent . . . insatiable.

At last he let her go. She could see his face dimly, a face from which all bitterness had been wiped. Pain was still there, but complete contentment lay in his eyes.

He lifted her hands and with a gesture which she remembered only too well, carried each one in turn to his lips.

'That was so wonderful, Celia. Darling, my sweet love, I love you so!'

'I adore you,' she said, with the simplicity which had always enchanted him.

163

'Heaven knows why,' he said. 'I'm a wretched person for any girl to love. Married . . . tied up . . . unable to do anything for you . . . or about you . . . what use is there in loving me, Celia?'

'I may as well say the same to you. Why do you love me?'

'I could give you a thousand reasons.'

She pressed her cheek against his shoulder.

'If only our love wasn't so hopeless, Guy. It seems so cruel that two people should feel like this about each other and be denied the right to love.'

'It's inhumanly cruel. There have been days and nights when I've thought about you and asked myself why I don't chuck everything and just carry you away.'

'You couldn't do it, darling, and I couldn't let you.'

He gave a heavy sigh.

'I suppose not. But to leave you again will seem to me a worse sin than leaving Frances.'

'I don't want you to leave me, Guy. I shudder at the mere thought. But we can never get away from the fact that Frances is your wife.'

'What a wife!' he said with a hollow laugh.

'Oh, Guy, I wish things weren't so bad for you.'

'They're pretty bad, darling, except when I'm working. I can lose myself in my work, of course. But once I start to think of you . . .

164

it's pretty bad. I even envy you being alone. It must be better than to have to share your life with someone you despise.'

'I'm sure of that. I couldn't bear to live with another man loving you as I do.'

He gathered her back into his arms fiercely.

'I couldn't bear it, either. I didn't think it was possible to love anyone as much as I love you. I love you so much that I want every bit of you . . . . all your loveliness and sweetness . . . your body, your mind, your soul. Celia, darling, *darling.*'

His lips were against her mouth once more. Drained of all powers of resistance, she returned his kisses. But came out of that maze of desperate passion only to realise that it was but a prelude to their second parting. He *had* to leave her. She *had* to let him go. And it would be madness for them to have any successive meetings. Sitting together in the car, with their arms around each other, they agreed upon that, miserably, but definitely. They loved each other too much to meet. It could only end in disaster. They were both only human. He must do the right thing and keep away from her.

'It'll be hellish,' he said, 'but a little easier, perhaps, now that I know you're all right. When you ran away that day, you left me in such terrible doubt. Anything might have happened to you.'

'Oh, darling, I thought it was best.'

'You were wonderful and brave. But it's better for me to know you're safe and well and that you're going to work in a place where you've got an old friend.'

'I'll be all right,' she whispered. 'You mustn't worry about me, Guy.'

'I'll try not to, darling. But it's pretty grim not even being able to hear from you.'

'I'm always with you in spirit, Guy. Always!'

'I feel that. I've felt you close beside me all these weeks.'

'And you've been with me.'

'That means a lot for us to be together in mind. I never forget you for a single moment. I do all my work for you now . . . everything I do is for you.'

'That will comfort me, Guy.'

'But, oh, my darling, how long the days will seem without you . . . without a hope of seeing you.'

She began to tremble. He wrapped the fur rug around her slight body and kept her in his arms. He kissed her hair repeatedly.

'My darling, lovely Celia!'

'Don't let's stay here,' she whispered, 'I don't think I can bear it. I shall only break down.'

'We'll go and have a meal somewhere,' he said, 'and then I'll drive you home.'

She nodded.

'Yes . . . yes, you must take me home very soon. And you must go back, too.'

166

He released her and switched on the engine. They moved forward through the darkness. And for a long while neither of them spoke. She sat close to him with her hand on his knee. Now and again he lifted that small cold hand to his lips.'

Celia thought:

'Days and weeks and months . . . *years* without him. It's such ghastly pain. Why doesn't pain kill one? Why can't one die? Or why don't I love him a little less and induce him to run away with me and ruin himself?'

But that was a thing that she knew she could never do, no matter what it cost her. She made an effort to master her pain. He wanted her to dine with him. He wouldn't want her to be miserable and dull and tearful. Men didn't like women to be like that. He would want to have a happier memory of her.

So, when finally they sat at dinner together at a small wayside hotel, she smiled and jested with him and they laughed together over their memories of the flood. She would not spoil the evening for him by letting the agony of her feelings come to the surface. He had never found her more fascinating. She showed him a side which he had never seen before. A bewitching, captivating side . . . a Celia of shining eyes, flushed cheeks and ready wit. A woman to admire and to adore. And she remained like that until the last moment before they said goodbye. The moment when he pulled the car up before the Bayswater boarding-house and she realised that her little hour of mingled heaven and hell was over.

Then the smile died from her lips and her large brown eyes looked into his, haunted, terrified. She was afraid of leaving him. Afraid of facing life without him and he knew it. He could not fail to know it, because he felt that same grinding fear and misery of losing her.

He caught her close and held her for a moment in a desperate embrace.

'I can't let you go, darling, I can't.'

'You must, Guy. And you must swear never to come here again. You *must*. For your own sake as well as mine.'

'Oh God, Celia.'

'Swear it.'

The sweat stood out on his forehead. He felt drained of vitality, of purpose, of everything but his overwhelming need of her. But he knew that she was right and he forced himself to utter the words:

'I swear it.'

'I'll love you all my life,' she said, chaotically, 'and I'll remember everything . . . till I die. Now, good-bye, darling, *darling!*'

She tore herself out of his arms, opened the door of the car, jumped out, slammed the door again. Then without daring to look back, ran up the steps and into the house.

CHAPTER TWELVE

Celia had been doing secretarial work in the offices of Rotherford & Sons, Cockspur Street, for a little over a month.

One fine mild morning in April found her sitting at her desk typing a letter for Tim, and typing it badly. She kept making mistakes, having to rub out, and finally she pulled the sheet out of the roller with an exclamation of disgust.

Her mind was not on her work today. As a rule she concentrated on her job and so far, according to Tim, she was a big success in spite of the fact that she had none of the technical knowledge of the other girls employed here. He had been right when he had said that she was methodical and efficient. And she had a memory which he found invaluable. It was Celia who made his appointments, saw that he kept them, reminded him of letters that must be written or answered, answered telephone calls and took messages from clients with a tact and charm which had done for her exactly what Tim had wished it to do—made her indispensable to the firm.

In another month's time Celia's salary was going up. And she had no qualms now about her future. She could see that she was safely with Rotherford & Sons for as long as she

169

cared to work in this way.

She felt that she owed an immense lot to Tim. She could not possibly have nicer employers or work in a more congenial atmosphere. Her life was not as poor Jan's— toiling in the dark and dreary atmosphere in the wholesale furriers in the City. This prosperous firm of architects had installed themselves in beautiful modern offices with great windows looking over the roof-tops of London. The latest form of heating and lighting had been installed. The carpets were thick and luxurious. The decorations the last word in modernity. The place was a good advertisement for the firm.

Celia worked at a desk in a small room leading out of Tim's private office. On the sill beside the wide window stood a bowl of iris, mixed with daffodils and narcissi.

'A few harbingers of Spring to show you that it's time we all leapt over the meadows with the little lambs,' Tim had said when he gave them to her this morning.

She was never allowed to be without flowers. And never without the cheerful flow of facetious but kindly humour from her 'boss'. He was undoubtedly still interested in her— she realised that and regretted it, more for his sake than her own. It was very pleasant to be treated so well, to be spoiled and fussed over, to be made to feel that she was of real value. But she did not want the personal element to creep into it. She could never respond to any overtures from Tim. She belonged to Guy Denver—as she had told him—utterly and forever.

Of course it was Guy of whom she had been thinking this morning, instead of keeping her mind on that letter which she had to type. She had not seen him since their brief passionate meeting of five weeks ago. And she had not heard from him. They were both keeping rigidly to the agreement which they had made, to remain apart. But that did not mean that he was forgotten by her for a single moment. And this morning he had been brought especially before her notice by something which she had read in the paper—just a paragraph about St. Gabriel's—the big London hospital, not far from Cockspur Street. A new wing had been opened yesterday by the Duchess of Kent— and the name of one of the most important consulting-surgeons bracketed with that of Sir Maurice Whitby, House Governor, and other notabilities in the medical world had caught Celia's attention. At the sight of that name— Mr Guy Denver—she had felt herself tremble and burn. She had cut out the little paragraph and put it in her bag. God, how she loved him! How she loved to know all that he was doing, and to follow his life. Yet what little opportunity she had of doing so. And there were times when she was forced to remember that woman, his wife. Frances Denver, as

Celia had once seen her—beautiful, arrogant, imperious in her costly furs, and with that faint sneer on her scarlet lips. That was the woman with whom Guy lived. But a woman whom, he had assured Celia, he never now held in his arms. Nevertheless, Celia thought of her with burning jealousy. What wouldn't she give to be in Frances Denver's shoes! And yet Frances had once nearly left Guy for another man. It seemed to Celia nothing short of insanity.

Her mind was wandering round another subject. Tim hated that Bayswater boarding-house in which she lived. He was trying to bully her into moving. He wanted her to live in a better place, he said. He had a friend in Chelsea with a little house—the wife of an Army officer who was out in Palestine, and who was hard-up. She would take Celia as a paying-guest and give her a real home. But Celia would not leave Jan.

'Jan looked after me when I was down-and-out and I'm not going to desert her, now that my prospects are better,' she repeatedly told Tim.

Tim continued to argue. In fact, Tim was a little too interfering altogether in her private affairs, and Celia was irritated because of it. Yet she could not help liking him, looking forward to her day's work with him. He always made her laugh. It was good to laugh even when one's heart was nearly breaking.

Despite her reluctance to do so, she had

172

gone out to several dinners and shows with Tim. He would not take 'no' for an answer, and Jan encouraged Celia warmly to accept these invitations.

'You're a fool to sit at home and brood over a married man,' was Jan's blunt analysis of the situation, 'Here's an attractive young bachelor with prospects and money running after you. Use your commonsense, lamb, and don't lose a golden opportunity.'

It was useless Celia thought, trying to explain what she felt . . . futile to try to make Jan or anybody in the world realise that although she might never see Guy again, her heart was his, and she could not contemplate the thought of marrying another man.

Just before lunch, Tim Madden called her into the next room.

She walked in prepared to do some work. But Tim was not in a working mood. Sprawled in his revolving-chair, he was circling round slowly, thumbs in his braces, blue eyes scowling and a look of dissatisfaction on his usually good-humoured face. All the windows were open wide. The April sun streamed in. It streamed upon Celia and made a nimbus of gold around her fair head. Tim stopped revolving in his chair and concentrated his gaze upon Celia, and her lovely hair. Pretty wasn't the word, he thought. She was delicious. Nothing of the heavy make-up necessary for Celia. Only a touch of powder, and an outline

173

of lipstick. She had a glorious skin and the longest blackest lashes he had ever seen. *And a figure to make any man's pulses race.* She was not as thin as she had been when he had found her in that state of complete dejection, in March. She was just perfect now—slim, graceful, and dressed with taste. He hadn't seen her in this dress before. Something new for the Spring, he supposed. Soft grey wool with a white puritan collar. She looked rather like a little girl of sixteen. Yet those large brown eyes of hers were still tragic and the eyes of a woman who suffered. It hurt Tim Madden to look into them. He was no psychologist and he treated most women as pretty playthings to be petted and given flowers and taken out in order to 'make whoopee'. But Celia couldn't come into this category and never would. There was so much dignity about her. Too much for Tim's liking.

'Browned off' he told himself, using his favourite expression. 'It doesn't matter what I do . . . "browned off"!'

'Do you want me, Mr Madden?' Celia asked, demurely.

'Yes,' said Tim, gloomily, 'yes, like hell I do.'

Celia coloured.

'Don't be silly.'

He stood up and straightened his coat. Taking a comb from his pocket, he passed it through his thick black hair.

'Spring is in the air, Celia, and you're still behaving like mid-winter.'

She shook her head at him.

'What *do* you want?'

'A little encouragement, honey.'

'Now, Tim, you know that this is the office ...'

'And that I'm your boss and that you're my typist and that all work and no play keeps Celia a good girl. Oh, yes! I'll believe you. But I won't agree with you. "All work and no play" gives Tim the willies. I tell you the sun's shining and it's "Oh, to be in England now that April's there ..." Is that right? I'm rather bad on quotations.'

'That's right. But I can't see what it has to do with you and me.'

He came near her and stood looking down at her from his great height.

'Don't you like me one little bit?'

She caught her lower lip nervously between her teeth.

'You know I like you and that I'm eternally grateful for what you've done for me. But ...'

'But I'm just about the most unattractive man on earth to you, eh?' he finished for her.

'Not at all, Tim,' she said gently. 'I think you're very attractive. But ...'

'To the devil with all these "buts".'

Celia sat down on the edge of his desk, feeling a trifle weak. Tim was so persistent. What could she do about it? How could she

175

make him understand that she could never find any man on earth attractive in the way that he meant? How could she explain that day and night she had before her the vision of Guy's thin tired face with those clever eyes and tender lips . . . that she could remember nothing but the touch of those sensitive surgeon's fingers . . . nothing but the wild hope that one day she might be with him again, a hope that refused to die even though there was nothing on earth to keep it alive.

Tim caught one of her hands in his.

'Celia, I'm not fooling. I talk a lot of tripe but I'm honestly in love with you. I was up in Lincoln. I still am. Isn't there a shred of hope?'

'Oh, Tim!' she said.

'Don't turn me down, Celia. I'm a confirmed bachelor unless you'll marry me. I could make you happy if you'd give me a chance. I'm moderately well-off these days. I can give you what you need. We can have a grand little flat, my car, some very good times and . . .'

'I know, I know all that,' she interrupted, 'and I'm frightfully touched and honoured by your proposal, Tim. But I can't marry you, my dear. I just don't love you and that's the unvarnished truth.'

'Let me teach you to love me, Celia.'

She tried to draw her hand away from his.

'Tim, you know there's someone else.'

'You've often hinted that,' he said, shortly, 'but surely you can't go on chasing a will-of-the-wisp all your life. He's married. You've said so. What can you do about it?'

She shut her eyes, the old pain racking her.

'Nothing, I admit.'

'Who is he? Tell me about him? If he's in love with you, why doesn't he divorce his wife and marry you? Good Lord, it wouldn't matter who I was married to—if I fell for you I'd leave my home for you tonight.'

Celia's long lashes lifted. She looked at him with a mixture of pain and regret.

'You're a dear, Tim, and I know you're sincere. But this man can't leave his wife. We neither of us really believe in divorce, and even if we did, it would be impossible, because he's a doctor. His reputation is at stake. That's the whole tragedy. I could never let him ruin himself for me.'

Tim dropped her hand. He found a cigarette, lit one, shrugged his shoulders hopelessly.

'That's just the sort of thing that *would* happen to you. Renunciation, sacrifice and all the rest of it. It's tough! I'm damned sorry for both of you. But if you know it's hopeless, why not try to give another fellow a chance?'

'My dear,' said Celia, 'I love Guy so much that I just haven't room in my heart for anybody else.'

'I see,' said Tim, 'so "Guy's" his name! God, but I envy him.

'You needn't. He isn't very happy, I don't

177

suppose.'

Tim took the cigarette from his lips and looked down at her intensely for a moment.

'I'm not very happy, either, Celia. I'm crazy about you. Don't turn me down altogether, darling. Let me take you round, and oh! I don't mean being engaged or anything if you don't want to yet, but let me see you and do a lot for you, and some day you might come to care for me.'

She was touched and flattered. She could not be otherwise. And Tim had a very handsome pair of eyes. She found herself half wishing that she could love him. How easy it would have made life! How pleasant to become engaged to a charming young man who could offer her marriage. How much better than living alone, grieving over a hopeless love. Yet the memory of that love was so precious that it outweighed any desire on her part to live her life as Tim wished her to do.

He had thrown away his cigarette and was close to her now. For a moment he took her in his arms. She placed two hands on his shoulders gently to ward him off. But he was insistent. He bent to kiss her. She turned away her lips. No man, *no man*, save Guy should ever kiss her on the mouth again. Tim's kiss landed on her cheek. With a sharp sigh he drew away.

'Browned off again! You're just the little

frigidaire, aren't you? I suppose I must resign myself to the inevitable, and forget it's Spring!'

He was the old Tim, laughing again but she detected the note of pain in his voice. She was desperately sorry for him. She knew that pain only too well—that awful ache of hopeless love.

'Oh, Tim,' she said, 'don't be upset about it and don't let it spoil our friendship, I'm so fond of you, really.'

'I'm *too* fond of you,' he said with a grimace, 'but believe me, baby, nothing can spoil our friendship. That's secure. And to tell you the truth, I'm like Wellington. I won't admit defeat. You may be more attracted by me in the summer. I'll frisk about with the lambs alone for a bit, and come back for another answer when the roses are blooming. And now, how about lunch? Could you frisk with me as far as the Berkeley Buttery?'

But Celia was forced to refuse even that request. She was meeting Jan at Lyons Corner House. Not so chic, nor as amusing, perhaps, as the Berkeley. But she was giving dear old Jan some lunch and nothing would induce her to disappoint her friend.

She went out into the April sunlight, a little saddened by her encounter with Tim. She hated to hurt him She could see that he was genuinely in love. And he meant to try again . . . nothing daunted! What a prospect for her! It made things a bit difficult in the office.

179

'Guy, Guy,' she thought, 'where are, you, my darling, and what are you doing this morning?'

How utterly hopeless it was even to try to put another man in his place.

She crossed the street, looking upwards a little, dreamily. The grey cupolas and stonework of the old buildings looked lovely against that blue sky. London was lovely in the Spring. It was quite good to be alive. Yet so desperately sad to have to live from day to day—on memories.

A bus came thundering along, a taxi to her left hooted. Celia was suddenly aware that she was stepping into a stream of traffic. Her thoughts had been elsewhere. She moved sharply to the right. And then too late, loomed the bus, and in her ears came a confused sound of brakes grinding, the screech of tyres skidding, and of many warning voices shouting on either side. She had one blind instant of panic. Then a mudguard caught her and flung her down. Instantaneously the golden April morning was blotted out for Celia. She pitched into a world of darkness from which she did not waken for a very long time.

She knew nothing of the chaos that followed her accident. The traffic jam . . . all vehicles held up by policemen. The crowd that surged around that grey prostrate figure, the pitying hands that lifted her, and made a pillow out of a coat for her fair young head. The sharp bell of an ambulance streaking down the road. The

180

ambulance-men in their white coats lifting her on to a stretcher. A policeman jotting down notes, opening her bag, trying to find her address. The jumble of voices:

'Poor young thing . . . is she dead?'

'Badly hurt, I'd say . . . '

'Such a pretty girl . . . '

'What was she doing, to get hit like that?'

'Where's she being taken to?'

'St. Gabriel's Hospital . . .'

And St. Gabriel's Hospital it was. The slim unconscious figure of Celia Hammond was carried into the new casualty ward in that new wing which Mr Guy Denver, surgeon-consultant, had helped to open only yesterday.

CHAPTER THIRTEEN

Guy Denver walked into his wife's boudoir and laid a small sheaf of bills on her desk. Frances was on her sofa waiting for her manicurist, two little pads of witch-hazel over her eyes, her recumbent form draped in a chiffon negligée which was trimmed with fur. She did not remove the pads from her eyes as she heard her husband's footsteps. She drawled:

'What *do* you want, Guy?'

'To hand you over two-hundred-and-fifty pounds' worth of bills for your clothes,' he said, drily, 'and to beg you to pay them as

181

soon as possible. They come in repeatedly and always to me.'

Frances' fingers with their blood-red nails then lifted the cotton wool from her eyes. She glowered at Guy:

'You never have anything pleasant to say when you come into this room.'

Guy answered in the same dry voice:

'It isn't very pleasant for me to be pursued by your creditors, Frances.'

She shrugged her shoulders.

'You're responsible for my debts.'

'You have a very generous allowance,' he said, 'which you frequently exceed and I've already increased it, backed up your overdraft, bought you a mink cape and . . .'

'That's right,' she broke in, 'throw your presents down my throat.'

He looked down at her, his face wooden. Never these days did he openly betray to his wife what he felt about her . . . what supreme contempt he had for her shallow and mercenary character. But there were times when he wondered how it was possible for a man to be so blinded when he is in love. For once he had thought that he loved this woman. When she had left him for de Poiret, he had been heartbroken. Yet now he realised that he had never loved her at all, never known her at all. All her charm had been on the surface. All her seeming affection for him had been a tissue of lies. And now the life they lived together was barely tolerable. They positively disliked each other. For as much as he despised her, so he knew that she hated him, because he was no longer her slave, and because he would give her no cause to divorce him. Now that she had been prevented from getting her freedom by her own actions, she would have liked to have found something to pin on *him*—some infidelity whereby she could act the aggrieved wife, get away with a third of his income, *and* ruin him in the bargain.

Inevitably his mind, his secret heart compared her with Celia. Celia, the brave, the loyal who would not take her happiness at his cost. And at times he wondered how to go on—and why he did not crack up under the strain of maintaining this ghastly marriage.

'My dear Frances,' he said, 'I don't think you can honestly accuse me of throwing my gifts down your throat. I'm not ungenerous to you, but there are limits—even to *my* income. If you continue like this, we shall be living away beyond it, and I do not intend that to happen. In my opinion it's a bad principle.'

'Oh, to hell with your principles—I'm sick of them,' said Frances, with an expression which took all the beauty out of her face. And she swung her feet down on to the floor, sat up and pulled the rose-coloured chiffon angrily about her shoulders. It tore under her sharp pointed nails and she added a *'damn'* viciously under her breath.

183

Guy turned and began to walk out of the room. He felt stifled in it. It reeked of the scent of flowers—Frances was always being sent expensive bouquets by young men who were her admirers—and of the strong French perfume which she used. There was not a single thing about her that attracted him any longer. And she knew it and it never failed to infuriate her, even though she no longer wanted him.

She called him back,

'Where are you going?'

'To the hospital. Don't keep me, please. I'm late already.'

'We work so hard!' she sneered.

One of Guy's eyebrows went up ironically.

'I prefer the hospital to the atmosphere of bickering which I get in this house.'

'If we bicker, it's your fault.'

'Do you really think that?'

Frances opened a shagreen box, took a Turkish cigarette from it and said, without ceremony:

'Give me a light.'

He chafed, anxious to be off to the hospital. He knew that she was only trying to keep him in order to irritate him. As he lit the cigarette for her, she flung him a derisive look from beneath her long lashes which were stiff and black with make-up.

'I can't say you've made much effort to be the loving husband since you came back from

184

your escapade in the floods.'

He remained immovable.

'I don't think we'll discuss that.'

'I honestly believe you're still in love with that girl.'

Then for an instant his calm deserted him. The colour rushed to his cheeks and his eyes became suffused. How dared she mention 'that girl' . . . his lovely, gentle Celia who had renounced him and their love because he was married to this heartless creature.

It was on the tip of his tongue to lash out at Frances, but he knew how futile a scene would be. She liked to taunt him about Celia and those days of the flood. She was always curious as to whether he saw Celia or not. Always accusing him of neglecting her for either Celia or some other girl. Yet, she knew that, except in his professional capacity, he never spoke to another woman. Knew too, that his attitude toward her was the result of her own unspeakable disloyalty and lack of consideration of him.

Controlling himself, he turned, walked out of the room and shut the door. He went out of the house to his waiting car. The chauffeur drove him down Harley Street toward St. Gabriel's Hospital. He found himself shaking a little and pulled out his pipe—the old pipe that helped to calm his nerves in moments like these. It didn't do to let anything Frances said, upset him. No! She wasn't worth it, and he

185

needed a clear head and a steady hand for his operating. But God! how tired he was—tired of the whole situation—weary unto death with the ache of longing for Celia and the effort of keeping away from her.

The glorious spring day held no delights for him. Physically he was not well at the moment. The strain of the last few months, coupled with heavy work, had been telling on him. He was losing weight and needed a holiday. Yet he did not wish to take one. He would rather go on with his job—fill in his days—make himself so tired that he could not think too much about Celia. If he took his well-earned holiday, what would he do and where would he go? He would find it intolerable going away with Frances, and if he went alone, he would have too much time on his hands in which to remember *her* . . .

There were moments when he contemplated driving himself up to the Fen district and offering to rent that little stone house in which he had lived with Celia. Sometimes the thought of that house drew him like a magnet. For it was a house in which he found himself—his real self—and learned what the companionship of a woman could mean—a true woman like Celia.

Yes, he would like to go back there. Yet could he bear it alone? Would it not require superhuman strength to stop him from sending for her? And if he sent . . . it would only put

186

her to torture of refusing, which he knew she would always do, for his sake alone.

He drew a hand across his eyes and sighed.

'Celia, darling, *darling*, will there be an end of this agony one day, or must it go on for us both forever?'

In the hospital, as always, he cast off personal griefs and troubles. He was just 'Mr Denver' . . . the cool, calm, practical surgeon, keen on his work, heart and soul absorbed in the feats of surgery which he performed each day, exhilarated by the lives that he saved.

There was plenty for him to do today, Sister told him as she walked with him down the wide, white corridor toward the operating-theatre. Two major operations, an appendix, and a case from the casualty ward which had just come in. They had had so many accidents today, the house surgeon was frantic. Would Mr Denver mind doing this casualty's arm? She had been run over and it looked as though her left elbow might be useless unless some quick and clever work was done on it.

Guy talked 'shop' with Sister, pausing for a moment outside the theatre to button up his white gown. The door of the theatre was ajar. It was in the new wing and Guy, himself, had designed it. It was a magnificent theatre and a joy to the surgeons with its great windows, the latest type of shadowless lamp over the operating-table, the glistening white tiles, enamelled cupboards and perfect form of heating and lighting.

Down the passage came a wheeled stretcher on noiseless tyres. Under the blankets a figure was lying. Guy glanced at it. He could see only a hand which was held by the nurse who walked beside the stretcher.

'What's this, Sister?'

'I think it's the casualty with the elbow.'

Guy stood aside to allow the man to push the case into the theatre. As the stretcher passed, he saw the face of a girl on the flat pillow. And suddenly, violently, the colour left his cheeks, then rushed back. His heart gave a shocked jolt. For he knew that face only too well . . knew every feature of it . . . had kissed every line . . . had threaded his fingers feverishly and passionately through that fair, silken hair which was spread on the pillow. It was Celia, *Celia*. Celia, white and unconscious looking as he had first seen her when he had drawn her out of her car on that unforgettable night of the flood. For the second time he saw her thus. But she did not know him. She was already succumbing to the drug which had already been given her before they started on the general anaesthetic.

Guy followed Sister into the theatre. He kept his gaze riveted on the marble face of the girl who was now being lifted onto the table under the lamp. Like one in a daze he heard his anaesthetist greeting him, took in the sight of the nurses, one of whom with a pair of forceps was lifting instruments from the boiler, another of whom was opening a drum of sterilised gauze and cotton wool.

'Celia,' he said to himself, 'oh God, *Celia!*'

The temperature in the theatre was very high but it was not just the heat which brought the sweat on to Guy's forehead. It had been a terrific shock to him to find that the first case on which he had to operate was the woman he loved—the woman who had occupied all his thoughts for weeks and months. He was conscious of tremendous anxiety. What had happened? He wanted to know all the details of this accident. How bad was Celia's elbow? Sister had said that unless the elbow was carefully attended to, she might lose the use of that arm. But that must never be. On no account must there be any irreparable injury to Celia. That slim lovely arm must be made whole. God, but how well he remembered it curled about his neck; how well he remembered putting his lips against the smooth pale skin. For a moment he stood wavering, asking himself whether or not he should perform this operation. Whether he had the nerve . . . or whether his personal feelings would override his professional skill. Then his brain cleared and he became alert and cool again. Of course he could do it. There wasn't another man in the world he'd trust her to. He was fully confident of his own powers as a surgeon. If that smashed elbow of hers was to be put right, then he *and he alone*, should do it.

He advanced to the table, and took the rubber gloves which a nurse handed him, still dripping from the disinfectant in which they had been dipped. His heart-beat slowed down. He was perfectly steady now. Steadily he could look at the beloved face of the girl lying on that table. The anaesthetist was putting a mask over her mouth and nostrils. The pungent odour of ether filled the theatre. He could hear the deep stertorous breathing from the patient. Sister had drawn the blanket away from the injured arm and was removing the temporary dressing.

Guy was no longer the anxious lover who stood beside that table, but the surgeon masked, begloved ready for work. It was the surgeon's eye which coolly and critically took in the sight of Celia's injury.

The operation which Guy Denver performed that afternoon was another triumph for him. Those who were watching said afterwards that never had Mr Denver worked with such delicate precision. For it was a delicate operation patching up the shattered nerves and sinews, removing splinters of bone, grafting on fresh skin. In the hands of a bungler, Celia might, certainly, never have held a straight arm again. But when she was taken back to her ward, still insensible of what had been done, and who had done it, she was a Celia who would not suffer from any permanent disability. The skill of the man who loved her had saved her from that.

It was Guy who suffered after that operation. For the first time in his career as a surgeon, he collapsed. Once Celia had been wheeled from the theatre, the world was suddenly blacked out for him. Doctors and nurses rushed to his aid, shocked and surprised. Of course they knew that Mr Denver had been overworking lately. He looked ghastly. Somebody else must do the other operations. He was not fit to carry on, this afternoon.

Guy lay in the matron's sitting-room, sipping brandy, ashamed of his fainting-fit. The matron, an excellent soul, and one of his devoted admirers, refused to let him get up for some time. He was as wax in her hands. He felt utterly weak and played out. He could think only of Celia. It was hard to control his desire to rush to her ward and see her again. He was silently grateful to the matron when she started to talk about the case.

'Sister said she never saw you operate so well, Mr Denver. A lovely piece of grafting on that casualty's elbow.'

Guy lay still, eyes closed. *'That casualty!'* If matron only knew, he thought, that she was the girl whom he loved—whom he would love all his life . . . Heavens! what an irony of fate that Celia should have been brought *here* for *him* to operate upon.

He questioned matron about the case. All she could tell him was that the girl's name was Hammond, that she had been located to an address in Bayswater and worked in an office in Cockspur Street. A Mr Madden had been on the telephone—her employer—and, matron added, she was to be moved into a private room at once. He said that he would be responsible for all expenses.

Guy sat up. His heart began to beat quickly. That must be the man who was Celia's old friend from Lincoln. Jealousy tore at him. So Madden was standing the expense of a private ward! Guy realised how little he knew about Celia, now . . . anything might have happened in these five weeks since he had seen her. Madden was keen about her. Perhaps she had succumbed . . . yet, no! . . . Guy speedily erased that fear from his mind. He could not and would not believe that Celia had changed. She was still his. Still his, *in her mind.*

'Now don't get up, Mr Denver . . .' began matron. But Guy was already on his feet, straightening his coat and smoothing back his hair.

'I'm perfectly all right now. It was abominably stupid of me to pass out like that.'

The matron gave a hearty laugh.

'I've seen many of you young men do it before. Don't worry! I'm surprised you don't go that way more often what with the strain and the heat in those theatres.'

He said:

'Where is my patient?'

'Private ward—No. 14.'

'I'll just go along and tell Sister what I want done for her in the morning. I'm rather interested in that case,' he said, briefly.

A few minutes later he was in No. 14, Private ward, standing beside Celia's bed.

He was alone with her. He had stood alone thus beside a thousand beds in this manner, looking down at a motionless figure lying under sheets and blankets that had no crease to them. A stiff, rigid hospital bed. Yet never before had he experienced such violent and varied emotions.

The blinds were down, shutting out the April sunlight. He could see Celia's face, dimly. It looked pinched and drained of colour. An agony of tenderness smote him. Poor Celia, poor little girl! Why should she have met with this accident? Why should fate deal her one blow after another?

Suddenly she stirred, put up a hand, and moaned. Her right hand, for her left arm was heavily bandaged, and in a splint. Guy bent over her and took that groping hand. The professional doctor gave place to the man who adored her. In a voice of deep emotion, he said:

'Celia . . . my *darling!*'

Her heavy lashes lifted. Still doped and drowsy, she looked up with blank gaze. Another little moan escaped her. She whispered.

'Oh! *Oh*, Guy!'

His pulses thrilled. He knew that she did not recognise him but that his name came instinctively to her lips. He bent his head and pressed the small hand which he held against his lips.

'I'm here, I'm here, my darling.'

The mist rolled away gradually from Celia's consciousness. She came back to a queer, distorted world. Her first sense was of pain . . . acute pain in her arm. Her next recognition was of the man who bent over her bed. For a long moment her dark dazed eyes looked up into his. Then she began to remember . . . first her accident, outside the office . . . then her brief return to consciousness while the house surgeon was applying a temporary dressing to her arm . . . Some message, too, that the nurse had given her from Tim who had said that she was to go into a private ward and that he would come to see her as soon as he was allowed. But why was Guy here? How came he to be by her side? She did not know. She was only aware of immense thankfulness at seeing him, at feeling the pressure of his hand.

'Guy—dearest,' she said, drowsily.

'Oh, Celia, my sweet . . . what a frightful piece of bad luck for you . . . poor little thing.'

Her mind became clearer.

'I don't mind,' she whispered, 'I'll be all right . . . but why are you here? How did you know?'

'Darling,' he said, 'this is my hospital and it was I who operated on your arm.'

She stared up at him.

'You!'

'Yes, by all the strange miracles you were brought to me. Thank God, for I think I can promise you that the elbow I'll be all right and that you'll have full use of your arm again.'

She was dumbfounded. 'A strange miracle,' he called it. Certainly it was that.

'So for the second time you've operated on me,' she said, slowly, 'and now I shall have another scar in memory of you.'

'Yes, another one, darling.'

Her fingers clung convulsively to his. She was growing more conscious of pain. Weakness brought the tears to her eyes and they rolled down her cheeks. He could not bear to see them. He took out his handkerchief, wiped them away; bent and kissed her forehead.

'You're all right, my sweet. You'll be all right. Are you in much pain?'

'Quite a bit.'

'I'll get nurse to come along and give you an injection. You shan't suffer more than I can help.

She tried to smile. She was still in a state of shock from her accident and he could see that she was not fit to cope with any situation. Pressing her hand, he tried to comfort her with tender words.

'I'll look after you, Celia. Everything shall be done for you that can be. It's a mercy you were brought here to me, darling.'

'Oh, Guy, I've wanted you so.'

'I've wanted you, too, my darling. It's been like death without you.'

'Do you still love me?'

'More than anything in the world.'

'That's how I love you,' she said under her breath.

'It's almost too much seeing you here like this . . . almost too much,' he said incoherently.

'You must be careful,' she said, suddenly alive to danger for him. 'You mustn't let them guess. Oh, you must be so careful of your reputation.'

'Still thinking of me?'

'Never of anybody else.'

'You're such an angel,' he said, 'and I'd give my life to be able to make you happy, yet I can't.'

Her fingers squeezed his.

'I've been given this happiness . . . seeing you, knowing that I shall be able to see you again. The pain . . . the accident . . . are worth it.'

Guy wanted with all his soul to gather her in his arms and hold her close. Instead, he had to be content with a long, hungry look and another swift kiss upon her hair. He heard footsteps. He knew that Celia was only too right . . . that he must be careful here in his hospital . . . Duty, career, Frances . . . those three hopeless barriers were still between them.

A nurse came into the room.

'Oh, excuse me, Mr Denver,' she said, when she saw the surgeon, 'there's a gentleman wanting to see Miss Hammond.'

'That'll be Tim,' said Celia. 'I don't want to see him yet. I don't feel well enough.'

'Give him that message, nurse,' said Guy.

The girl—she was a probationer—looked at him nervously.

'Can I say a word to you, please, sir?'

'Certainly,' said Guy.

For a moment he held Celia's gaze. They exchanged a long intense look. Then he forced himself to say in a formal voice:

'I'll have a look at you in the morning, Miss Hammond. Nurse shall come now and give you something to make you sleep.'

'Thank you,' she whispered, 'good-bye.'

Her gaze followed the beloved figure as he left the room. After he had gone, she lay still, giving herself up to the pain . . . the physical pain which seemed so much more bearable than the mental agony which she had endured since her separation from Guy. It was, indeed, strange and wonderful that she should be here in *his* care.

Outside in the corridor, the probationer was telling Guy that Miss Hammond's friend had been a bit troublesome. He had told another nurse that if he couldn't see Celia, he insisted upon speaking to the doctor in charge of her case.

'Right,' said Guy, shortly. 'I'll go down to the waiting-room and see Mr Madden myself.'

He found a very tall young man with rather a ferocious expression marching up and down the hospital waiting-room. As Guy entered, Timothy Madden stopped pacing and greeted him eagerly:

'You the doc who's looking after Miss Hammond?'

'Yes. I operated on her a few hours ago.'

'Is she all right?'

'Perfectly. The arm was badly smashed, but I think we've made a good job of it.'

'Is she in much pain?'

'She's having an injection now. She won't be allowed to suffer any more than can be helped.'

Obvious relief shone in the blue eyes of Tim Madden. He heaved a sigh.

'Thank God! Now I can breathe again. My name's Madden—Tim Madden—Miss Hammond's a very old friend of mine and she works in my office.

Guy said:

I'm Guy Denver.'

'I say . . .' began Tim, then stopped abruptly

198

and took a quick glance at the surgeon. *'Guy,'* he repeated sharply.

'Yes.

'You're not the . . . surely you can't be the doctor who . . .' Tim stopped, stammering, uncertain.

'The doctor who what?

'Well, who was shut up in that house with Celia in the floods.' The faintest colour darkened Guy's tired white face.

'Yes, I happen to be he.'

'Oh!' said Tim.

They were silent a moment, looking at each other. The wary, critical, almost suspicious look of two men who realise instantaneously they are both in love with the same woman.

Guy was thinking:

'Not a bad boy . . . honest . . . successful . . . and palpably in love with Celia . . .'

And in Tim's mind ran the thought:

'So this is the married man whom Celia loves . . . the man who's standing between *us*. Clever, attractive . . . but *damn him* . . . what right has he to hold Celia's love?'

Guy spoke first.

'Has Miss Hammond mentioned me to you?'

'Yes,' said Tim, in a short voice.

Guy felt uneasy. He was not sure quite how much Celia had spoken about him to her employer. At the same time, he felt a hopeless sadness envelop him. His position was so desperate. Here was a nice young man able to offer Celia marriage . . all that she deserved. And he, *he* had nothing to offer, no right even to care for her. Nevertheless he would not have been human if he had not felt bitterness toward Tim. Tim in whose office she worked. Tim who saw her every day and could ask her out any night he wished. Tim, whom she might eventually turn to and marry.

A stifled feeling overcame Guy. He had not really recovered from his collapse of a few hours ago. He felt that he had better go home, take a sleeping draught and get to bed in order that he should be fit for his work tomorrow. He had an important case. A royal personage coming for a consultation. He could not afford to miss that. Nor to make a mistake. If he was successful, it would mean that he would be more than ever in the public-eye and that eventually he would be offered a title. Sir Guy Denver! Frances would like that! But, oh, God, how little it all meant to him. What a mockery was the whole of his life's success without the woman he loved at his side.

'I thought I'd just let you know, Mr Madden, that Miss Hammond is in no danger and that you have nothing to worry about,' he said, shortly, 'and now as I am busy, will you excuse me?'

Tim hadn't the slightest wish to detain him, although there were a lot of things he would like to have said. For instance, he wanted to tell Guy to 'lay off' . . . to give Celia a chance . . . it was damn bad luck her being brought to his hospital and in *his* care, too! An amazing coincidence.

'When can I see Miss Hammond?' he asked.

'Tomorrow,' said Guy. 'She isn't really fit to see anyone tonight.'

Tim picked up his hat and umbrella.

'Right,' he said, 'perhaps you'd let Miss Hammond know that I'll come tomorrow. I gave the nurse some flowers for her. I'll send in some fruit this evening.'

'That will be nice for her,' said Guy, coldly.

'Well, thanks very much,' said Tim equally coldly, and made a hasty exit.

Guy stood alone a moment, fumbling for a much-needed pipe. Bitterly he thought :

'Why don't I stand in that young man's shoes? Why haven't I his chances? Oh, Celia, my Celia . . . perhaps never really to be mine!'

Before he could leave that room, a girl came in. A big, raw-boned girl wearing a shabby coat and skirt, a felt hat, and a cheap fur around her neck. She literally rushed in and stormed him.

'Are you one of the doctors? Do you know about Miss Hammond? Is she all right? I'm in such a state . . . of all the frights when they gave me the message . . .'

She broke off, holding a handkerchief against her lips. Her eyes were scared and wet. She had been crying and was careless of a blotched face and shining nose.

Guy knew at once who this was. Celia's friend, Jan. And immediately he liked her. Liked her because she was genuine, and her love and anxiety for Celia shone out of her honest eyes. Gently he said :

'Are you Miss Leith?'

Jan stared.

'How on earth did you know?'

'I've heard a great deal about you.'

'Who are you?'

'One of the surgeons here. I operated on Miss Hammond's arm a few hours ago'

Jan did not even bother to ask his name. She did not connect him with the doctor whom Celia loved. She clutched his arm and said:

'Oh, my Lord, tell me she's all right.'

'Of course she is. Very much so. And that arm's going to be all right, too.'

'Was that all it was—her arm?'

'And a few bruises here and there.'

'Not her poor head again?'

'No,' said Guy with a ghost of a smile, and a pang at the thought of that fair sweet head which he had doctored in the past. 'Her face and head weren't touched, fortunately. The taxi got her in the arm.'

'Poor darling,' said Jan with a gulp. 'Poor lamb! Oh, doctor, you don't know what a darling she is and how little she deserves this sort of thing.'

'I do know,' he said, sighing.

'She lives with me,' said Jan, blowing her nose violently.

'You shall see her,' said Guy. 'Follow me. I'll take you along to her room.'

'Isn't she in a public ward?'

'She was. But after the operation, they moved her to a private room, at the request of Mr Madden.'

'Eh, there's a bonny lad for you!' said Jan in her strongest Lancashire accent, 'the best friend she's got.'

Jealousy smote Guy Denver again but he put it aside.

'I'm sure he is—a very good friend.'

Outside the door of No. 14 of the private ward, he left Jan. 'Don't stay too long. She'll be getting drowsy. She's just had an injection.'

'I only want to see her for a minute,' said Jan, 'but I just couldn't sleep tonight until I heard her speak. I've been picturing her a mangled corpse and I'm half silly.'

Guy patted Jan's shoulder.

'Don't you worry. She's no mangled corpse. Go in and see her for yourself.'

Jan paused with her fingers on the handle of the door.

'You've been very decent to me. What's your name?'

'Guy Denver,' he said, shortly, and then moved away before she could speak to him again.

Jan, open-mouthed, stood staring after him.

'Guy Denver!' she repeated to herself, and then added: *'For mercy's sake.'*

Denver! *The* doctor. Celia's beloved! But of all the things to have happened . . . for him to be in the hospital to which she had been brought. For her to be under *his* care! It didn't seem to Jan at all right. Her heart sank at the thought of Celia back in contact with that man who was married and could never be any good to her. The poor kid! As if she hadn't had enough . . . as if she hadn't wept enough tears over him in her time! And now when she had gained some sort of peace, and found a boyfriend like Tim Madden, in Jan's opinion it was nothing short of a catastrophe that Guy should have crossed her path again.

Jan tip-toed into Celia's room. Like all strong healthy people who have never had much to do with illness, she was a little awed by the dim atmosphere, the strong odour of disinfectants and of the ether which still clung about the patient's bed, and petrified because Celia looked so still and straight in that high white bed.

This morning when Celia had said good-bye to Jan, she had been looking her best in her new grey spring outfit. They had laughed together over some joke before they had parted. One never knew what was going to happen in this world, thought Jan. Just *fancy* Celia getting run over!

She advanced to the bedside and uttered

her friend's name, almost beseechingly.

Celia, on whom the drug was working, opened her large dark eyes with difficulty.

'Guy,' she whispered.

Jan swallowed hard.

So that man's name was on her lips, was it? Drat the whole business!

'It's Jan, you poor lamb,' she said, leaning over Celia.

Very slowly Celia reached the state of recognition.

'Hullo . . . Jan.'

'Are you all right, ducky?'

'Yes . . . all right.'

'What did you want to go and give me this fright for?' Celia smiled faintly.

'Sorry . . . so silly of me.'

'I call it acting like a loon! What were you about? Had you had a couple of quick ones?'

Celia shook her head.

'Well, you've given me a nice old turn,' said Jan, wiping her eyes, 'but I feel better now I've spoken to you. Lord! I shall miss you tonight. I suppose you'll have to stay here for some time?'

'The doctor thinks . . . a week or two . . .'

'Hum,' said Jan, 'the doctor, eh? Looks a bit fishy to me, getting yourself run over so as to have *him* taking your pulse and fussing around you.'

Celia forced back the effects of the sedative and became more alert.

'Oh, Jan . . . then you know?'

'That *he* is here? Yes. I've just met him.'

'Don't you think he's sweet?' asked Celia, naïvely.

'I thought he was pretty good,' said Jan, 'but it won't do, and . . .'

'Don't lecture me, now,' broke in Celia, 'I shan't see much of him . . . let me be happy while I can.'

That brought a lump to Jan's throat but she was not going to let Celia know it.

'I'll just get you out of here and home again as soon as I can,' she said gruffly.

'All right.'

'And look at the flowers! What a bouquet!' said Jan, pointing to a huge bunch of mauve and pink carnations, 'Who sent you them?'

'Tim,' said Celia, with an effort.

'I thought as much. Well, he's the one to concentrate on, my lamb.'

Much as Celia loved Jan, she wanted her to go away. She wanted to stop thinking about Tim, about everyone, save Guy. A few minutes ago, Guy had leaned over this bed and kissed her hair. With the memory of that kiss she wanted to sink into sleep. She had had so much pain, mental and physical. It would be good to sleep . . . perhaps to dream of him.

Her eyelids closed. The heavy lashes curved against her cheeks. Jan stood looking down at her anxiously. How white she was. How lovely and innocent she looked, too, lying there so quietly.

'Poor lamb . . . poor little lamb!' Jan thought.

Bending, she touched Celia's brow with her lips.

'Good night, ducky, I'll come and see you tomorrow, and mind you hurry up and get better. It won't be too bright in the old home without you.'

She walked away and was annoyed with herself because she had to dry her eyes and blow her nose vigorously again as she moved down the long hospital corridor and out into the street.

CHAPTER FOURTEEN

It was one of the night-nurses who first discovered the fact that the patient in No. 14 of the private ward was the girl who had been so romantically shut up with Mr Denver in that house up North during the January floods.

The night-nurse had a good memory. At the time of that flood, the hospital had buzzed with the story of its most prominent surgeon being marooned in the Fen country. Nobody else seemed to remember that the girl's name had been Celia Hammond. But the young night-nurse did remember, and forthwith the information spread right through the nursing-staff of St. Gabriel's. Tongues wagged freely. Over the inveterate cup of tea, plenty was said. Not necessarily in disfavour of Guy who was a great favourite, and whose wife was cordially disliked. Frances had at one time or another been forced to organise bazaars or balls in aid of the hospital and treated the nursing-staff with a chilly hauteur and disdain which had earned her no popularity. But there were no bounds to exaggerations of the story by the time it finished circulating through St. Gabriel's. And inevitably it was said that Mr Denver was 'keen' on Miss Hammond and that 'they bet the pair of them would make hay while the sun shone, now she had been brought into his hospital.'

Celia had been in St. Gabriel's for ten days before any such gossip reached her. For ten days, blissfully ignorant that she was the centre of attraction and that her name was being linked with Guy's, she was almost happy. She saw him night and morning, her darling, beloved Guy. There were no dressings to be done on her arm. It had been put into a plaster-splint where it must remain for at least six weeks. There was really no need for Guy to visit her, but he did so. Morning and night he found time to look in to No. 14. Sometimes there was a nurse in the room, or a sister came with him which was unfortunate, and meant that he must merely be formal to the patient. But most times he came alone, and then she knew the rapture of holding his hand, and listening to all that he had to tell her.

Those were golden moments to be remembered through the long hours when she was without him. Moments when he was no longer the tired, harassed doctor, but an eager boy again, madly in love with her. Moments when he would steal a swift passionate kiss and say those words which she would never tire of hearing:

'I love you, my darling. I love you!'

Tim Madden said the same words—in a different way. Tim also visited her daily, was able to do all the things which Guy dared not do. Fill her room with flowers. Buy her expensive fruit. Send her the latest magazines and books. Tim sat every evening beside her bed after office-hours and said:

'You may be the result of an accident, but you look ravishing, and no amount of the frigidaire-business is going to stop me from telling you that I'm crazy about you. Only . . .'

Poor Tim! Celia had no answer for him except a shake of the head and a protest. All the responsiveness in her was for Guy. It was for Guy that her heart beat so madly and for whom her large eyes shone with warmth and mistiness, and all the passion of a woman in love. It was really for Guy that she sent Jan out to buy that new, attractive bed-jacket—the most expensive she had ever owned—palest blue quilted silk with a big blue bow, which made her look ridiculously young and—as Tim had told her—quite ravishing.

But the happiness which Celia knew, waiting for Guy's visits and enjoying them, was short-lived. For there came a day when a talkative probationer making her bed, let the cat out of the bag.

'We're all so thrilled about you, Miss Hammond. 'Celia smiled at the girl.

'Why on earth?'

'Well, just to think that you were shut up all those days in the flood with Mr Denver.'

Celia's heart missed a beat. The tell-tale colour burned her face and throat. The probationer, tucking in the blankets, went on:

'We all adore Mr Denver. He's terribly attractive, don't you think? I think he's so like Leslie Howard to look at. Too divine! Must have been too marvellous to be marooned like that, with him. Weren't you thrilled to find that you had been brought to his hospital?'

Another silence. Celia's face was no longer pink. It was rather white. Her mind was working feverishly.

Oh God! So *that* story has got round! Everyone was talking! The papers had done enough harm as it was, and his wife would get to hear that she was here. That would cause a fresh scandal. The sooner she left St. Gabriel's, the better!

For the rest of that day, Celia lay and fretted. Her arm was better. The pain in the elbow was negligible these days. But Guy had said that she must remain in the hospital for another week. It was not only the arm but the shock of the accident which had affected her. Yesterday when, for the first time, she had put her legs over the side of the bed, they had felt much too light for her body and she could hardly stand. She was certainly not fit and it was more interesting here than it would be in that little back room in the boarding-house, with Jan. Besides, she could not go back to work until her arm was out of the splint, and she could type again. And although Tim talked about sending her away to the sea for a change of air, at his expense, she had no intention of allowing him to do such a thing.

She had made up her mind to remain in St. Gabriel's—wanted to, because it meant that she could see Guy.

But the probationer's chance words had shown her the danger of the whole situation.

She must tell Guy, tonight.

By the time he came for his usual good night visit, Celia had worked herself up into a state of acute nerves and depression. He found her looking flushed and distressed.

Standing by her bed, he held her hand between his own, kissing it repeatedly.

'Darling, what is it? What's worrying you?'

She looked up at him with large miserable eyes.

'I've got to leave here, Guy. I've got to get

211

out at once.'

'But why, my darling? Aren't you comfortable? Has anything gone wrong?'

'You don't realise what's being said.'

He dropped her hand and stood looking down at her, a frown knitting his brows. As a matter of fact, he knew exactly what was being said. He had heard the gossip—not from the nurses here—but from his wife. Frances had attacked him this morning just before he started work.

'So your precious girl of the flood is merrily installed under your wing at St. Gabriel's!' she had said. 'But how thrilling for you, and no wonder work is so attractive.'

A few sharp questions had informed him that the hospital was alive with gossip. Frances had received her news through the wife of another doctor on the staff.

He set his teeth as he looked at Celia.

'Oh God!' he said savagely, 'why can't they leave us alone?'

Celia swallowed hard.

'They never will. Our names will always be linked now. And it simply won't do. It's essential that there should be no scandal about you.'

He felt hopeless, cornered. She was so right in what she said, and yet there were moments—and this was one of them—when he would gladly have bartered reputation, 'position, everything for the sake of having

212

her with him. She meant everything in the world to him now. He was conscious of the fact that she grew nearer and dearer to him every day. There was something between this girl and himself—some strange magnetism, some inexplicable depth of understanding and sympathy which bound them together in spirit even when they were apart. He must always love her. He could not help himself. And it was death for him to know that she was as inaccessible as the stars and that all hope of being with her was as remote as those stars.

She saw the hunted look on his face. She knew that he was feeling as thwarted, as cheated of love and happiness as she felt herself. Her own suffering was so acute that she loathed the idea of his pain. Yet she could do nothing to allay it. In fact, it was her duty to increase it by removing herself from his path once more.

She broke out passionately:

'What can I do, Guy? What can I do? It's such a desperate position.'

'You're right,' he said, 'it *is* desperate!'

He began to walk up and down her room, hands in his pockets, face gaunt and miserable. His gaze lit on the bunches of roses and iris on her window-sill; on the big gilt basket of peaches and grapes. He knew who they were from. That young man who loved her and wanted her to marry him. And he knew that he had no right to stand between them—or at least to decrease Tim Madden's chances of winning this girl by forcing his own personality upon her. She loved him. That was all too evident No woman had ever loved him more unselfishly, more grandly, than Celia. Love— the very essence of it—lay in the depths of those dark, marvellous eyes of hers. Love burned her lips when they clung to his. She was all his for loving, and he could not take her or her love. He ought to renounce her completely. It was only fair to her—and to Madden.

Was there ever a man in such a wretched position? It was sheer agony to leave her now, to contemplate the possibility of her turning to that other fellow. Guy was only human. He tried to do his duty by Frances—by his job— but he was flesh and blood, and he loved Celia. He felt that any sort of torture would be preferable to that of relinquishing her to the embrace of some other man.

He paused in his restless pacing and came to her side again. There were shadows like bruises under his eyes but he forced himself to smile.

'We're up against it, I'm afraid, my sweet.'

She, too, was heavy-eyed, drained of colour and vitality. She lay back on her pillow and shut her eyes.

'Sometimes I can't bear it,' she whispered.

'Don't say that, Celia. You've got to help me. I don't feel very strong. For heaven's sake help me, darling. If you weaken, I shall. I can try to stand it. A man can stand these things, but I can't bear the thought of your unhappiness.'

She struggled to regain her courage, her philosophic acceptance of the position. That cry of his wrung her heart. She knew that she must be strong in order to help him or their love would spell defeat instead of victory.

She opened her eyes and held out her hand.

'I'll be all right, Guy. You mustn't worry about me.'

He caught that little hand and crushed it to his lips. 'I love and adore you above all other women. I shall never cease to worry about you, darling.'

'And you know I shall always love you.'

'You mustn't,' he said between his teeth, 'that's what you mustn't do. That's what I've got to forbid, Celia. It isn't fair on you.'

'If I can't have you, I'd rather have nobody.'

'But I don't want that. There's this fellow Madden . . .' Guy deliberately tortured himself '. . . he wants you to marry him. He could look after you. For God's sake, give him a chance.'

She caught her breath sharply.

'You *want* me to?'

'That isn't fair. You're not to ask me that.'

He looked ghastly. She knew perfectly well in her very soul that he hated the thought of what he, himself, suggested. And being a woman in love she exulted in the thought.

'You *can't* want to. I know you don't.'

'Oh, Celia, Celia, you've got to put me out of your mind and heart,' he said in an anguished voice. 'It would be so much better for you, darling. You're so young; you've got your whole life before you. Madden's a good fellow . . . and, oh, *hell.*'

He dropped her hand, broke off, pulled a handkerchief out of his pocket and wiped his forehead. He felt as though he was running a race for life and losing it.

Everything in her yearned toward him. She had a terrible temptation to put out a hand, draw his head down and cover his face with kisses. It was so wonderful to know that he loved her this way, and it would have been so easy for her to act the temptress rather than help him to do the right thing. She restrained herself only because of *him* . . . knowing that it was in her power to ruin him or to keep the standard flying . . . that standard of honour and decency by which he had always lived. She had a moment's blinding picture of what might happen if they were both mad enough to lower that standard, and go away together. She could see Guy, turned out of his profession . . . the General Medical Council would have no mercy on him now, because she had become his patient . . Guy, divorced, disgraced, living with her somewhere in exile. He might go on loving her. Their passion might never die (hers would not, anyhow).

And they might have some sort of peace and happiness together. But it would be a tarnished happiness. Every time she looked at him she would realise that she had been the cause of his ruin . . . that she had removed from him the noble work, the fine name that he had taken a lifetime to build up. In time, it might creep in between them and slowly poison their love—wreck their peace. It might even end in him hating her. Whatever happened, she could never, *never* allow that to happen. No neither of them must ever weaken. The force of her thoughts drove a cry from her.

'Guy . . . Guy, go away and never see me again, I implore you.'

'If you say so . . .' the words were dragged from him.

'You know it's got to be.'

'Yes, I know it.'

'I must leave the hospital at once.'

'You're not fit to.'

'I'll get moved to a nursing-home, then . . . Tim will help me . . . I'll do anything to avert a scandal,' she said, chaotically.

He did not answer. He stood there dumb and wretched, marvelling at the flame of courage that burned so fiercely in this frail girl. At last he said, slowly:

'All right. Perhaps you'd better go.'

She felt choked, agonised. She felt that if he stayed here in this room a moment longer, all her resistance would be sapped from her. She never felt anything more crushing than her present sense of despair. Her first renunciation of him had been bad, but this second parting seemed even worse, because she loved him a thousand times more and was even more conscious of his need for her.

She fixed her burning, longing gaze on his face, hungry for the pressure of his lips against her mouth, longing for his arms to go around her and hold her close. But even that last embrace was denied her. There came a knock on the door. With an effort which seemed to cost all her strength, she said: 'Come in.'

A nurse put in her head and said in her bright, professional voice:

'Here's a visitor for you, Miss Hammond.'

Into the room came the big bulky figure of Tim Madden, armed with more flowers and a large box of chocolates.

Sick at heart, almost fainting, Celia lay back on her pillows and tried to force a greeting. Like one in a daze she saw Tim and Guy nod to each other frigidly. Then Guy said:

'Well, I'm glad you're so much better. I don't think there's any need for me to see you again. You'll have to keep that arm in the splint for another month. I . . . I think I may be away, so I'll get one of the other surgeons to take it out of the plaster.'

'Yes . . . thank you,' came from Celia's dry lips.

Guy Denver did not trust himself to look

again at that beloved figure in the bed. He knew that all his life he would remember her thus. With the little blue silk coat around her shoulders, her fair silky hair tumbled about her head, those big brave eyes shining at him.

The door closed behind him.

Tim, sensing an 'atmosphere', advanced to Celia's bedside, somewhat embarrassed.

'How about a nice chocolate for the poor injured child?' he said in an attempt at joking.

But she did not answer. Her eyes were tight-shut and her teeth clenched. He saw her hand opening and shutting as though with a vast effort to control herself. He was filled with mingled compassion and anger. There had obviously been a 'scene' between her and that surgeon-fellow. Damn him! *Damn him* for the hold he had over Celia. The poor kid looked ill—much worse than when she had first been run over.

'Look here, Celia,' said Tim, putting the chocolates and a large bunch of lilies-of-the-valley on the bed, 'it's time you got out of this place. I don't care what you say, I'm going to have you moved to a convalescent home in Brighton or Eastbourne or somewhere. You can be taken down in my car and a couple of weeks by the sea'll make a lot of difference to you. I'll get on to your friend Jan's employer, and see if I can't get her a holiday, too, and let her take you away.'

Celia did not answer. She was beaten—

exhausted by the tumult of feeling which had just flooded her. She could think only of Guy . . . Guy who had gone . . . gone without even touching her lips in farewell. Gone, saying in that deadly formal fashion that he 'would not be seeing her again'. The words beat in her brain. She wanted to cry . . . cry passionately, resentfully, bitterly, and yet no tears came. In that dumb, exhausted fashion she lay there listening to Tim who was saying what was to be done with her.

When at last her lashes lifted and she looked at him, he was horrified by the expression in her eyes. He said:

'Oh, God, Celia, don't feel like this about things! What's the use? I know it's this damn doctor you're in love with . . . it's getting you down, and you oughtn't to be here. That's why I want you to go. Won't you believe me? Won't you help yourself—and him—by going?'

That tore an answer from her.

'If it'll help him—yes. And I suppose it will.'

'Well, obviously,' said Tim, 'it can't be good for either of you to go on meeting. It's crazy.'

'I know it's not good for his reputation,' she whispered, 'they're gossiping in the hospital. And his wife is a menace.'

'I shall take you out of it tomorrow,' said Tim, grimly.

'I can't let you spend all that money . . .'

'If you talk about money, I'll pull you out of bed and drop you out of the window,' he said.

She gave a laugh that broke on a sob.

'I wish you would. It's a big drop and I'd pass clean out. I'd *like* to pass out, Tim. I wish that taxi had knocked me right out . . . no, I suppose that's wicked . . . but oh, Tim, I can't bear it, *I can't bear it!*'

And now the tears came in a hot torrent. With her face pressed against the pillow to stifle the sobs, Celia wept in anguish for her hopeless love, her lost lover. Tim held her hand, horribly sorry for her, yet feeling powerless to help; wondering why fate should store up so much mental agony for this girl who had never done any harm to anybody on earth.

He let her cry, and when at length she was calmer, he said:

'I can't bear to see you like this, Celia. It gets me right down. I haven't a laugh left. Not a joke!'

She turned to him, her wet crumpled handkerchief pressed to her quivering lips.

'I'm sorry. I've disgraced myself. And you're so good to me . . . so awfully good.'

'I think you'd better marry me and have done with it.'

She did not answer. But she drew the back of her hand against her swollen eyes. So great was her despair in that moment, she began to ask herself whether it mattered what she did. Perhaps she *ought* to marry Tim. Guy had said so. Perhaps it would be better for Guy if she

221

did. It might make things easier for him to know that she belonged to another man, and was right out of his reach, rather than think of her as the unmarried girl who was more accessible.

Tim seized on her silence.

'Won't you give it a thought, Celia? This is scarcely the moment to press my suit, but if there *is* a lot of gossip about you and this chap, I think it would be a good thing for him if people thought you and I were engaged.'

That was clever of Tim. There was truth in what he said, she thought bitterly. It *would be* much better if people spoke of her as Tim Madden's future wife. It would soon stop tongues from wagging. Frances Denver herself could not nag Guy about her after that.

Celia was not in a fit state to think things out just now. She was driven almost beyond endurance. Her nerves were at concert-pitch. She was thrown mentally from one emotional reaction to another. Her main thought was for Guy . . . for his good. Suddenly, wildly, she said what Tim had been wanting her to say for the last six weeks.

'Yes, very well. If you want me to marry you, I will. You must be mad! You know I love another man . . . you must be crazy. But if that's what you want, all right, I'll do it.'

His square, dogged face flushed. This was an easier triumph than he had anticipated, and he accepted it with a slight feeling of shame.

Feeling that he had taken advantage of a bad moment. Taking her hand, he patted it in an almost brotherly way.

'Darling, I won't be a bore. I'm not going to burden you with long lingering kisses or anything of that sort. Just look on me in a platonic light until you feel better about things. But if you can say you're engaged, it will make things easier, won't it?'

Celia drew a deep breath. In a very small voice, she said: 'Yes, Tim . . . I . . . suppose it will.'

Then quite quietly, she fainted dead away and Tim rushed frantically to find a nurse, and that was the prelude to his engagement.

CHAPTER FIFTEEN

It was singularly unfortunate, perhaps, for both Celia and Tim that the injured arm behaved in a fashion which made it impossible for Celia to leave St. Gabriel's as soon as they would have wished.

Following Celia's fainting-fit, her temperature went up, added to which the arm began to throb and it was evident to the house-surgeon who saw her much later that night, that there was something wrong and that the arm would have to come out of its plaster-splint.

The house-surgeon, a nice young man named Turner, said cheerily:

'We'll have Mr Denver to see to this first thing in the morning.'

Celia said nothing. Tim had long since gone but the bulky shadow of Tim remained in this room, reminding her that she was now his affianced wife. Whether she had accepted him in a moment of hysteria and misery, whether or not she had done right, she had no time to analyse. She was merely sunk in a state of wretched apathy from which she was roused only by the thought that the arm was giving trouble and that Guy would be called upon to see her again.

Whilst every instinct in her yearned to see him, she knew the inadvisability of another meeting which could only bring agony to them both. Desperately, she said:

'Must we worry him? Couldn't you tackle it?'

Dr Turner was flattered but he laughed:

''Fraid not. Mr Denver did the work and he never gives a job of his over to others, besides which, I wouldn't like to tackle it. You've no idea the genius Mr Denver brought to bear upon that nasty little mess of yours.'

'Mr Denver's so marvellous,' said the nurse who stood at the opposite side of Celia's bed.

Celia shut her eyes tight. She longed to say:

'Oh, go away both of you, and leave me alone and *don't* mention that name to me any

224

more . . .'

Dr Turner prescribed a hypodermic for the night to quieten the pain and send Celia to sleep.

'Nothing to worry about,' he said genially, 'these things do flare up sometimes—a little pocket somewhere . . . may want draining . . . Mr Denver will soon have you right.'

Mr Denver! *Mr Denver!*

Celia put a hand across her eyes and bit hard on her lower lip. Apart from the physical discomfort of her injured arm, her nervous system was so jagged that she wanted to scream aloud. There was so much self-control necessary. She was thankful when Dr Turner and the nurse went out of her room. What time was it? She did not know. It seemed hours since Guy had left her. Hours since Tim had been here and had seized the psychological moment in which to make her promise to marry him.

Her eyelids closed. The hypodermic began to work. Blessed relief from pain and misery gradually stole through her. In the drowsy state preceding sleep, she thought only of Guy. Her jangled nerves quietened down and her sense of awful misery decreased. She had done the best for him. Tomorrow everybody here would know that she was going to marry Tim.

She had done the best for him.

Guy, Guy, where are you now? With your wife . . . trying to do your duty. Duty . . . *duty.*

(Awful word that stood out and refused to be banished!) Guy, do you suffer as much as I do? Do you feel this agony of hopeless longing in every pore of your being? I hope not, for your sake. I want you to be happy, I could have made you happy, Guy. I understand you now . . . all your needs! We should have had a lovely life together! Even if we had been poor, we would have washed up dishes and laughed, like we did together in the flood. How long ago that seems! It must have been in another life that I met you . . . that you pulled me from that bridge and slept on the floor beside me in that little stone house. How quietly you slept! I could hear your breathing in the watches of the night and by candle-light I saw the outline of your beloved face. You were bitter and miserable and disillusioned. But I made you forget it. You were happy with me, Guy. You would always be happy with me, because we were made for each other. We are like two halves, which must inevitably form the perfect circle . . . complete . . . enchanted . . .

Guy, darling . . . oh, darling, I love you so! Don't go from me forever. Stay with me, Guy. Oh, Guy, why didn't those waters rise and drown us both in the flood before we could suffer this way . . .?

No, I mustn't think like that. You have your great work. You're a great man. Our need for each other is tremendous but even greater is the need that all your patients have of you.

226

You couldn't abandon them for me. You'll go on being brave, and so will I.

Darling, darling . . where are you? I'm so lonely and it's so dark and so difficult . . . Guy . . . *Guy.*

Celia's over-burdened brain, going round and round in a hopeless maze was blotted out by a merciful oblivion. The drug had done its work. She was asleep.

She was awakened early. One of the nurses brought her a cup of tea. And the moment consciousness returned, all the old agony returned with it. And now a physical pain superseded her mental troubles, because the trouble in the arm was acute. The nurse seemed to know that Celia had to undergo another operation and the name 'Mr Denver' came out, as usual, over and over again.

There came a moment when Celia snapped at her . . . rare for Celia to lose her temper. That was when the young nurse said: 'Oh, *I do* think it's romantic . . . him operating on your arm after that adventure you had together in the floods . . .'

A white-faced, tense-lipped Celia answered:

'It isn't romantic at all. Just a coincidence. And, by the way, when you've found out what time my arm is to be opened up, please telephone my fiancé.'

She hated the word even while she said it, but it had the desired effect. The nurse flushed, and exclaimed :

'*Fiancé!* I didn't know you were engaged, Miss Hammond.'

Celia, with a temperature, aching in every limb, heart-aching, too, said shortly :

'Well, I am . . . to Mr Madden.'

The nurse left her. Celia sipped her tea and thought:

'Now it'll get all round the hospital, and it should put things right for *him.*'

It didn't seem very fair to Tim to talk that way, but that was Tim's fault. He knew what she felt and insisted on the engagement.

If only that arm hadn't played up! If only she could have felt as well as she did, and Tim had been allowed to take her out of St. Gabriel's, how much easier everything would have been.

The next hour was sheer misery for Celia. She dreaded seeing Guy again. Yet knew that he must come and before he came, half-a-dozen nurses put their heads in the door to congratulate her on her engagement.

'How lovely!' they said.

'What a thrill!'

'You lucky girl!'

'Mr Madden's so good-looking . . . don't you adore tall men?'

'Aren't you a dark horse! None of us knew . . .'

'Mr Denver had better make that arm straight or he'll, have Mr Madden to deal with. . . .' (laughter).

228

Laugh! Go on laughing! thought Celia—all of you. Go on telling me how lucky I am and what it all is. Who cares? What does anything matter now. It's all so ironic and so *dreadful.*

She bore up as well as she could. There was Jan to tackle. Dear old Jan rushed in for a few moments before going to her work. She seemed delighted about the engagement although bitterly disappointed that the arm was giving trouble and that she could not have her beloved Celia home again yet.

'Just another bit of bad luck,' she grumbled, thrusting into Celia's hands a bunch of violets which she had bought from a man outside the Underground. 'Still, I suppose it doesn't matter you staying here, now that you're engaged to Mr Madden?'

'No, it doesn't matter,' said Celia, wearily.

'What made you decide to do it, lamb?'

'Don't ask me now, Jan darling. I don't feel well enough to discuss affairs.'

Jan eyed her friend critically. Celia did not look well, that was certain. Great eyes ringed with black in that white little face. Was it all the arm, or was she still desperately unhappy about the doctor? Jan felt anxious for her. Yet if she had agreed to get engaged to Tim Madden, there seemed hope. Tim was a rattling good sort. He'd pull Celia out of this morass.

Jan departed.

'Must love you and leave you, ducky. Got a

sale on this morning. I shall get Mr Madden to buy a nice mink coat for you and I'll get the commission.'

Celia smiled wanly. Jan blew her a kiss and made her exit.

Celia struggled not to think any more. That was the only thing to do—to stop thinking and let life go on. It was like a great cruel river into which she had fallen and which was carrying her along . . . the water swirling over her head . . . she couldn't stop . . . couldn't alter her course. The river was too strong.

Dr Turner put his head in the door.

'Feeling groggy?'

'Not too good.'

'We'll soon have you right. I spoke to Mr Denver on the phone a minute ago. He was disappointed to hear that the old arm has got to come out of the splint, but not surprised. These things do happen.'

'Yes,' said Celia, tonelessly.

But she wondered what Guy was really thinking . . . how he was reacting to the idea of seeing her again . . .

She was not really surprised when, half-an-hour later, Guy walked into the room and announced that he had no intention of doing the operation.

Ill though she felt herself, she was still capable of being alive to the fact that he looked ghastly. Probably he hadn't slept all night. He was stern and tight-lipped. Yet at

230

the back of his eyes there was an agonised tenderness waiting to break through.

He managed to see her alone. He said:

'It was all right doing the arm when you were brought in unconscious that day. I made myself do it. But I couldn't manage it a second time. I'm going to hand the job over to Miles-Goring. He's on the staff here and a fine surgeon. It's only a small job . . . there's a pus-pocket which has got to be opened and drained. You'll be all right in a few days. But I can't face doing it, Celia.'

Her heart-beats seemed to shatter her thin body.

'I understand,' she whispered.

Then he pulled his right hand out of his pocket and she saw that it was bandaged.

'Oh! what have you done?'

'A little white lie,' he said grimly. 'A subterfuge, my dear, so as not to do this job. I told them I cut my finger and that's why I've got to chuck work for a couple of days.'

'I hate to be the cause of you abandoning your work.'

'That's all right. I'm due for a holiday and forty-eight hours off duty won't hurt.'

'Are you going away?'

'I think perhaps I'd better. I shall go alone, of course. I just want to think of you.'

Her big sad eyes looked up at him with passionate tenderness.

'Oh, Guy!' she whispered.

The tenderness broke through the mask of severity. He seized her hand and kissed it in the old lover-like way.

'My darling child!'

Her fingers clung to his feverishly. She was hot and her cheeks were scarlet. The doctor in him was troubled about her. Her temperature was right up.

'Are you in much pain, my darling?'

'It's pretty bad.'

'You're being done at half-past ten. You haven't much longer to wait. You can trust yourself absolutely to Miles-Goring. He's an awfully good chap and I've told him that you are a special patient of mine.'

'Am I?' she whispered, with a ghost of a smile.

He took in the sight of her hungrily . . . the beautiful fairness of her hair, the transparency of her complexion, and the glorious velvety depth of those great gold eyes which haunted him day and night.

'Oh, my little love,' he said, 'if only you were mine to look after . . . if only I needn't leave you . . .'

A violent pang went through her. Suddenly she remembered Tim. She forced herself to say:

'I want you to know . . . before you hear it anywhere else . . . that I'm going to marry Tim.'

Guy dropped her hand. His thin, tired face

232

changed from white to red and then back to white again. For an instant he looked like a man who had received a mortal thrust. She saw that look and cried out:

'Oh, Guy, darling, darling, I *had* to do it. He begged me to last night, and I thought it best . . . with all the gossip in the hospital . . . best for you.'

Silence a moment. Then Guy said in a savage undertone:

'I won't have you marry this man or any other as a sacrifice to me. I won't have it. Do you hear?'

'It isn't only that.'

'You don't love him. You love *me.*'

Hot, shaking, unnerved, she answered from the depths of her heart:

'I know that I love you! I *worship* you. But it's best for me to marry him. Guy, Guy, you must believe it's best.'

'To think of you in another man's arms . . .'

'You mustn't think about it,' she broke in in a tortured voice.

He put two hands to his head. He felt that it was going to burst. In that moment he was racked with ungovernable jealousy . . . a jealousy which he had no right to feel. It was more than flesh and blood could stand, loving this girl so much and contemplating the thought of her in Tim Madden's embrace. For a moment all ethics of right and wrong were discounted. He experienced the most insane desire to force Celia to go away with him . . . away from everybody in the world to a place where neither of them would be found again by anybody they had ever known.

Then two great tears gathered in Celia's eyes and began to roll slowly down her cheeks. She said :

'We agreed last night that we must part. Don't, *don't* make it hard for me, or it'll *kill* me.'

That brought him to his senses. He could bear his own pain but hers he could not endure, and he knew that he must help her. Unless he did, she would be lost. He had no right to be jealous. She had done this thing for him . . . and perhaps for herself. Perhaps she might find it easier to carry on knowing that she was bound to another man. It made the gulf between them so wide, so deep, that it could never be crossed.

Conquering himself, he took her hand again and held it tightly between his cold, nervous fingers.

'It's all right, darling. Forgive me. Just for a moment I could scarcely bear it. But perhaps it *is* all for the best. Don't cry, Celia. I can't bear your tears, darling. Please don't cry.'

She choked, tried desperately to smile.

That smile nearly broke his heart. He said:

'It'll all work out, darling. Don't worry any more. Give Madden my good wishes. God knows I wish him luck—and you. If I thought you were going to be happy, I'd be happier myself.'

'We'd better not talk about happiness,' she whispered.

'We must both try to get something out of life . . . some peace of mind,' he said. 'Meanwhile, I shall take a holiday, longer than forty-eight hours . . . I think I'd better stay away from London for a bit. I don't think I dare risk seeing you again.'

Footsteps sounded in the corridor. Celia heard them and a feeling of complete panic seized her. In another moment this room would be full of people . . . nurses . . . doctors . . . the men waiting to wheel her to the theatre . . . Guy would vanish. Vanish not only for the moment, but forever. She burst out passionately:

'Oh, Guy, *Guy.*'

He bent and took her in his arms for a fleeting moment, held her against him, crushed his lips to her piteous mouth.

'I love you. I'll love you all my life, but for God's sake be brave, darling. Be brave and be happy . . .'

He tore himself away and left the room before anybody else could enter it. And that was not the end of torture for Celia. In came her special nurse to fuss round and condole with her, because 'Mr Denver had cut his hand. What a shame it was! Mr Miles-Goring was a wonderful surgeon but as Mr Denver had begun the job, it was such a *shame* he couldn't finish it . . .'

Celia had little to say. She was too miserable and exhausted. The tears would keep on rolling down her cheeks. Nurse thought that she was just suffering from the effects of fever and the pain in her arm. She wiped the tears away and tried to be bright and cheering, which nearly drove Celia mad.

'As soon as you come round, we'll have your young man to see you. It must be such a thrill for you just to have become engaged and it'll make all the difference to you knowing that he'll be with you. Sister was on the phone with him a little while ago and he sounded so upset about the arm, and said we must phone him as soon as the op's over. He's that very tall young man with a square jaw who comes to see you every evening, isn't he? Aren't you a lucky girl . . .'

No answer from Celia. Her eyes were tight-shut. Her bloodless lips pressed together. She had reached/the stage when she could not even be irritated. She was sunk . . . sunk . . .

Then came Mr Miles-Goring. A distinguished man with a slight look of Guy about him which gave her a pang. But he wasn't Guy. He had none of Guy's wonderful magnetism. He was much more cut-and-dried and, naturally, not at all personally interested in her. She was just another case and not a very interesting one at that. Opening up the

236

arm was child's play. Nevertheless, he was courteous and endeavoured to be reassuring with a proper bedside manner.

'We'll soon have you right again: Not afraid, are you?'

'No,' she said.

And she wondered what he would have said if she had told him that she wished passionately that she could die under the effects of the anaesthetic which she would be given. That she would give anything not to wake up again. And if she said that, of course, he would be both alarmed and shocked. With the rest of the world, he would tell her that she was wicked to wish any such thing. There was so much to live for. Hadn't nurse just said what a lucky girl she was with Tim as a future husband?

'God, God!' said Celia, to herself, 'help me to get through this and come out sane.'

CHAPTER SIXTEEN

'It's wonderful,' said Jan Leith, 'what a spot of money can do!' She was sitting beside Celia on the glass-covered verandah of a big hotel in Brighton. They were drinking coffee after lunch. On the Front before them, a steady stream of cars passed to and fro; the promenade was thick with pedestrians. This was Easter week and a gorgeous April day. Across the blue sky, little white clouds scudded merrily, in a wind which whipped the greeny blue sea into snow-crested waves. The fresh salt air was good to breathe.

Jan felt that it was good to be alive. What she had just said was true enough, in her estimation. Certainly it was wonderful what a 'spot of money' had done for her. It had obtained for her this amazing holiday with Celia. A holiday that was like a dream. Just a few discreet words with her manager and Tim Madden had fixed it all without trouble. The manager was only too delighted to grant Mr Madden a favour since he had purchased a very handsome ermine wrap for his fiancée.

That ermine cape sat snugly around Celia's shoulders today. Her fair hair was perfectly coiffured—she had spent a couple of hours with the hairdresser in the hotel and come out looking, as Jan said, *too* 'ducky' with Victorian curls on top of her head. She was altogether a fashionable young woman these days. Tim was spending money on her freely and refusing to take 'no' for an answer when Celia gave it. His pride in her was limitless and his generosity equally so.

But Celia did not share Jan's enthusiasm. What money could do was grand—in a way! But it couldn't make a woman happy when she was in love. Only possession of her lover could do that. And the more Tim gave Celia, the

238

more embarrassed she felt. She had no right to take his gifts—no real right to marry him. But she had chosen this way out . . . and she was trying to keep to her bargain.

It seemed to her two years rather than two weeks since she had had that last operation on her arm and come down here in Tim's car, with Jan.

Of course she was much better in health. The arm was still in a splint and would be for some time, but it was healing nicely, and this time Miles-Goring had assured her there would be no further complications.

She had had a fortnight of the laziest possible existence here, with Jan to nurse and fuss over her. Jan hardly allowed her to lift a finger to do anything for herself. They were out most of the morning; rested after lunch; and, so far, every evening, Tim tore down from London in his car to dine with them and spend the evening.

They were not to go back to that gloomy, shabby boarding-house in Bayswater. That was another arrangement which Tim had made. Without waiting for protests from Celia, he had taken a tiny Service-flat in her name near Hyde Park. There, Celia was to live with Jan until their marriage.

'And after that what about me as a housekeeper?' Jan had once said jokingly. 'I'm sick of the fur-trade, and I'm a very good cook. What Lancashire girl isn't? How about Mr and

Mrs Madden taking me on as the domestic help?'

To which Tim had replied:

'Not a bad idea, Jan. We must see about it.'

For there was nobody, now, whom Tim admired more than Celia's friend. He was enormously impressed and touched by her ceaseless devotion to Celia. When he left Celia with Jan—he knew it was with somebody who was as anxious to take care of her as he was, himself.

But Celia, thinking about that word 'marriage', felt only dark fears for the future. How *could* she marry dear old Tim, nice as he was? How could she lie in the arms of any man when her spirit, her soul, was with Guy? Where Guy was or what he might be doing now, she did not know. Once more he had vanished from her ken. Once more they were physically separated as though an enormous wall barricaded them from each other's sight. Yet he was still with her . . . always at her side . . . always she remembered every expression on his face . . . every inflection of his voice.

How *could* she marry Tim? Yet every day placed her under further obligation to him! She felt that she was in a trap—a trap of her own making. But at least she was glad that the announcement of her engagement must have stopped any scandal about Guy and herself.

'More coffee, lamb?' said Jan.

Celia shook her head.

'Heigh-ho, heigh-ho,' said Jan, 'it's Saturday and our Timothy will be down after lunch. He's going to take you out in the country for a run, my dear, so he said last night. I shall go on the Palace Pier. If there's anything I love, it's going on the Palace Pier.'

Celia smiled.

'Careful, Jan! An unchaperoned girl on the pier . . .!'

Jan grinned like a schoolboy.

'Eh, but I wish your fears had some foundation, my dear. I never get looked at twice. If I got looked at *once*—I'd make a dash for the man.'

'Idiot,' said Celia, with a deep note of affection.

'In my next life,' said Jan, 'I shall be born with a face and figure like yours, my lamb.'

Said Celia, bitterly :

'Do you think it's brought me any real happiness?'

Jan frowned. She knew perfectly well that Celia was unhappy within herself, and that all her efforts to be gay and happy when Tim Madden was around, were a strain. The poor kid was still in love with that doctor. What a curse to be born with such a loyal nature! Yet Jan, of all people, could appreciate loyalty.

A shaft of sunlight fell upon Celia. Looking at her, Jan thought how much her friend had altered since she came out of hospital. She looked older, more mature, much more beautiful. Suffering had removed the extreme youth from Celia's face and ennobled it. She was positively lovely these days, Jan reflected, but there was too much sorrow in those great brown eyes, too much repression in her lips.

Celia put on a pair of blue-rimmed dark glasses.

'How lovely the sun is,' she sighed, and leaned back in her chair and thought:

'Somewhere, this same sun is shining on Guy. Where is he? What is he doing? How, is he feeling? Oh, my darling Guy, do you think as often about me as I do about you?'

She looked sadly at her left hand. Such a lovely ring on her engagement finger. She had told Tim that she liked rubies, so he had found her an old-fashioned ruby ring. There were diamonds encircling the beautiful red stone. It was exquisitely set in platinum and looked well on that slender hand of hers. But what of that other ring which must soon replace it! That plain band which would tie her to Tim, forever? She winced at the mere thought. Tim would not wait too long. Two months at the most! He wanted her for his wife by June, when he got his summer holiday, and he had planned to take her down to the South of France.

It was a tragedy, she thought, that life should be offering her everything on a platter except the one thing she wanted. And Guy, Guy must feel the same. He, too, had

242

everything but love. And that was the only thing that really and truly mattered.

'Take a look at this!' said Jan, breaking in upon Celia's reflections. 'Society-woman with boyfriend, stepping out of a car that screams "Hollywood".

Celia removed her glasses and glanced through the glass windows. Quite close to them, a long white Mercedes-Benz had pulled up before the hotel entrance. The driver, a tall, dark man who looked to Celia un-English, was helping his companion out, whilst the commissionaire, who had just opened the door, stood deferentially by. It was upon the woman whom Celia concentrated her gaze. There was something vaguely familiar about the tall, slim figure in the smartly tailored tweeds. She wore violets pinned to the short mink cape over her shoulders. For the moment all that Celia could see was a head on which was perched a brown felt hat with a veil. A diamond clip on the brim caught the sun and flashed as she moved.

'Where have I seen her before?' Celia said.

Then the woman raised her head and Celia's heart gave a sharp jolt. One look at that pale, haughty face with the dark eyes and brightly rouged lips, was sufficient.

'Good God!' exclaimed Celia.

'What is it?'

'That woman,' said Celia, breathlessly . . . 'is . . . is Guy Denver's wife.'

Jan swung round and took another look at the couple who were now coming on to the verandah. Her eyes grew round and inquisitive. 'Eh!' she said, with her slight Lancashire drawl, 'that's a coincidence. Mrs Denver, is it?'

'Yes,' said Celia in a low voice and hastily put on her dark glasses again. She had no particular wish to be recognised by Frances Denver. Her heart was beating rapidly and her face had lost its colour. It was not really much of a coincidence that Frances should come to this hotel which was one of the largest and the most popular on the South Coast. So many people came down from town for lunch or dinner. But a dozen questions darted through her mind.

Who was the man? Was it by any chance Paul de Poiret back in the limelight? That was a French car. She could see the 'F' on, the back of the Mercedes, and she had thought, as soon as she had seen the driver, that he was a foreigner. What was Frances Denver doing down in Brighton with a man who was not her husband? *Did Guy know?*

Jan saw how white Celia had grown. She knew the sight of Guy's wife was affecting her.

'Listen,' she said, abruptly, 'how about you coming up and lying down for half-an-hour before our Timothy turns up?'

Nowadays she always alluded to Celia's fiancé as 'our Timothy'.

Celia rose.

'Yes, I think perhaps I'll go up,' she said, unsteadily.

As she and Jan walked through the vestibule, Celia was forced to remove her glasses, because after the dazzling brightness of the sea-front, she was almost blinded in the dark lounge. As luck would have it, she walked straight into Frances Denver who was on her way to the ladies' room.

Frances threw one casual glance at the slender girl with the fair curls, then a second much more interested one. She stopped and spoke to her.

'Well, *well!* if it isn't our heroine of the flood.'

Celia stood still. That cold, sarcastic voice cut so unpleasantly across her memory. It brought back the pain of that day when she had left Guy . . . virtually turned out of his house by this woman. Frances added:

'Are you staying here?'

'Yes,' said Celia, and turning, indicated Jan: 'May I introduce Miss Leith.'

'How d'you do?' said Frances in her most chilly voice.

Afterwards, Jan told Celia, it was all she could do from making one of her most blunt and unpleasant rejoinders. But instead, she passed on to the lift. She thought Celia might find it less embarrassing without her.

'By the way,' Frances Denver said to Celia, 'I believe I have to congratulate you on your

245

engagement, haven't I?'

'Yes.'

'Just in time, my dear.'

Celia's hands clenched.

'What exactly are you inferring, Mrs. Denver?'

'No inference, believe me. A plain statement. It was just in time. In the medical circle, your name was being very much linked up with my husband's.'

Celia felt hot, then cold. She thought that Frances Denver must, surely, be one of the most unpleasant women in the world. What could it profit her to be so spiteful? It was not as though she loved Guy or wanted him. Celia could not bring herself to utter any apology, any explanation. She stood there, flushing violently, at a loss for words.

But Frances Denver was never at a loss for words. She was enjoying the discomfiture which she was making Celia feel. Certainly she had no further use for Guy. Especially as Paul had reappeared on the scene. Paul, with whom she was as much in love as ever. And she was of the mind that he was a little more in love with her this time. Since his return from Paris, to launch a new play of his which had just been translated into English, he had re-opened the old intrigue with a vengeance. But she was still not at all sure that he wished to stand as co-respondent in a divorce case. She felt a cold, malicious fury against Guy and this girl for renouncing their love—and especially against Celia whose engagement had killed any hopes that Frances might have entertained that Guy would commit himself.

'Of course,' she added, 'there is still a lot of scandal. That flood story will want some living down, even though you *are* going to be married.'

Then Celia found words:

'I hope and believe, Mrs Denver,' she said with difficulty, 'that there will be no harmful gossip attached to Mr Denver's name. It would be utterly undeserved.'

Frances' red lips curved into an unpleasant little smile. Her gaze travelled up and down Celia.

'Would it?'

'I think you know that,' said Celia.

'My dear girl, I know nothing about your affair with my husband. It was too subtly managed.'

Anger welled up in Celia. How dare she insinuate this sort of thing . . . *how dared she?* And yet when Celia remembered how much she and Guy loved each other, and the passionate nature of the few meetings they had had, she felt tongue-tied. She could not altogether repudiate Frances Denver's suggestions. She loathed listening to them. She loathed this sordid conversation between herself and Guy's wife.

'And for all I know,' continued Frances,

'you and Guy are still in communication.'

Said Celia, white and breathless:

'That's utterly untrue. Please remember I'm going to marry Mr Madden . . .'

'But you'll admit that you *were* in touch with Guy until quite recently.'

'I'll admit nothing, and I see no reason why I should stay here and listen to this sort of thing, Mrs Denver.'

Frances shrugged her shoulders.

'Oh, please don't think I mind any more. I have other interests. I see no reason why I should sit down and wait until Guy chooses to amuse me. If you like to phone him up and ask him down for lunch—do! But just be discreet and don't upset him by mentioning that you saw me here with Mons. de Poiret. I'm supposed to be with a sick aunt!'

Laughing, she turned and walked away, leaving Celia completely shaken. How *could* she? Was she lost to all sense of decency? Had she thought for nobody except herself? Did she not see that her own line of conduct must reflect upon Guy's name?

And that was the woman to whom Guy was bound. The woman with whom he must live for the rest of his life. Celia moved towards the lift, her mind and heart in chaos. Those few chance words with Frances Denver had reopened the old wound unbearably. The thought of Tim was wiped out. She could think only of Guy and wonder what he would say if he knew that his wife was meeting Paul de Poiret again. It was too awful to think that a woman could behave like Frances Denver. Deceiving anybody as fine, as worth-while as Guy. Telling him that she was visiting 'a sick aunt'! And for all the world to see her here in Brighton. Of course nobody would tell Guy. But they would pity him in secret. It was humiliating to think that Guy should be the object of pity.

'And I adore him,' Celia thought passionately. 'I'd give *my life* for him. It just isn't fair.'

Up in the big sunny bedroom which she shared with Jan, she burst out with the whole story. Jan received it in disgust.

'I've no use for such as Mrs Denver! The wife of a decent man and especially a man in the public eye—to let him down like that! Shame on her!'

'And to let down Guy, of all the men in the world,' said Celia, pacing up and down the room.

'She's got a nerve,' said Jan. 'How does she know you won't tell the husband just what you've seen?'

'She's too clever for that. She knows perfectly well that I wouldn't want to hurt or worry him.'

'I don't think it would hurt him much.'

'No, but it would worry him because he's made up his mind to try to live in peace with his wife and she isn't giving him a chance.'

'Well, if she's on with this Frenchman again, she'll find herself being divorced before long.'

'God!' said Celia, under her breath, 'if *that* happened . . .!' she broke off, breathing fast.

Jan looked at her. Those scarlet cheeks and gleaming eyes told their own pathetic story. Wild hope followed by wild despair.

Jan marched up and took Celia firmly by the arm.

'Listen to me, lamb. If you're thinking that you see a chance of that doctor getting free . . . you ought to tell Timothy so straight away. It wouldn't be fair on him. You, of all people, couldn't do a thing like that, Celia.'

'Like—what?'

'Well . . . chuck your fiancé at the last moment.'

Then Celia broke down. Sitting on the edge of her bed, she burst into tears, holding her uninjured arm across her eyes.

'Oh, God, Jan, I wouldn't want to let Tim down. I never really wanted to become engaged to him—you know that. I was driven into it, and I've tried to keep to my bargain. I'll go on trying, only I can't stop loving Guy. This kind of thing is too shattering. It breaks me to pieces, Jan. If Frances Denver does anything crazy and Guy gets his freedom, and I've tied myself up to Tim, *it would kill me.* It would kill him, too. It would be too ironic and terrible!'

Jan sat beside her, holding her in her arms,

stroking her hair, as she had done so often in the past, when her Celia was in tears.

'Poor lamb! Poor darling! I know how hard it all is. Hush, don't upset yourself like this! What will Timothy say when he sees you've been crying your eyes out. Don't let what that wretched woman said upset you. You can't count on her conduct setting the doctor free, anyhow. If you throw Timothy over, it may all be for nothing.'

Celia sobbed:

'It's a mess—an awful mess! Sometimes I can't cope with it, Jan.'

'Well, if you have any suspicions that you won't carry through with this marriage, the sooner you tell our Timothy so, the better.'

Celia raised her face. It was haggard and desperate.

'I'll talk to him today. I'll tell him everything that's in my mind. It's only fair to him—I agree with you. And yet, don't you see what a corner I'm in? Because if I break my engagement now, that woman *might* try to reopen the scandal about Guy and me. She's all ready to.'

'It's certainly difficult,' said Jan, 'but she can't pin anything on you, or on him. You've both acted absolutely honourably.'

The telephone bell rang. Jan answered it, then put down the receiver and turned to Celia:

'Our Timothy's downstairs waiting for you.'

Celia rose from the bed and wiped her eyes.

'I'd better do my face and pull myself together.'

'And I shouldn't say anything to him while you're upset. Wait a bit, lamb. Don't wreck your life—and poor old Timothy's hopes—just because of a few words that hateful woman has said.'

CHAPTER SEVENTEEN

As soon as Timothy Madden saw Celia, he knew that something was wrong. She was looking lovely and she had made up her face so that the traces of tears were no longer there. But she had a strained look and there was still a certain moisture in her eyes. She had been looking so much better that he was troubled to see the change in her.

'What have you been doing to yourself, honey?'

She tried to laugh, determined to do as Jan had advised and say nothing about her present mood . . .

'Nothing! Too much sun all of a sudden.'

And hastily she put on the concealing dark-glasses and followed Tim out of the crowded lounge. All the time her gaze moved furtively around, seeking for Guy's wife—yet dreading to see her. But there was no sign of either Frances or her companion.

Tim had eyes only for the slender figure at his side. He was desperately in love with Celia these days. But he was disciplining himself rigorously. He had made no attempt to act the lover, so far as kisses and caresses were concerned, since their engagement. He had maintained the 'affectionate brother' attitude, knowing that it was what she wanted and no matter how difficult he found it.

At times he deceived himself into the belief that one day she would turn to him; that he would be rewarded for his tireless devotion. There were moments when she seemed so soft, so sweet, content to be with him. But many other and more frequent were the moments when he saw facts as they were rather than as he wished them to be. Celia did not love him and never would. Celia still loved that doctor. Tim knew it and the thought drove him mad with jealousy and at the same time made him agonisingly sorry for her.

Passionate love that must be suppressed and that had no outlet was a terrible thing . . . a grievous, gnawing ache with which he was only too familiar. He told himself that a man could stand it. But Celia, so fragile, so gentle, how could she endure the pain? Sometimes out of sheer selfless sympathy for her, he wished to God he could lead her to the man she loved and say:

'For God's sake take her away and make her happy.'

But he was continuing with this engagement and the plans for his marriage, still hugging a forlorn hope that all would be well in the end.

He had enjoyed doing all that had been done for Celia these last few weeks. He wanted to spend every penny he had upon her. He was proud of her beauty and her charm. He liked to see the other men in the hotel turn to make a second glance at her. She moved beautifully. He liked her in that tweed suit with the dark blue chiffon tucked-in scarf and the blue silk handkerchief tied around her fair head to protect the curls from the. Brighton breezes. Those small feet were perfect in the blue suede shoes. God! she was adorable. How intolerable to know that her heart was elsewhere.

'Let's get into the car and go for a long country drive,' he said, abruptly.

She gave a nervous little laugh.

'You're very stern today.'

'Fed up,' he said, in a curt voice which she rarely heard from him.

'Why, Tim?'

'With everything.'

'I don't think I've ever heard you say that before.'

'I don't think I've ever felt before quite as I feel today.'

She dragged her thoughts away from her own troubles and concentrated on his. He was settling her in the car now, wrapping a rug

254

about her knees, and he climbed in beside her, lit a cigarette and started off down the Front.

'It's such a lovely April day,' said Celia, 'one oughtn't to feel fed up.'

'That's true enough. Especially when you've got the most heavenly girl in the world sitting beside you.'

She gave another uneasy laugh.

'Then what's bothering you, Tim?'

'You, my dear,' he said, grimly.

The colour sprang to her cheeks.

'I don't want to be a bother to you, Tim.'

'Well, you are—a hell of a bother. When you look like you do today, I know damn well we're never going to make a success of life together—that's all.'

Her heart sank. It sank, not for herself, but for him. The big, cheerful Tim was so much more sensitive than she had ever given him credit for. So quick to perceive her moods and react to them. Perhaps because he loved her. She knew that she would be like that with Guy.

He turned the car off the Front, drove up Second Avenue, and Convent Hill, and on to the Dyke Road. He did not speak again until they were at the Dyke itself. Near Saddlescombe he pulled up by the side of the road and switched off the engine. For a moment neither of them spoke. Tim let down all the windows and pulled back the sunshine-roof of his car. Up here it was glorious with those moving billowy clouds racing above

255

their heads across the blue April sky; a sky that merged into the green of the Downs; the roving Sussex Downs, windswept, beautiful, immortal.

In the distance a grey windmill looked as though it was a child's toy. To their right, a solitary rider guided his horse over the springy turf, followed by a black-and-white dalmatian. On the other side, a farmer with a collie at his heels, drove a flock of sheep toward their pen.

'Lovely and rural—spring at its height, God's in his heaven and all's wrong with my world,' said Tim, bleakly.

Celia shook her head.

'Dear, *dear* Tim, I can't bear to see you in this mood, Do tell me what *is* wrong.'

He looked at her with blue, discontented eyes.

'I'm all for quotations. How about that Omar one?'

'Which one?' she smiled, and her smile seemed to go straight to his heart because it was so sweet and yet so impersonal. She was always impersonal with him. What a lucky fellow that doctor was to have won her love. What heaven it must be to know a Celia who would become a burning flame in a man's embrace.

He began to quote, half angrily, half humorously:

' "Ah, love, could thou and I with sorry fate conspire, would we not take this world of ours

256

and shatter it, then remould it nearer to the heart's desire!" '

Celia looked down at her engagement ring. There was deep grief in her eyes.

'My dear, I agree. It would be lovely—but we. can't.'

'We certainly can't, otherwise you'd have to fall in love with me, which would suit *me*. Then you'd marry the other fellow which would suit *you*. A complete tearing in two of Celia which is a hopeless proposition.'

She twined her ring nervously round her finger.

'Why don't we drive on?'

'Do you want to avoid a discussion?'

She raised large, sad eyes to his.

'Not if you feel it's going to bring us anywhere, or do us any good.'

He threw away his cigarette and seized her hands.

'Listen, darling, we've been engaged less than a month. During that time I've never kissed your lips, do you realise that?'

She changed colour and her lashes flickered. Her throat felt dry and hot.

'I know. You've been so marvellous. Marvellously patient.'

'But it can't go on, can it, my sweet? I've got a fairly optimistic nature, but as a rule I've got what I've wanted. I thought I'd got it when you promised to marry me, but I'm not so sure now.'

She swallowed hard.

'I've disappointed you, I know.'

'Don't talk as though you've committed a crime. You can't make yourself love someone whom you *don't* love; my dear.'

'I'm so terribly fond of you, Tim, *and* so grateful.'

'I know that. But I don't ask for gratitude and I need more than fondness. I'm in love with you, Celia. Are you never going to be able to feel anything but fondness for me?'

She was silent a moment, her heart beating unhappily. She had long expected this discussion to come. Why should Tim put up with giving all and taking nothing? And what use to shrink from all that an engagement entailed, only to plunge finally into marriage, then become his absolute possession? She must either do this thing properly or not at all, and she knew it. She dreaded the issue of their analyses. She had only two alternatives; either to tell him that she could never love him and give him back his ring, or force herself into giving him a semblance of love—enough at least, to satisfy him.

If he ended this engagement, out of sheer impatience and disappointment, she would lose all that he offered. But that did not seem to enter into the problem with her. The only thing that mattered was Guy. What effect would it have upon Guy if she allowed this engagement to come to an end? Would

Frances use it as a weapon against him? At the same time, what earthly right had *she* to use Tim as a pawn in a game which she was playing on behalf of another man?

Desperation seized her. The man at her side knew that the was undergoing a violent mental struggle. He could see it in her face; feel it in the trembling of the small hands which he was holding. He knew long before she gave her answer that she would do what was best for him, or for Guy Denver, or for anybody in the world rather than for herself. She never thought of herself. It maddened him. He said:

'Can't something be done to put things right for *you?* Don't think of me. Think of yourself. What do *you* want? Answer me truthfully, for heaven's sake.'

'Oh, Tim, don't torture me.'

'That's the last thing I want to do, But isn't it going to torture you if I claim what might be called "my rights" as a lover? How, for instance, are you going to feel if I say that I've done the brother-act long enough and that I want this . . .'

He pulled her suddenly, roughly into his arms. She felt his lips, hard, demanding against her mouth. The contact with her drove Tim mad for a moment. He held her so that she could not move. During that kiss, Celia alternated between a frenzied desire to push him away, and a ghastly feeling of disloyalty to Guy—Guy who had been the only man on

259

earth to kiss her in this way. In her anguished mind and heart she was conscious of the impossibility of continuing with this affair. It had been wrong from the very start. Unfair upon Tim and grossly unfair to herself. She endured that embrace while it lasted, but when Tim's arms fell away from her, he saw that she was as white as death and there was an expression in her eyes which put the last nail in the coffin of his hopes.

'That's made you loathe me, hasn't it?' he asked between his teeth.

'No, no,' she said, 'I could never loathe you. I . . . I'm devoted to you . . . I . . .'

She broke off, stammered and put her face in her hands. Tim got out of the car and slammed the door. He was shaking. It took him a few moments to get a grip on himself; to fight his own battle. He walked away from the car for a moment, a grim, blank look on his square face. When he returned to Celia, he found her still sitting there with her face hidden. In a changed voice that had lost all its harshness, he said:

'Listen to me, darling. You won't be asked to do that again, so don't be frightened.'

She uncovered her face. Her eyes were brilliant with tears.

'Oh, Tim, I'm so unutterably ashamed.'

'What of?'

'Of disappointing you. Of being such a coward. If I was a bit stronger and braver, I'd have carried this thing through but—'

'Oh, don't be absurd,' he broke in, and climbing into the car, took one of her hands and patted it. 'You've been stronger , and braver than nine women out of ten in similar circumstances. You've never been dishonest with me, Celia. You told me right at the beginning that you didn't care for me this way. I had no earthly right to get a promise out of you at the time I did. You were ill and miserable. I've been a swine.'

'You haven't. You've been absolutely marvellous. The trouble is that I don't know how I'm going to repay it all,' she said, piteously.

'Talk about paying back, and I'll never forgive you, Celia. Anything I've done for you has been because I've wanted to, and it's given me a tremendous "kick" doing it.'

The tears began to roll down her cheeks.

'You're so good and now I've spoilt everything.'

He took out a large blue silk handkerchief and wiped away the tears.

'I've been living in a fool's paradise, honey, thinking we'd shake-down as a married couple. It would have been hopeless, and it's better to face up to it now rather than afterwards.'

She made a gesture of despair.

'I've spoilt everything,' she repeated.

'Nonsense. I'm not going to walk out in a "high dudgeon". I'm your friend for life, just as I always have been. I've just got to learn to look at you in a different way. And meanwhile, you're to go on convalescing—just as you are—and then come back to the office and do some more work. I've lost a wife, but I'm keeping a damned efficient secretary.'

She could not answer. It was all too much for her. She could not bear to think that she had hurt Tim, and yet, like him, she saw the futility of continuing with their engagement. She had not meant to break it. He, himself, had brought about this crisis. She drew off her ring and blindly handed it to him, only to have him push it back into her hand.

'For Lord's sake don't start giving me back my presents. If you do, I'll give them all to Jan. What do you think I want the ring for? To give to the next blonde whom I'm foolish enough to fall for!'

'Oh, Tim.'

'Listen,' he said, 'we can't just sit here and weep together. It's wasting a fine day. Let's pretend we've been married for twenty years and that we've settled down to a nice benign sort of friendship and that we're going out for the day.'

Impulsively she leaned up and touched his cheek with her lips.

'I think you're the grandest man in the world.'

'Is that what a wife would say to her husband after twenty years?' said Tim, gruffly, to hide his emotion.

'I'm sure one day your wife will say it to you.'

'Well, what can I say to you?' he ruminated a moment, then added: 'Oh, well, my dear, I think you've kept your figure pretty well, especially as you're the mother of ten!'

That made her laugh.

'Tim, you *are* an ass.'

'Let's drive to Worth Forest,' he said, 'and find a place for tea. Later we'll go back and take old Jan out to dinner.'

'Ian will be simply horrified about this.'

'I like Jan,' said Tim, 'she has none of your beauty—blast it—but she has a damn fine figure. I'm not sure I shan't abandon you this evening, and take Jan out alone.'

'How thrilled she'd be,' said Celia. 'She thinks there's nobody in the world like you, Tim.'

His masculine pride revived somewhat. Celia's lack of response had given him an inferiority complex which did not suit him. It was nice to know that even dear old Jan was capable of being 'thrilled' because of him.

'I *shall* make a pass at Jan,' he said, 'and you shall be left out in the cold.'

'Where I belong,' said Celia, mournfully.

'Where you have no right to be! And I only hope to God you'll get what you want one of these days.'

She did not answer. But as the car moved

on through the April sunlight, all her thoughts and emotions became focussed once again upon Guy, moving about him in an intolerable circle of hopeless longing.

CHAPTER EIGHTEEN

Guy Denver came back from the nursing-home where he had been operating that Saturday afternoon, handed his case to his secretary and sat down at his desk.

It had been a long and difficult operation, and all his nerves were on edge. He was weary—unutterably weary. Not only bodily; there seemed a weight on his soul these days which was forever increasing. A weight which had been there since he had said good-bye to Celia. A weight that was crushing all the joy out of his life, taking away from him even pleasure in his work. Nothing seemed to mean very much these days, neither the work nor the attempts which he made to enjoy the hours of relaxation.

He knew only too well that the significance of it was the existence of an overwhelming love for Celia. It had grown to such proportions that it swamped everything else. He had heard it said many times that love was neither as necessary nor as all-embracing in a man's life as in the life of a woman. He no longer credited the truth of that statement.

Celia *was* his life. The memory of her was undying, like a torch, perpetually burning in his mind and his heart. Forever he would bow before the shrine of her courage, her self-abnegation. And through the long days and nights since their final farewell, he had lived purely mechanically, every pulse-beat reminding him of her, of countless little things about her. The marvellous look in those large brown eyes when he was about to kiss her. The touch of her small hands about his head. The scent of her hair, the lilt of her voice, the way her lips would tremble suddenly into a smile. He could forget nothing about her. He was wholly in love and the thing was a ghastly tragedy because he knew that she returned that love. Yet they must remain apart. He ought not even to *think* of her with longing. He was married to another woman. He was not free to love, Yet love he must, no matter what laws or barriers separated them.

This weight on his spirit seemed today more intolerable than ever. He had had a difficult week. More unpleasant scenes with Frances who seemed to grow more selfish, more exacting, more unpleasant to live with in the circumstances, rather than make any effort to meet him half-way. A little friendliness, a little real consideration would have done so much to help. But she had nothing for him these days but demands—or sneers. What she was getting out of life privately, in concealment from him, he did not know. He could not watch her every movement, neither did he wish to. She was always out. She had no use for him. That made it all the more bitter and ironic to know what Celia would have felt in his wife's place.

He forced himself to keep to his bargain, not to see Celia again. But the hardest part of that bargain was the lack of contact with her. He knew nothing about her. The last news he had heard was from Miles-Goring who had reported that the arm was doing well and, of course, Guy was aware that she had left the hospital.

He had had a few hellish moments when he had seen the announcement in the papers of her engagement to Timothy Madden. He could not bear to imagine her engaged to Tim. Neither could he bring himself to visualise the marriage between those two. It was too much for him. But he tried to believe that what she had done was for the best and in all sincerity he hoped that the step she had taken would bring her some peace, some happiness.

For him, he felt, that there could be no more of either. Only this going on from day to day, blindly and doggedly doing what was required of him.

Frances had said that she was away for the week-end visiting relations. Guy was expected tomorrow in Hertfordshire to stay the night with one of his old Cambridge friends who had a charming house down there. It was a place where he was always welcome and he *could* get out and play some golf on Sundays. But even golf these days was an effort, and staying with John Harrison and his wife merely a painful reminder of what happiness there *could be* in the world. The supreme contentment that can exist between a really happily married couple. John and Silvia Harrison adored each other—as he and Celia would have adored, Guy told himself bitterly—and they had two marvellous children. Why should such chances be given to some and not to others? Why should one be burdened with disappointment and suffering whilst another found fulfilment of his dreams? Where was the justice? Where the answer to the problems? There seemed none, and Guy Denver, at one time the most keenly ambitious and philosophical of men, found himself these days lost in a hopeless fog which choked and baffled him.

If he could only see Celia, he thought, at times—just for a moment make sure that she was well and content—just for a moment assuage some of this terrible longing by holding her in his arms, he might go on with fresh courage. Yet no! To see her, to touch her would merely revive the old agonising fire which might eventually annihilate them both.

There was nothing for it but to put up with the present position.

The secretary placed before him a list of

people who had telephoned. Guy looked at it moodily. Nothing very pressing. It could all wait until Monday. Perhaps he would ring up John and invite himself down to Hertfordshire this evening, now that he had finished earlier than he had anticipated. It would be good to get out of London. The Harrisons had a beautiful garden. He would like to be in it and feel the April sun warm upon his face.

He dismissed his secretary and rang for his manservant.

'Pack my case, Albert, I shall be going down to Mr Harrison before dinner.'

He bathed, and changed into grey flannels and a tweed coat. Down in the consulting-room again, he took a tin of tobacco from a drawer in his desk, filled his pouch and then his pipe. The clock on the desk told him that it was close upon six o'clock. Plenty of time to drive down to the Harrisons before dinner.

Albert came into the room with a telegram on a silver salver.

'This has just come, sir.'

With pipe in the corner of his mouth, Guy ripped open the orange envelope. Now who the devil could be wiring him? Then as he read what was typed on that narrow blue ribbon across the white page, his tired face flushed hotly, and the blank look in his eyes was replaced by an almost terrible animation.

He took the pipe from his mouth and laid it on the mantelpiece.

'Good God!' he said, aloud.

Then conscious that the man was waiting for an answer, he sent him away. There was *no* answer to this, except one that would be made in person.

He read the telegram again, twice, three times.

'CANNOT GO ON LIKE THIS MUST SEE YOU IMMEDIATELY PLEASE WAIT FOR ME WILL BE WITH YOU THIS EVENING CELIA.'

That message, so totally unexpected, and worded so urgently, flung Guy into a terrific state of excitement and anticipation. In the face of such a message he could not be strong; he could not ignore it and fly from the house and from danger. Celia needed him. Celia was coming here. That was enough for him. Whatever happened he must wait and see what she wanted of him. Feverishly he re-read those startling words.

'CANNOT GO ON . . .' What did that mean? Was she finding her engagement to Madden impossible? Was she going to ask him, Guy, to take her away? Good God, that was not possible, not after all that she had said about not ruining his career. For one blind and emotional moment, Guy Denver asked himself what he would do if Celia had weakened and was about to make that request of him. And with every instinct in him crying aloud for her,

269

he believed that he, too, would be weak; that he would agree to abandon everything for her, and go with her.

But of course she might demand no such thing. Probably it was just that she wished to see him. Had he not a moment ago been thinking the same thing? Hungering for a glimpse of her.

Where was she? When would she come? How long would he have to wait? He saw that the wire had been sent off from Brighton. She must have been convalescing down there. Would she come by car or by train? When would she be here?

The Guy who stood there holding that telegram with shaking fingers, was very different from the weary, half-alive doctor who had walked into the same room an hour ago. The old boyish light had returned to his face. His heart beat madly. He felt almost choked at the thought of Celia walking into this room, into his arms. Celia, his *Celia*.

At any moment she might come. Walking to the bell, he rang it and gave an order to Albert to telephone to Dr Harrison's house and say that an urgent case was keeping him, and that he could not, after all, go down there until tomorrow morning.

'And by the way, Albert,' added Guy, trying to speak casually, 'a—a Miss Hammond will be calling here, at any moment. Show her straight in here, will you?'

270

'Yes, sir,' said the man and departed.

Guy put his pipe in his mouth again, and, smoking, walked up and down his room, up and down, deaf, dumb, blind to everything but the thought of Celia who was coming to him. It was like a miracle, like an answer to his wild, unspoken prayers. Yet what could they hope to gain by this interview? What could be the result except another anguished parting. *Unless* . . . but he allowed himself to think no further.

It was exactly an hour later that the sound of the front-door bell made Guy pause in the middle of the room, which he was still pacing, and stand like one glued to the spot, his gaze riveted on the door. Was this she? Surely it must be, by now?

The next moment the door had opened and Albert announced:

'Miss Hammond.'

Then she was here, as he had pictured her, and Albert had closed the door upon them, leaving them alone. She was here as he had pictured her a hundred times in the past bitter weeks of loneliness and depression. Only a hundred times more beautiful. A Celia dressed as he had never seen her, expensively, smartly, with a mink cape over her shoulders, hiding the arm which was still in a sling; a small hat perched high on the fair Victorian curls, which he thought ravishing.

Her eyes were caught and held by his. The

flame in those eyes was still there, just as he used to see it, and as he had dreamed of it. The warm leaping flame to answer his.

He took a step toward her.

'Oh, God,' he said, 'oh, God, Celia.'

She answered, breathing his name scarcely above a whisper. 'Guy!'

And then she was in his arms, warm, fragrant and yielding, yielding to that long fierce kiss of passion and worship which he pressed upon her upturned mouth. It was a moment so intense that they were both shaken to the depths by the very intensity of it. When it ended, they were white, trembling, clinging to each other like two lost souls, submitting so voluntarily to the devastating tempest which consumed them. Without speaking they clung for a long while. Then her frail body seemed to sag against him and looking down at her, he saw that her eyes were shut and that she was near to losing consciousness.

Filled with indescribable tenderness—a tenderness which outweighed even the violence of his desire—he picked her right up in his arms, knowing that he loved her better than anything or anybody in the world. He carried her to the sofa and laid her down upon it, putting a cushion beneath her head. He drew off the small hat, loosened her cape and, kneeling beside her, stroked her head and her cheeks, murmuring broken endearments.

'Celia . . . my darling . . . Ah! but it's good

to see you again. Almost too much . it *is* too much for us, Celia. We belong . . . we belong to each other body and soul. There's never been anything like this in my life . . . nothing near it . . . it's so lovely and so terrible . . . oh, my darling!'

Her eyes opened again. The colour was returning to her face. With an arm curved about his neck, she asked no questions, except one . . . the only one which held for her any real interest or meaning.

'My darling, do you still love me?'

'You know that I do. When I kissed you just now, you must have known.'

'Yes, yes. But I want to hear you say it.'

'I'd say it every day, every hour of my life if could. I *will* say it. Now that I've got you here, I'm never going to let you go again.'

She looked up at his face. She had never seen Guy look quite like this before. He was like a man intoxicated. Beyond reason, having no power to reason. If ever he had loved her, she knew that he loved her now. It was unbearably sweet and yet the old barriers were still there and almost as soon as she was out of his arms, it was as though ropes of steel caught her, dragging her back from him, away to the old solitary desolation.

She struggled into a sitting position. Holding on to his shoulder, she leaned close to him, her fair hair tumbled about her fevered face, her thin body shaken with her heart's

273

dizzy beating.

'I love you,' she said under her breath, 'and it is almost too much, as you say. Oh, God, it's wonderful to see you again.'

'It's a miracle,' he said.

He sat at her side, an arm about her, holding her jealously, possessively, as though defying anything or anybody to separate them again. Once again her lips were raised to his, and they kissed desperately.

Then at length when that first wild intoxication of their meeting died down a little and they could breathe more normally, they began to talk on a practical plane. She said:

'I came as soon as I could, after getting your wire.'

He drew away from her, looking at her with puzzled eyes:

'My wire?'

'Yes.'

'But I didn't send you a wire, darling. *You* sent *me* one.'

It was her turn to stare.

'I—wired you . . .?'

'Yes . . .'

He put his hand in his pocket and drew out the slip of paper.

'There it is. It got to me about half-past-six.'

Celia read the message which was signed with her name. The frantic beating of her heart quietened. A queer sort of coldness came over her.

'I didn't sent send that wire, Guy. I didn't write it,' she said.

He gave an unbelieving laugh.

'But, my darling, that's preposterous! You must have sent it. Haven't you just come from Brighton?'

'Yes.'

'And are you going to tell me that you didn't send that wire?'

'I didn't, Guy,' she said earnestly, shaking her head. 'I assure you that I did not. Why should I deny it?'

Baffled, he shook his head.

'I don't understand.'

With slim, shaking fingers, she opened her bag and drew yet another wire from it.

'Don't tell me you didn't send this!'

He read it over her shoulder.

'MUST SEE YOU URGENTLY DO NOT PHONE BUT COME TO HOUSE AS SOON AS YOU RECEIVE THIS IMPERATIVE
—GUY.'

'We-ll,' said Guy with a long-drawn breath, 'there's some thing extremely peculiar about all this, my dear. I did *not* write *that*.'

They stared at each other, uncomprehending.

'I just didn't hesitate when I got the message,' said Celia. 'I presumed that you had some good reason for asking me not to

275

telephone you. It was enough for me that you wished to see me so urgently, and I just caught the first train.

'The same applied to me. I just waited until you came.'

'But it's astounding,' she said, slowly.

He gave a short laugh.

'It's somewhat odd. I think somebody's been playing a practical joke on us: Somebody who apparently *wanted* us to meet.'

Then he saw Celia flush and bite her lip.

'What has struck you?'

'The truth, I fancy,' she said in a voice that trembled. '*Somebody who wanted us to be together* . . . yes . . . I think I can tell you who organised this so cunningly.'

'Who?'

'Your wife, Guy.'

He got up and looked down at her with clouded eyes.

'Frances! But why the hell . . .'

He broke off, as he grasped her meaning and added:

'You mean Frances sent those wires— gambling on the fact that we'd both comply with them—in order to get us here alone? You mean she's still hoping to link our names—to make trouble?'

'I don't see that there can be any other explanation of the telegrams.'

'But Frances isn't in Brighton—that wire was sent from Brighton.'

'She *is* there,' said Celia, 'that's exactly why I have formed this conclusion. She is there, and she saw me in the Imperial Hotel this afternoon.'

In a few rapid words she proceeded to describe to Guy her meeting with Frances, and described also the escort and the Mercedes car.

Guy said quickly:

'Paul de Poiret. So *he's* on the scene again!'

'Yes, and presumably your wife wants her freedom but *not* at her own expense.'

'The old low game,' said Guy between his teeth. 'Good heavens! how any woman could be so unscrupulous.'

'Of course nobody knows that I've come to you,' Celia made haste to say. 'As it happens I did not tell Jan where I was going. I just walked out and said that I'd let her know when I would be back.'

'What did she think of that?'

'Only that I was upset or fed-up, or something. I'd just . . . ' her voice faltered a bit . . . 'I'd just had a scene with Tim and broken my engagement.'

Guy's heart leapt.

'Broken your engagement!'

She raised her eyes to his . . . eyes full of infinite love, and yet dark with distress.

'Yes. I couldn't go on . . . those words in the telegram were true enough . . . I *had* to tell Tim I couldn't marry him. Only I would never,

277

never have come to you like this. You must believe that. Oh God, I've made a mess of things. I knew I would! Here is your wife using every dirty trick to pin something against you and just when I've broken with Tim, it won't look too good, will it?'

She sat there, beating one small fist against the other, her face a study in despair, but Guy would not let that look remain. He sat beside her again and gathered her into his arms.

'The whole world can go to hell. Frances with it. I don't care what she does now,' he said recklessly. 'I can't let you suffer any more and it's too much for me. She's done this thing and brought us together . . very well . . . let her get on with it. I cannot and will not stand another parting from you, Celia.'

For a moment she surrendered feverishly to his kisses, drinking them in, glorying in the white-hot flame of passion that consumed them both. It was a terrible love, this love that ran so high between them. A devouring torrent 'of emotion against which their puny struggles seemed of no avail. They could not even detest the trick that had brought them together. For a few unreasoning moments they could only be thankful for it; sit there in each other's arms rapturously, man and woman loving as they were meant to love, without repression and restraint.

But it could not go on, that fever of caressing, that glory of surrender. There

278

must soon return the full knowledge of their situation as it really was, so fraught with danger.

'Guy, Guy,' said Celia, 'for heaven's sake let us keep our heads. Much as I love you, I'm not going to forget what it would mean to you if we took this plunge—as that unspeakable woman wants us to, just in order to gain her own ends.'

Pale and shaken, the man sought refuge in his pipe . . . lit it and smoked it in silence for a moment, stooping forward slightly, elbows resting on his knees. He could not bear to look at Celia. He had never been more conscious of weakness . . . of the mad longing to 'cut and run' and to put an end to all this suffering.

'Always it has rested with you, darling,' at length he said in a low voice, 'yours has been the strongest will, the bravest spirit, the guiding light. I'm done, Celia. I'm in your hands.'

She answered against all her instincts which inclined so passionately towards him.

'Then you're safe. You're safe, my darling, because I can never allow you to destroy yourself for love of me, and neither will I allow that woman to destroy you.'

He put his pipe in his pocket and turned to her.

'Celia,' he said in a voice full of emotion, 'I can't begin to tell you what I think of you; how fine I think you are. You make me ashamed.'

She shook her head.

279

'You don't understand. If I was thinking of myself, I'd be hopelessly weak. It's all for you, Guy. You, *the doctor!* Oh, my dear, there are moments when I with you were a stockbroker or a bank-clerk—or any ordinary man, not in the public eye. Then I might very well run away with you and let the water close over our heads.'

He took her hand and put his lips against it.

'I've done nothing to deserve such love. I can only tell you that from the bottom of my heart, I'm grateful and I adore you.'

She drew away her fingers and stood up, making some attempt to smooth her hair. Her eyes were shadowy with strain.

'I ought to go, Guy darling. I must catch the first train back to Brighton. Now we know that Frances has done this—it is possible that *she* is on her way back here, hoping to catch us out. There's nothing she would like better than to find us locked in each other's arms . . .' Celia broke off with a short unhappy laugh.

Guy stood up, hands thrust in his coat pockets. His eyes and lips were grim.

'The difference between you two women is almost unbelievable. I thought Frances was bad but I didn't think she'd go to such lengths as this.'

'Mind you, we are taking it for granted that it is her work. But I don't see who else could have sent the wires because nobody else knew our movements.'

280

'Of *course* it's Frances. I suppose she hasn't heard by any chance about your broken engagement?'

'No. That's just a coincidence. When she does know, it will give her another weapon—that's why I mustn't be found here.'

'You shan't be,' said Guy, 'but, my darling, you don't look fit. I can't allow you to rush down to Brighton without any food, or rest.'

'I shall be all right. I'm much better, really. And this . . . she touched the sling and gave him a fleeting smile . . . 'quite all right now. Next week I'm to have it out of the splint.'

He bent and kissed the fur-cape which she had let fall over the injured arm.

'My darling, lovely one!'

'Oh, Guy,' she sighed, 'how awful it is that two people who love each other as much as we do should have to spend all their times together saying good-bye.'

'It is hard—very hard, Celia. But you've been so brave and good, my dear. There must be some sort of reward, surely?'

'My reward is to know that you're all right,' she said. That's why I *must* defeat the object of those telegrams. No doubt Frances thought that once we met again, alone here this evening, we wouldn't have the strength to separate.'

Guy gave a grim laugh.

'She judges people on her own rotten standards. Not that she wasn't damn nearly right. I damn nearly *did* run away with you just now.'

Celia gave him her hand with another, touching little smile.

'Will you drive me to the station?'

'Oh, God,' said Guy, wearily, 'why can't I drive you to the other end of the world where people would leave us alone?' For a moment she leaned her fair head against his shoulder. 'Wouldn't that be heavenly!'

He took her wholly into his embrace and kissed her many times, passionately, tenderly, most reluctant to let her go again.

'Celia, my darling, my dear one, what will be the end of it all?'

With her lips against his cheek, her eyes shut, she abandoned herself to his caresses.

'I don't know, darling. It'll work out, I suppose. For all we know, Frances may get tired of trying to divorce you and allow herself to be divorced.'

'After this trick, I'll have her and de Poiret watched,' said Guy savagely, 'I won't lose a single chance of getting my freedom. She's forfeited all rights to my respect or consideration. I despise her. And I hate myself for ever having loved her. But I didn't love her really, Celia, I know that now. I was fascinated by her looks and that charm which she can exert over men when she chooses. I know now that I've only loved one woman . . . will only love one woman all my life. You, Celia, *you*.'

282

Their parting was not brief and sensible, as they might have wished or planned in a practical moment. It was like all such partings—long drawn-out and miserable.

It was only with difficulty that Celia kept her poise, her strength-of-will. The future terrified her. Inwardly she was in wild revolt against leaving Guy and returning to that Brighton hotel.

Her engagement was broken. Come what may, she had taken that drastic step and at least she need not dread marriage with another man. But she had nobody in the world, save Jan. Nothing but her job . . . and only the vaguest, more forlorn hope that Guy would one day be free to come for her.

She was broken and weeping by the time she left that consulting-room. Somehow or other Guy brought himself to permit her to leave. They were both at breaking-point and he knew it. His heart was sore and heavy when he looked at Celia's face. It had been so lovely, so radiant, when she had first entered this house. Now it was pinched and drawn and those glorious brown eyes of hers were swollen, wet with tears.

'God!' he thought, 'one pays a heavy price in this world for adhering to the path of honour and duty!'

He walked through the hall like a man whose ankles are fettered, dragging his feet. Every step brought him nearer to the parting.

There would be just a quick drive to Victoria, then another of those anguished good-byes with which he was now all too familiar.

But when Celia was weak, he tried to be strong. Now that she was trembling and in tears, he sought to strengthen and comfort her.

'Don't worry, my darling. It'll be all right. Something will happen, I feel sure—something to bring us together.'

She handed him the telegram which she had received down in Brighton. How astonished and thrilled she had been when she read it, she thought, wretchedly. It had come soon after Tim had driven her back to the Imperial Hotel from the Dyke. With Jan they had been sitting in the lounge, smoking and talking. Jan, having received the news of Celia's broken engagement with obvious disapproval. But, dear old Jan, she had been thrilled enough when Tim had suggested that she should go out with him alone that evening. Celia had left them still making their plans when she rushed to the station. They had been mystified by her sudden decision to go to London and not a little worried. But she assured them all was well and that she would be back tonight.

She had not really known what to expect when she *did* see Guy. But here it was . . . it had ended in the old *impasse*. It never seemed to end in any other way.

'You can give this wire to Frances and tell her that the trick was successful—but only up to a point,' she said, with a bitterness that Guy had never yet heard from her.

He made no answer. Words failed him on the subject of Frances. But he wouldn't wait until Monday to tell her what he thought of her. No doubt for safety's sake, she would go to the aunt in Eastbourne later tonight. Well, he would ring her up there, and have a few knife-edged words with her.

It was close upon nine o'clock by the time Celia reached Brighton again.

She had had no dinner. She did not want any, but Guy's last service had been to take her to the buffet and make her drink a small brandy-and-soda before she caught her train.

In the taxi, rolling along the Front, she thought of his tenderness, his care for her, and how absolutely she loved him. During the journey down, she had thought of nothing else. Now she felt almost emotionless, as though the grief within her had become a solid burden which could not be relieved by tears. It was, indeed, as though she had no more tears to shed.

She felt cold and sick. Her arm was aching which it always did now when she was overtired. Dully she wondered what sort of an evening Jan and Tim were having. She wanted to reach the hotel and go to bed without seeing Tim again. She did not even want to talk to Jan.

Once in her childhood she had seen a dog

which had just lost its master, creep into a corner, sit on an old coat of his, and die there, refusing food and drink. That exhibition of dumb sorrow had agonised her and been her first experience of real misery. It was queer that she remembered that incident tonight. Because it was what she would like to do; to creep by herself into a corner and just die. It was so difficult to go on living—without *him.*

She could at least be thankful for Tim's sake that he did not feel quite this way about losing her. He was unhappy, of course. Bitterly disappointed that she was not going to marry him after all. But his was a different temperament. He skimmed more lightly over the surface of things. His nature was gay and resilient. She knew that he would accept the situation philosophically, and that he would soon find consolation in one of his many 'blondes'. Thank God for that! She would hate Tim to feel as she or Guy were feeling. And it was all too clear to her that there could never be another man in *her* life. However lonely that life might be, it was henceforth dedicated to Guy.

She was incapable of thinking, and almost beyond suffering by the time she reached the Imperial Hotel. She was conscious only of exhaustion.

The head-porter who knew her, touched his cap as she entered the vestibule.

'Miss Leith isn't in, I suppose?' she asked.

'No, miss. She and the gentleman went out before dinner and haven't come back.'

'Good,' thought Celia, 'now I can go to bed and try to sleep.'

She let her tired gaze rove round the brilliantly-lighted lounge. An orchestra was playing. There were people in evening-dress at most of the tables, drinking after-dinner coffee. And so the world went on—Celia thought—a gay world that had no time for an individual's personal grief.

'Guy,' thought Celia, desolately, 'Guy, how am I going to bear it without you?'

She became aware that the porter was speaking to her.

She paid little attention to what he was saying until she realised that he was trying to convey to her some piece of news which he thought might interest her.

'What was that?' she asked, vaguely, 'what did you say?'

'About that couple, miss, who were here for dinner this evening. Terrible tragedy it was.'

'What couple?'

The porter, relishing a piece of drama, launched into details.

Surely she remembered . . . earlier in the afternoon a lady and gentleman had come for lunch in a big white Mercedes car. Everyone had looked at the car. From France it was. And the gentleman was believed to be French.

At this point in the story, Celia's exhausted

brain grew clear and she became suddenly, intensely interested in what the man was telling her.

'Yes, yes, I remember that car. In fact, I know who the lady was,' she said. 'Well, what about them? What happened?'

'A horrible accident, miss.'

Celia stared at the man. She felt herself going white, then red.

'An accident. But where . . . how . . . what happened?'

He went on with his story. He had told it so many times this evening and was enjoying it to the full.

During dinner it had rained a bit, he said. Maybe she had noticed? After all the Saturday traffic, it had got a bit oily on the roads—and slippery. The Mercedes had been on its way out of Brighton, on the Lewes Road, going much too fast according to the police, and they skidded just beyond Moulscombe and crashed into a Southdown bus . . .

Celia's heart was beating so quickly now that she was afraid that she might faint. Indeed, she had to catch the porter's arm in order to steady herself. He broke off in his story and looked at her with some concern.

'Aren't you well, miss?'

'Go on,' said Celia, feverishly, 'what happened? I tell you I know the lady—what happened?'

'I'm sure I hope I'm not upsetting you, miss,

288

if she's a personal friend of yours . . .'

'Go on,' Celia repeated wildly.

The lights of the lounge were going round her. It was as though two bands were pressing her head. She tried to keep control of herself. And before the man finished his story, she tried for decency's sake not to *hope* that she would hear the worst. She said to herself:

'I mustn't wish it. I *mustn't!* It would be awful of me. No matter how bad she is, or how much Guy wants to be free, *I mustn't wish it.*'

And then the porter said:

'Afraid it was all U.P. with the poor lady. The gentleman was saved by a miracle. Badly cut and a fractured rib, but he was on the right side. The bus caught the poor lady. She was dead when they pulled her out.'

Again he tapped. And this time to catch Miss Hammond just before she fell, and to call anxiously to the girl at the reception-bureau to help him. It seemed that the story had been too much for Miss Hammond. There was now another piece of drama to thrill the head-porter. A nice commotion in the lounge as they carried Miss Hammond into the lift and up to her room . . .

CHAPTER NINETEEN

It had been on a golden spring morning, when the first daffodils were out, that Tim Madden had once summoned his personal and favourite secretary to his office and told her that he was in love with her.

It was on another such golden morning, a year later that he sent for her again. But not to make that same avowal. For love of that kind was over forever between Celia Hammond and Timothy Madden. During this year in which she had continued to work in his office, a real and enduring friendship had existed between them.

A friendship that would go on until the end of time. They both knew that. But they would not be able to see each other much longer. Their lives lay in opposite directions. Today was Celia's last day in the office. And tomorrow she was going to Egypt. For in Egypt, Guy was waiting for her and they were to be married out there.

The Celia who walked into her 'boss's' room carrying the letters she had just typed, was a very different being from the Celia of a year ago. That girl had known grief and despair; all the agony of separation from the person she loved most on earth. She had fought a bitter inner-conflict from which there was no peace. But the Celia of today was finished with conflicts, with pain and bitterness. Her separation from Guy had continued only because circumstances had made it impossible for them to be together for a year following Frances Denver's sudden and violent death. Such a separation was of a kind which they could both bear. They had never really been out of touch. They had fed their hunger on the glorious hope of the future, on letters, telegrams, photographs, all countless little things which bring infinite satisfaction to temporarily parted lovers.

Celia laid her work on Timothy's desk. He sat back in his swivel-chair and grinned at her.

'The last little service, eh? I'm going to miss you, Celia. I shall never find another secretary to take your place.'

'Oh yes, you will, Tim; and I'm sure my successor will be much more efficient.'

'Perhaps efficiency isn't everything. I've liked the nice personal *feeling* that's between us. I shall miss that. The next girl will be only a machine.'

Celia sat on the edge of the desk.

'You've been wonderfully kind to me, Tim. I shall never forget it, and neither will Guy.'

He looked at her without sadness, and was without jealousy that he could now hear that name. He was immensely glad, too, that she could utter it with such a warm note of happiness in her voice, and such a warm sweet look in her eyes. She deserved to get the man she loved. No woman had ever loved a man more, and Timothy Madden knew it. He knew something else, too. That Guy Denver was one of the straightest and best fellows on earth. Before Guy left London, Tim had got to know and respect him. It was no wonder to him nowadays that Celia felt the way she did about her doctor.

Time does a lot of things . . . a lot of kindly helpful things. It had been kind to Tim and had helped to ease down the old longing which he had once felt for Celia. It had brought him another love. A love for Jan Leith. For, as he had told Celia many times this last year, he had learnt the value of spiritual attraction as well as physical. He had finished with his 'blondes', his pretty play-girls. He had found something he liked better and something that he knew would last. The marvellous spirit that was within Jan. That grandness in her character which made a man forget that she was neither very pretty nor very polished, but just a homely, bright-eyed Lancashire girl.

The relationship between Tim and Jan was a queer one, and sometimes it made Celia smile. But it also made her glad, because Jan was so happy. Jan was just frankly head-over-ears in love with Tim. It had never entered her modest head that he might transfer his affections from Celia to herself. The fact that he sought her company nowadays, and made it obvious that one of these days he was going to seek it permanently, was a never-ending wonder and ecstasy for Jan. And Tim did not treat her as he had treated Celia; half afraid of saying anything, doing anything, in case he made himself unpopular. He knew what Jan felt and he responded wholehearted; and always with a jest, a touch of humour, of tender bullying.

'What a face!' he would say then ruffle her hair and kiss her at the same time . . . or:

'Oh, Lord, am I going to hear that dialect for the rest of my life? It's shocking! I shall go deaf on purpose . . .'

But another kiss . . . and Jan wouldn't worry. She adored him, and she showed her adoration. All her past philosophies about 'letting a man see who was master' were forgotten. Jan was Tim's slave. She would have done anything in the world for him.

The two girls had continued to live together during this past year and for the most part, the outings with Tim, had meant a trio. The three of them had got on remarkably well.

After the death of Frances, Celia had only seen Guy once or twice. There was still public opinion to think of and those who did not know the inner history of the whole affair, would have thought it queer had Guy started to devote himself to another woman as soon as his wife was laid in her grave.

So he had done what he had considered

293

the only thing possible. He had resigned from his London hospital and from London life. A chance had come along which would take him abroad and he had thought it best to take it.

A new British hospital was due to be opened in Alexandria. They wanted a 'big man' at the head of it. And Guy Denver was 'bigger' than they had ever hoped for. They accepted his services eagerly. There would be plenty of work for him to do, and Egypt's beautiful seaport was a fine place to live in with a fine climate. A place where Celia could eventually join him, and where they would both enjoy their lives to the full.

For ten months now Celia had not set eyes on Guy. But she knew that he was well—better perhaps in health than he had been for some time—and that he was enjoying his work in Egypt and, as he told her in his letters, every day that he worked was just a preparation for her.

She had some new snapshots in her bag to show Tim, today. They looked at them together. There was pride in every note of Celia's voice as she pointed out the beautiful garden of the villa which Guy had just bought overlooking the harbour. The villa which was to be her home.

And there was a snapshot of Guy, in a group, in the grounds of the new hospital. With a pencil-point, Celia indicated two Egyptians wearing the customary robes and *tarboosh.*

'Guy's always talking about those two. They're his personal sort of bodyguard and devoted servants. I'm not interested in them. Only in that nurse just behind the doctor. *There's* a really pretty girl for you!'

'Trying to make me jealous?' she laughed.

'You couldn't be,' said Tim, shaking his head. 'You know that lucky chap out there is just counting the hours until you join him.'

'I think we're both counting them,' said Celia, softly.

'And so you go tomorrow?'

'Yes. I go tomorrow.'

'And Jan and I will stand on the platform at Victoria and see off that boat train, and then go back and sob together.'

'You're not to sob,'.said Celia, 'or I certainly shall.'

'I don't think there's much to sob about, really,' said Tim. 'You're going to be darned happy and much as we'll miss you, we're going to be happy too, one day.'

'I hope so, Tim.'

'It's damned awful,' said Tim, gloomily, 'that I, who have been noted for my lovely girls have got to spend the rest of my life with a wife like Jan. What the devil did I want to go and fall for *her* for?'

'She isn't as plain as all that,' said Celia, staunchly.

'She isn't plain at all. She's got a grand pair

295

of eyes. Isn't it time we all went out to lunch, anyhow? And afterwards, you're not to come back to the office. You're to go home. You've got plenty to see to. We'll have our last binge tonight —all three of us.'

Celia put a hand on his shoulder.

'There's so much to thank you for, Tim. I can only hope one day that you and Jan will come out to Egypt and stay with Guy and me. That would be one of the nicest things to look forward to.'

'You've got Egypt on the brain,' said Tim, 'isn't it wonderful what a craze a girl gets for a certain place when the right man's in it! Now Jan simply *worships* Cockspur Street.'

'You're a conceited devil if ever there was one,' said Celia. 'Anyhow, I admit that I've got a craze for Egypt and I'm proud of it.'

'Well, jolly good luck to you, old thing, and let's hope the March gales don't blow and that the ship doesn't rock so that you don't arrive green in the face.'

'I don't care if I do. I've got a doctor and a hospital waiting for me at the other end.'

They left the office laughing together. It was the thought of that doctor and of that hospital, and the life to which she was going which filled Celia's mind and heart, flooding her very soul with warm, glorious contentment during the week that followed. The days and nights of that journey to Alexandria were nothing short of delirious for her. Days and nights bringing her ever nearer to her heart's desire. Nearer to an ambition which she had once thought could never be fulfilled; to a joy which both she and Guy had thought they must forever deny themselves.

She was so immensely glad now that she had waited . . . that she had never weakened in her resolve to say good-bye to Guy while his wife was alive.

Fate and the gods had been kind. Guy had been given his freedom in a way which had been least expected. And it was a way that Celia never cared to dwell upon. Frances Denver's death had given Guy to her, but she would not have wished the wretched woman to end her days so terribly. Besides, Guy had once loved Frances; she had been his wife. For a long time after the accident, Guy and Celia had both felt the sinister shadow of her end, and avoided any discussion of the affair.

But now all that was passed. They could forget Frances. They could think of themselves at last, and of the fulfilment of their dreams.

They were to be married the day after Celia's boat reached Alexandria . . .

To be married to *him.* Whenever Celia dwelt on the thought, her heart missed a beat and she felt half choking with sheer happiness. How lovely to know that she could belong forever to her Guy! How lovely to feel there were to be no more barriers, that there need be no further partings, tears, agonies.

As she told Guy, afterwards, she really remembered very little about her journey to Egypt. She was in such a daze of happiness. There was the send-off from Tim and Jan, at Victoria. Good-byes, hugs, kisses from her two great friends, the tears that came in spite of happiness—for it is always sad to say good-bye to a friend before a long journey. Her pride and pleasure in her brand-new trunks labelled '*Alexandria*'. Her new clothes . . . the fur-coat, which she was wearing . . . a last present from Tim . . . a wedding present, he called it. A big bunch of violets pinned to her furs, a glorious bouquet pressed into her arms by both her friends, and which she was to put in her cabin. Books, magazines, papers, everything that they insisted upon giving her in order to make her journey a cheerful one.

After that, thirty-six hours in the train, and then—Marseilles. And the big white liner of the Khedival Mail Line waiting to put out to sea. Five days on board, during which Celia spoke to nobody, because she wanted to be alone with her thoughts of the man who would be waiting at the other end. Each twenty-four hours brought warmer weather, calmer seas. Then Malta . . . and sunshine . . . not the feeble warmth of the March sun in England, but the hot, vivid sunlight of the Mediterranean. And finally the never-to-be-forgotten harbour of Alexandria. Celia's first glimpse of the Egypt which was to mean her future home.

The beautiful white city, the brilliant blue sky and the blue sea; the green fringe of palm-trees, the motley crowd on the docks. Egyptians with striped robes and scarlet *tarboosh;* black-faced Nubians from the Upper Nile wearing white turbans. Greeks, French and English; a sprinkling of khaki . . . the Army. And finally, as Celia walked down the gangway, that one face and figure which was the *only* one that mattered. Guy who waited for her . . . Guy, in grey flannels, his face burnt dark-brown as she had never before seen it, looking ten years younger, and as handsome and as eager as a boy. Guy, whose hands took hers and clung to them and whose eyes looked down into hers with unforgettable emotion.

'Oh, my *darling*,' he said. And it seemed all that he could say.

Her heart was full to overflowing. With the warm Egyptian sun drenching her, and all the strange sounds of Alexandria revolving around her, she felt that she was in a new wonderful world . . . a world of dreams rather than of reality. She said under her breath:

'Don't kiss me here . . . wait . . *wait*.'

He understood. Still holding one of her hands, he walked with her to the Customs. A couple of natives fought for her luggage.

'As soon as we've got through the Customs, darling,' Guy said, 'we can go straight to my villa. I want to show you our home before we go on to Dr and Mrs Elvey, who are going to look after you tonight.'

'Grand!' she said, happily.

They did not even kiss once they were in the car. They both seemed to wish to wait . . . it was sufficient to sit side by side, talking, drinking in each other's gaze.

Guy had never seen Celia as she looked today and he told her so. She was ravishing in that pale-blue suit with a blue felt hat on the side of her fair head. She had put on a little weight and it suited her, although it did not detract from that air of grace and fragility which he had always found enchanting. She was young and lovely and essentially his, and tomorrow she was to be his wife.

'Everything's fixed, darling,' he told her, 'we're to be married at twelve tomorrow and then we are going up the Nile for our honeymoon. I've got three weeks. Elvey is taking over at the hospital in my place.'

'It sounds too good to be true. Do you like your job out here, Guy?'

'Very much. It's more hospital work than private practice, but it's very interesting, and I'm in love with Egypt. I think you will be too, when you've lived here for a bit and got used to it. There are people who find it dirty and unattractive, but there's something about it that "gets" me.'

She squeezed his hand and laughed.

'It's "got me", already.'

'And so have I, thank God,' he said. 'Oh,

Celia, it's unbelievable to see you here . . . to know that you're here with me at last.'

'It's been a long time, hasn't it, Guy?'

'So well worth waiting for, darling.'

'Tell me more about our honeymoon.'

'We're going up the river in one of those little Nile boats. It takes quite a long time, and it's perfect at this time of year. The sunsets are a dream. We shall go through Luxor, to Assuan. You shall see the Tombs of the Kings and the ruined Temples of Karnak and Luxor, and all the ancient wonders of this country.'

'It sounds thrilling. But I doubt if I shall look at anything but you.'

'Then it'll be a waste, because I shan't look at anything but you.'

They both laughed.

'How's Jan?' he asked.

'In great form, dear old Jan! It's so marvellous for me to know that Tim's actually going to marry her one day. I never thought he would. She isn't his style at all. But she's so endeared herself to him that he just can't do without her.'

'They must come out here for their honeymoon.'

'That's what I told them,' said Celia.

And now they were at Guy's villa. Celia looked at last upon her future home; looked at it with a feeling of awe, as a child might look at the illustration of a favourite fairy-tale. For it seemed too magical and too wonderful to be true.

Hand in hand Guy and Celia walked together through a sun-drenched garden with tall date palms, beds of English roses in full bloom, and great scarlet flowers which Guy told her were poinsettias. The villa was Moorish in design, its tall windows looking down the hill to the blue sea. The white walls were purple with bougainvillaea, and golden with bignonia blossom.

The air was still, warm, velvet-soft. There was a mysterious beauty here which later Celia grew to associate definitely with Egypt.

And now they were indoors, alone for the first time since she had left the boat. Alone in a spacious lounge which was full of flowers. She only vaguely saw all the possessions which were to be hers. For she could concentrate upon nothing but Guy, and that passionate marvellous look in his eyes when he took her into his arms.

'Welcome to Egypt, my darling, and to your future home,' he said.

For a moment she could not speak. She took off her hat and threw it on to a chair. Locking her arms about his neck, she lifted her transfigured face. She said:

'I am yours. I always was . . . I always will be. My darling, *darling* Guy.'

And with the first touch of his lips against hers, she knew that her long waiting, and her journey had, indeed, come to an end. And Life

302

as they had both wanted to live it ever since they had exchanged their first long kiss, was beginning.